THE CHICKEN HANGER

THE CHICKEN HANGER

A novel

BEN REHDER

TCU PRESS

FORT WORTH, TEXAS

Copyright © 2012 by Ben Rehder
Library of Congress Cataloging-in-Publication Data

Rehder, Ben.
  The chicken hanger : a novel / Ben Rehder.
    p. cm.
  ISBN 978-0-87565-436-2 (pbk. : alk. paper)
1. Illegal aliens--Fiction. 2. Mexican-American Border Region--
          Fiction. 3. Prejudices--Fiction. I. Title.
  PS3618.E45C48 2012
  813'.6--dc22
                                            2011019635
TCU Press
P. O. Box 298300
Fort Worth, Texas 76129
817.257.7822
http://www.prs.tcu.edu

To order books: 1.800.826.8911

Designed by Vicki Whistler

To Mary Summerall

From whom I am still learning

ACKNOWLEDGMENTS

Many people helped in various ways with this manuscript. I'd like to thank Becky Rehder, Helen and Ed Fanick, Jill and Emelio Rodriguez, Mary Summerall, Meredith Deutscher, David Parker, Toodie Sweeten, Jane Chelius, Mike Farris, John Barber, John Burger, and Stacia Hernstrom. Also, much appreciation to Dan Williams, Judy Alter, Susan R. Petty, Melinda Esco, Vicki Whistler, Sarah Bird, Jim Sanderson, and Karla O'Donald, with special thanks to Rileigh Sanders. Last, my deepest gratitude to Steven L. Davis.

"The laws should be rigidly enforced which prohibit the immigration of a servile class to compete with American labor, with no intention of acquiring citizenship, and bringing with them and retaining habits and customs repugnant to our civilization."

—PRESIDENT GROVER CLEVELAND,
FIRST INAUGURAL ADDRESS, 1885

martes

ONE

RICKY DELGADO SAT in the waiting room of the small medical clinic and wondered whether he smelled like chickens. It was, of course, a valid concern. Did he carry the stench of live poultry? He'd had a chance to wash his face and hands before bicycling over from the plant, but without a full shower, the odor tended to linger. There were four other patients in the room, but one of them—an old Asian man—appeared to have a cold. He was sniffling frequently and blowing his nose into a stained handkerchief. He was too congested to smell anything. The rest of them? Maybe. Ah, well. Nothing much Ricky could do about it.

It was five minutes before five in the afternoon. Ricky had been waiting for two hours. He had tried to nap, sitting there in the chair, but he couldn't, so he'd thumbed through the magazines. Now he knew how to create his own potpourri, should the mood ever strike him. He'd also learned a revolutionary technique for developing awesome abs in just ten minutes a day.

℥

By five thirty, he'd been moved to a small examination room. A nurse—a pretty Hispanic woman—took his temperature and frowned.

"One oh three," she said in Spanish. "How long has it been this high?"

"I don't have a thermometer."

"When did you start feeling bad?"

"Maybe a week ago."

"Been staying home from work?"

Ricky shook his head. He wished he had more energy to talk. This was a nice woman. There weren't many like her in Rugoso.

"Anyone you work with been sick lately?"

"Not that I know of."

She wrapped the Velcro cuff around his arm to measure his blood pressure. Started pumping the little bulb. "Any other symptoms?"

He could tell from her accent that she was born on this side of the river, probably here in Texas. But her parents probably weren't.

"I cough a lot. And my chest hurts sometimes."

"Hurts how? When you cough?"

"No, it just ... aches."

"You cough up any mucus?"

"No."

"Are you congested? Your nose runny?"

"Maybe a little."

"When you blow your nose, is the discharge yellow? Green?"

"No."

"Do you ever get sinus infections?"

"I don't think so."

She nodded and unwrapped his arm. "One eighteen over seventy-five. Not bad." She made some notes on a chart that contained all his vital information:

Age: Twenty-seven.

Height: Five-eight.

Weight: One fifty-two.

Allergies: None.

Insurance: *Yeah, right.*

"You taking any medication?"

"No, nothing."

"Okay, just hang loose for a few minutes," she said. "Dr. King will be in shortly."

As she was shutting the door, he said, "Hey, miss."

She paused.

"What's your name?"

She smiled. "Cristiana. Cris."

❧

The doctor bustled in at six fifteen, a very important man, reading the chart, then rolling the little stool over beside Ricky. Didn't introduce himself, just started feeling around on Ricky's neck. Poking underneath the jaw line. Feeling the lymph nodes. He still hadn't said a word.

He looked into Ricky's eyes with that lighted scope, which was unpleasant, then he looked into Ricky's ears with a different tool. "You speak English?" he finally asked.

"Sure."

He looked down Ricky's throat, then he stood and got behind Ricky and put the stethoscope to his back. Moved it around and asked him to cough a couple of times. Had him lie on his back.

"How long have you worked at the plant?"

The plant had a special arrangement with this doctor. They mentioned that to Ricky on his first day. *If you get sick,* they said, *go see Dr. King. He offers a discount to Kountry Fresh employees.*

"Eight months," Ricky said.

The doctor was squeezing on Ricky's abdomen, feeling around for something.

Ricky said, "It was either that or get my master's degree."

He liked to have fun with these people sometimes. Say things they wouldn't expect. Bullshit a little. Joke with them. Sometimes it made a difference.

The doctor said, "Have you had any sort of illness that weakened your immune system?"

"No."

"Are you on any medication?"

"No."

The doctor shined the light in Ricky's eyes again. "Does this light bother you more than normal?"

"Yeah, a little. Sunlight does, too. I forgot to tell the nurse about that."

"Okay, I'm going to draw some blood, but I'm pretty sure it's the flu. Take some aspirin or Advil for the fever, and I'll give you some samples of this new antiviral, but it probably won't help much. You waited too long to come in."

ഔ

The nurse, Cris, caught him just as he was walking out the front door. She stuck her hand out. "Here, take this."

It was a small, rectangular cardboard box containing a new thermometer. One of the fancy digital models.

"Thanks."

She made a no-big-deal gesture. "We have plenty. The drug reps give us all kinds of freebies. You need to keep an eye on that fever of yours. Okay?"

She smiled again, and Ricky could feel it all the way down to his toes.

ഔ

Thirty-three miles away, south of Laredo, a man named Clayton Dupree said, "What we need is some night-vision goggles. I think a lot of 'em are moving through after dark."

Herschel Gandy didn't reply. Just kept scanning the low brush-covered hills with a pair of high-dollar Zeiss binoculars. It was two hours before sunset, and they were sixteen feet in the air, in a deer blind. The tower lifted them high above the dense scrub—the *guajillo* and *guayacán*, the cat claw, sage, and prickly pear. A harsh and forbidding terrain. Thorns on damn near everything. Then you had your rattlesnakes and lizards, scorpions and tarantulas, and plenty of wild game, too. Turkey and pigs, dove and quail. And white-tailed deer, of course. Some of the biggest bucks a man could ever place in his crosshairs—and the Gandy Ranch, on the eastern banks of the Rio Grande, had more than its fair share.

But deer season hadn't started just yet.

"They love the full moon," Clayton said. "Don't have to use flashlights then. Helps 'em navigate." He raised his own binoculars, and Gandy thought they appeared out of place in Clayton's large, calloused hands. Like some sort of anachronism. Clayton had the hands of a blacksmith or a muleskinner or a prospector sifting through hundreds of pounds of river silt a day. He was tall and lean, with sun-baked skin and a slight limp from an encounter with a bull when he was seventeen. That was twenty years ago, back when they were kids, and it seemed like yesterday. Gandy had been there when the bull tossed Clayton like a sock puppet, then crushed his knee with a front hoof. Ruined Clayton's rodeo career. Still a hell of a ranch hand, though.

Gandy focused on a *sendero*—a long clear-cut alley through the dense scrub—coming from the southwest. The path of least resistance. That's where the *mojados* would appear, if they showed at all. *Mojados.* The illegal aliens' own term for "wetback." Easy to tell which *senderos* they'd been using recently, because of the footprints and the garbage. Junk-food wrappers. Soiled toilet paper, sanitary napkins, and underwear. Plastic grocery sacks caught on thorny plants, waving like surrender flags. Water jugs that would decompose in, oh, maybe a thousand years. A huge fucking mess, and that was the least of it.

The wetbacks would cut a fence rather than climb over it. Like a lot of locals, Herschel specifically left his front gate open, hoping the wetbacks would leave the fence alone on the highway side of the ranch. But no, they cut that fence regularly, too.

If they could catch a calf or a goat, they would kill and barbecue it right on the spot. They'd break into homes and steal food, or anything small they could hock later. And those were just the average Juans heading north for day labor, or the *señoritas* coming over here to have babies, because babies born here automatically became American citizens. It was a whole different story with the drug runners. They were laying siege to this country, and nobody seemed to notice. Christ, most of them carried automatic weapons nowadays, making their way across private land like an invading army.

All of the illegals acted as if they belonged here and there was nothing a man like Herschel Gandy could do to stop them.

Wrong on both counts.

౬౨

Ricky pedaled slowly but steadily along the shoulder of César Chávez Memorial Highway, grateful that he didn't have to go back to the plant today. But Wayne would expect him first thing in the morning.

After eight months at Kountry Fresh Chicken, Ricky had a reputation as the fastest hanger in the plant. Maybe the fastest anywhere. Thirty birds a minute, which was about as quick as it got. He'd done the math. He was almost as good with numbers as he was with English. It came to eighteen hundred chickens every hour. Eighteen thousand in a ten-hour shift. Five days a week. Four and a half million chickens a year. And he was just one worker in one small plant in south Texas. Where did all those birds go? It boggled his mind. The citizens of this country had an amazing appetite for chicken. And everything else.

The job was the worst he'd ever had, which was saying something. He'd dug sewer line ditches through limestone, shingled houses in the August sun, picked fruit until his fingers bled. None of that was as bad—or paid as steadily—as live hang. That's what it was called.

Chickens entered in crates, and Ricky had to grab the birds, one at a time, and hang them by their feet on shackles passing by on an overhead conveyor belt. From there the birds went to the kill room, where their necks were sliced with a circular saw. After that, Ricky wasn't sure of the details, but he knew there were scalders—tanks of superheated water—to kill bacteria and make it easier to remove the feathers, which happened after the head was cut off but before the feet were cut off. Then the bare carcasses passed through a device that would singe the last fine feathers. Then evisceration, then into the chiller, then cut-up and deboning. It was like an assembly line, except it was a *disassembly* line.

In live hang, you had to hang at least twenty-three birds per minute. Less than three seconds for every chicken. Fall below that mark and you were in trouble. Because the chickens kept coming. They never stopped.

The live hang room was kept almost totally dark—it was supposed to calm the birds—but still, they'd shriek and peck at you, flap and flail, feathers flying everywhere. You'd lift them onto the hooks, and they'd piss and shit from sheer terror. By the end of the first hour, you were covered with it. Yes, you wore protective gear—a smock, goggles, gloves, plastic cones to protect your forearms from their angry beaks—but the filth and grime found their way past all that eventually.

It was always hot in there, too, even now, in October. So hot in the past week that Ricky couldn't always tell what was fever and what wasn't.

He was disappointed that he was sick right now. He wanted to be well when Tomás arrived.

∞

Right at dusk, Clayton sat up a little straighter and said, "There we go."

"Where?" said Gandy. He raised his binoculars.

"Two hundred yards. They just come over that rise. Three of 'em." Clayton had always been an amazing spotter, even with his naked eye, even at dusk.

"I still don't see 'em."

"Off to the right, in the shadows."

"What're they wearing?"

"Jeans, all of 'em. Green shirt, red shirt, blue shirt. Still wet from the river."

Gandy scanned up and down the *sendero*, not seeing shit, and then ... okay. Yeah. There they were. Skinny little fucks. None of them over the age of twenty-five. Maybe even teenagers. Dressed just as Clayton had said, and each man had a backpack—the kind that students carry—swinging from his hand. Toting food and water, no doubt. No weapons that Gandy could see. The men were moving slowly, wary now, because they'd seen the deer blind looming ahead.

"They're wondering if anybody's up here," Gandy whispered. "Now they've stopped. They're talking."

"Probably don't even know when deer season is," Clayton said.

"Wondering if they should go back," Gandy said.

He could feel his heartbeat picking up.

The wetbacks had only two options, move forward or retreat, because trekking through the brush was unthinkable for anything on two feet. The men would be lost in minutes. Come tomorrow, when their water ran out, they'd be goners. Sometimes Gandy wondered how many sun-bleached skeletons lay undiscovered on his twelve thousand acres.

Come on, boys, Gandy thought. *Just a little closer. Give me an easy shot.*

And here they came. Slow. Apprehensive. Looking for any movement, or any sign of danger. But the rear and side windows of the deer blind were closed, so Gandy and Clayton were cloaked in relative darkness, especially now that the sun had sunk behind the hills.

Gandy reached for his Sako .270 leaning in a corner of the blind. Raised it—careful not to bang the muzzle against the roof—swung it level, and rested the tip of the barrel on the sill of the open front window.

There was a round in the chamber. Always was. What good was a rifle that wasn't loaded? Gandy flicked the safety off with his right thumb. He pulled the butt of the rifle in tight to his shoulder and peered through the scope. Also from Zeiss. Cost nearly four grand, but it was worth it. Incredible visibility in low-light conditions. Built-in rangefinder. Took him less than three seconds to find the lead wetback in the glass, and to gauge his distance at one hundred and sixty-two yards. Piece of cake, but Gandy wanted him even closer. He wanted all of them to see the flame leap from the barrel when he shot.

He waited, and still they came. One hundred and fifty yards. One twenty.

One hundred. Perfect. There was a slight breeze swaying the tower blind, but nothing he couldn't handle.

He aligned the crosshairs on the man's nose. Placed his finger on the trigger. The copper-jacketed bullet would turn the guy's brain to porridge. Gandy figured he could probably drop the other two with torso shots within six or eight seconds. Man, it was tempting. Who would know? Who would care? Who could blame him for defending his country?

He took a deep breath, held it, and centered the scope on the man's gray backpack. Checked the range again. Eighty yards. Showtime. He squeezed the trigger, and the rifle roared and bucked in his arms. The sound in the blind was overwhelming. Before it even faded, Gandy was jacking another round into the chamber. The wetbacks, of course, were running, making a mad sprint back the way they'd come.

Gandy took aim and sent another round screaming over their heads. Then another. And another. Then the three men disappeared over the ridge.

Clayton said something, but Gandy couldn't make it out, because his ears were ringing like a goddamn fire alarm. He felt so ... *alive*.

"What'd you say?"

Clayton was grinning. "It don't matter how many times we do that, it never gets old."

miércoles

TWO

YOU START WITH NOTHING. No home, no vehicle, no clothing except what you're wearing. No clear sense of where you're going or how you'll get there. Like a hurricane victim, but you *chose* this, because it's better than what you had before. If you're lucky, you know somebody who knows somebody who'll help you out, maybe even let you stay with them for a few weeks until you make some better arrangements. Then you begin putting your new life together, one piece at a time.

Ricky's bicycle was his most valuable possession. The owner had left it unlocked in front of the Wal-Mart three years earlier, when Ricky had first come to Rugoso. It was an old single-speed Schwinn, neglected, but nothing that couldn't be salvaged.

First, he took it apart. The handlebar stem and the seat post had a fair amount of rust on them, and there were pitted spots elsewhere, so he sanded the entire frame and repainted it with spray cans of Rustoleum. Now it no longer looked like the same bike, so the owner would be less likely to recognize it. One of the pedal cranks was bent, but Ricky was able to straighten it. One of the inner tubes had a slow leak, but he patched it. The chain was in bad shape, but he found a replacement at a garage sale for fifty cents.

That's how he'd met Howard, a nice old man who lived about three blocks from Ricky's trailer. Howard had a big garage sale once a month. In the weeks between, he went to other peoples' garage sales, yard sales, moving sales, rummage sales, estate sales, any kind of sale. That's where he got the items he sold later. He looked for bargains and knew how to make money. He'd buy an entire box of books for five dollars, then sell each book for a dollar apiece. Or he'd buy a suitcase full of clothes for eight or ten dollars, then turn around and sell the suitcase alone for that amount, and sell each item of clothing for a dollar. Pretty smart. Howard said he made three or four hundred dollars a month that way, tax free, plus it gave him something to do. Occasionally Howard bought "big ticket" items like washing machines or lawn furniture, if he thought there was a profit to be made. A fresh coat of paint could double the value of a wrought iron patio set. Howard stored some of those items on his front porch, which upset some of his neighbors.

The bicycle chain Ricky bought from Howard was too long, but Howard lent Ricky a hammer and a punch to remove a couple of links. Then, a few weeks later, he gave Ricky a bag of mismatched tools—crescent wrenches, some sockets, a pair of pliers, vise grips, a couple of screwdrivers. He wouldn't take any money for them.

Howard said, "You work at the plant, right? Live in one of them trailers?"

"Yes, sir."

"Yeah, well, you're gonna need some tools, believe me, living over there."

Ricky thanked him, then said, "How did you know where I work?"

Howard chuckled. "You got feathers stuck to your boots, son."

℘

At sunrise, the man in the green shirt sat on a small hill above the highway and pulled cactus thorns from his lower legs. Dozens of them. Some were too deep to remove. This was not a good start. He had hoped to cross the road before daylight. A low-flying helicopter had passed over ten minutes ago, but it appeared to be gone now.

The man in the red shirt came up the hill, bent low, and squatted nearby. "How soon?" he said.

"Now, before it gets any lighter."

"How far to Rugoso?"

"About twenty-five miles." They needed to travel in a northeast direction, using the sun as a guide. If you carried a map or a compass, *la migra* would accuse you of being a *coyote*.

"Think we can make it before dark?"

"That's what I'm hoping."

It was an ambitious undertaking—most *mojados* were happy to cover ten or fifteen miles a day—but twenty-five miles was possible if you pushed yourself. Plus, a smaller group with no women or children could move more quickly. But the man in the green shirt was wondering if their injured companion, resting at the bottom of the hill, would slow them down. Could he cross fences quickly? How much water would he consume? He'd lost his own water, which already made him a burden.

"He wants to use your phone to call his brother," the man in the red shirt said.

"What for? Nobody can risk picking us up here. Too many checkpoints. We'd all get caught."

"He wants to tell him what happened."

That might be wise, letting his brother know the situation. Just in case.

"We're already running behind."

"It's not his fault."

"If he can't keep up, we'll have to leave him behind."

"Of course. He knows that."

"Says here that bats aren't blind," said Danny Olguin.

Warren Coleman, in the driver's seat of the Chevy Tahoe, didn't know what to make of that. Why did everybody think bats were blind if they weren't? He'd thought so himself. Why would an inaccurate notion like that persist? He found it somehow troubling. "You sure?"

Danny, in the passenger seat, sipped some coffee from a styrofoam cup, then continued. "'All bats have well developed, functional eyes and can see, although their eyesight isn't as acute as other mammals, and they do not see colors.'" Danny liked trivia and odd facts, misconceptions, and strange-but-true kind of stuff. Ripley's. Various chapters of the Guinness record book. Paul Harvey.

Warren continued to stare through the front windshield. He liked traffic check better than linewatch, but at the moment, there was little to see. Traffic was light. Mostly eighteen-wheelers carrying who knows what. Merchandise. People. Drugs. Couldn't stop them without cause.

Later, they'd work the drags for fresh prints. Warren used to enjoy cutting sign, because it was such a cat-and-mouse game. The illegals had their little tricks: wearing socks over the shoes, or using a piece of brush as a broom, sweeping their tracks away as they walked. Or they'd walk backwards for a stretch, thinking they were being clever, but that was easy to spot. Occasionally they'd go so far as to strap old cow hooves to their soles, but Warren had never seen a cow with just two legs.

Danny said, "Says people *think* bats are blind because they use a form of sonar called echolocation to find what they're looking for."

Interesting. Warren didn't mind the distraction. So far, he'd learned that lacrosse, not hockey, was the official sport of Canada, that tidal waves had nothing to do with tides, and that there were really only forty-six states in the U.S., if you wanted to get technical, because Kentucky, Massachusetts, Pennsylvania, and Virginia were commonwealths.

Danny was reading from a paperback called *Myth Information*, which he'd picked up at a garage sale for a quarter. To fight the boredom, he said. And traffic check *could* be boring sometimes—except for the brief moments when it absolutely wasn't. It was like deer hunting, which Warren had never enjoyed that much. You watch and wait, and just when it seems nothing is ever going to happen, a deer steps out from the brush and you get a few minutes of heart-pounding action.

They'd parked the SUV—white, with the familiar horizontal green stripe—along the east shoulder, tight against the fence line, facing north. Before them lay a long, desolate ribbon of U.S. Highway 83. By noon, it would be shimmering with heat waves, even this late in the fall. But now, at seven thirty in the morning, the sunlight was just beginning to tinge the upper branches of the mesquites on the other side of the highway. The dense wall of scrub, which stretched for miles in every direction, appeared impenetrable, but it wasn't. There were narrow paths that had been packed hard by thousands of aching feet. How many generations had followed the same route?

Warren forgot about bats and wondered, not for the first time, *What the hell are we doing here?* It seemed the height of foolishness and futility. Like standing in a massive thunderstorm and attempting to catch raindrops in a thimble. You might catch one or two, but how many were getting past you? Warren had been doing this for nine years now, and he truly had no idea if he was making a difference. And how would you judge that, anyway? By whose standards? From whose perspective? His supervisors gave pep talks, talking about what a great job they were all doing, but Warren wasn't so sure. Back when he'd been a city cop in Hebbronville—"Patrolman Coleman" they'd called him—he'd never felt that he was wasting his time.

"Well, hell," Danny said. "The guinea pig ain't a pig—which, duh, I know that—but it ain't even from Guinea. What the hell is up with that?"

Danny was from Midland. Twenty-seven years old. Divorced, with a little girl named Emily. He'd spent four years overseas in the army, then came back and signed up as an agent. A rookie. Despised the waiting, loved the chase. Warren remembered those days.

No more than sixty yards to the north, three men emerged from the brush on the west side of the highway. They didn't see the SUV tucked in the shadows. Warren didn't move. The men began to hurry across the pavement, and now Warren raised his binoculars, but casually, not quickly. Danny didn't look up. Two of the men, carrying backpacks, made it across, but one was a straggler, moving as if he'd had enough of this crazy venture. He cradled one hand close to his belly.

Say something. Go after them. It's your job.

The binoculars were powerful enough to give Warren a good look at the straggler's face. Just a boy, really. Young, handsome. With a bloody cloth wrapped around his left hand.

The two other men waited for their injured friend to catch up, then they climbed the barbed-wire fence and slipped into the brush on this side of the highway. Total elapsed time: maybe twelve or fourteen seconds. If Warren had been looking down when they'd crossed, maybe fixing a cup of coffee or fiddling with the radio, he'd have never seen them. Like they'd never even been there. That thought gave him some comfort, that it would've been easy to miss them altogether. He lowered his binoculars. The illegals were long gone.

"Oh, come on," Danny said. "This can't be right. They're saying Betsy Ross didn't make the first American flag."

Ricky woke the next morning feeling a little better. His fever was down a degree and a half. Maybe the antiviral medication was working after all, or maybe it was just the Advil.

Mornings in the trailer were usually chaotic, because Ricky had five housemates—all of them day shift employees at Kountry Fresh, though none of them were hangers. But right now the trailer was silent. Ignacio, Ricky's roommate, was already up and gone. They shared the bedroom at the west end of the trailer. Trino and Oscar, the Salvadorans who'd been here since their country's civil war, had the bedroom on the opposite end, and Ruben and Victor, the Guatemalans, stayed in the center of the trailer, in the part that was meant to be a living room. They were all gone, too, because it was ten minutes to eight, and Ricky was running late. He quickly donned some jeans and a T-shirt and headed out the door.

When he clocked in at the plant, at five minutes past eight, there was a note, written in a woman's hand, taped to his timecard: *See Wayne immediately.* Ricky got a bad feeling in his stomach. He had heard the stories from the other chicken hangers, and he knew that going to see Wayne Skaggs, the operations manager, was never a good thing. Was he going to get scolded for being five minutes late? Maybe Wayne wanted to ask about Ricky's visit to the doctor, although that seemed doubtful.

Ricky made his way past the kill room, past marinating and mixing, and through a steel door into the administrative side of the building. It was much quieter over here, and it smelled of good coffee. He followed a clean, well-lighted, air-conditioned hallway, passing several open office doors. Some of the offices were occupied—white men sitting behind desks, wearing nice shirts and neckties, working on computers or talking on phones. Ricky knew some of their names, but not all, as they rarely appeared in the processing area. What did they do all day? They never laid a finger on a chicken, so how did they keep busy?

At the end of the hallway was Wayne's office, with Carmen, his secretary, sitting at a desk just outside. Carmen was often the topic of discussion among the men in the processing rooms. She had shiny black hair and straight, white teeth. She always wore high heels, short skirts, and blouses that clung to her body in a pleasing fashion. Carmen was from Laredo, a first-generation *norteamericano*, and she spoke Spanish and English equally well. But if you could get by with just English, as Ricky could, she refused to speak Spanish with you. Not a word. You could speak Spanish to her, but she always answered in English. Ricky had heard that Carmen earned fifteen dollars an hour, and he wondered if that could be true. She answered phone calls and did paperwork. How could that be worth so much more than the actual job of processing chickens?

When Ricky approached, Carmen was typing, her painted fingernails flying over the keyboard. Well, that was something Ricky couldn't do. He figured typing had to be worth some money. He noticed the large diamond ring on her left hand. Everybody knew that she was engaged to be married in the spring. Her suitor was a gringo, of course. She had a photograph of him on her desk—a big white man wearing camouflage, posing with a deer he had killed. He was an insurance salesman.

Carmen stopped and looked up without smiling. Ricky couldn't recall ever having seen her smile. *She'd be even more beautiful if she would only smile,* he thought.

"I had a note to see Wayne," he said. In English.

ॐ

Herschel Gandy lived in a four-thousand-square-foot home in the center of the ranch, with a crushed-gravel driveway running nearly three miles to the nearest pavement, the state highway.

He was in his office, on the phone, talking to one of his hunters—Walter Sevier, a man who'd leased from the Gandy family for nearly twenty years—when Clayton Dupree walked in carrying a gray backpack. It looked familiar.

"Best herd I've seen in years," Gandy told Sevier, who was a complainer. Sevier had shot some amazing deer on the ranch—including three that made the Boone & Crockett record book—but that was never enough. He was always asking for new perks. A better blind. Remote-control feeders. Satellite television—complete with adult programming—in the lodge. But if you gave him what he wanted, and then you raised the lease fees to cover the costs, look out! More complaining.

Today, as usual, Sevier was asking for something—better scouting cameras, "not those crappy ones we have now"—and Gandy was putting him off by talking about deer. He'd already described the "monstrous" twelve-pointer he'd seen the previous week, and he wasn't stretching the truth. Plentiful rains earlier this spring and summer had helped the deer thrive. Thicker, healthier vegetation, on top of supplemental protein feed, meant healthier deer, which meant better antlers, and that's what it was all about. Big racks. A head that would look good hanging over Sevier's fireplace, or in his executive office in downtown Dallas. The tactic worked—Sevier quit harping about new cameras—and Gandy said he looked forward to seeing him in a few weeks.

He hung up and said, "Swear to God, that guy gets a boner that lasts from November until January. We got any new shots from the cameras?"

"Plenty."

"E-mail him a couple. Give him something to fantasize about until opening day."

Clayton responded by saying, "We might have a problem." Sounding strange.

"Yeah? What's up?"

Clayton lifted the backpack by one of the shoulder straps. There was a large, dark stain just below the zipper that ran across the top of the pack. In the center of the stain was a small, ragged hole. A bullet hole.

Clayton said, "That's blood, Herschel."

Gandy didn't say anything at first. Just stared at the backpack. The stain did look like blood, though it had gone from red to brownish-black. "Where'd you find it?"

"Right where them three wets was standing. I was filling feeders this morning and I saw it."

Gandy was wondering about his riflescope. Had it gotten jostled at some point? A blow could've knocked the aim off. And what about the slight breeze that had been swaying the blind? That could've ruined the shot. "You find anything else?"

"I took Sherlock down there and turned him loose. He didn't find nothing."

There were hundreds of feral hogs on the ranch, and hunters enjoyed using Clayton's scent hound, a big Catahoula named Sherlock, to track them. Sherlock had a nose like a radar system. If there were a body in the brush, he would've found it.

"Hell," Gandy said, "that kid might've cut his hand on some barb wire, or on a cactus. Any number of ways that blood coulda got there."

Clayton didn't say anything, but he didn't look convinced.

"Well, shit," Gandy said.

"Maybe we should call somebody."

"Yeah, like who? The sheriff? The Border Patrol?"

"Either one."

"What for?"

"Tell our side before they tell theirs."

"They ain't gonna tell anybody anything."

"I wouldn't be so sure."

"You're paranoid," Gandy said.

"I hope so."

"We'll just sit tight. Wait and see."

"Maybe we should have a story ready," Clayton said.

Which was probably a good idea. Gandy knew the truth wouldn't necessarily suffice. Thirty years ago it would've, or even twenty, but not today. "Like what?"

"Say I hollered at 'em in Spanish. Told 'em they was trespassing. They hollered back, yelling insults. One of 'em dug into his backpack ..."

Gandy liked where this was going. "And came out with something that looked like a handgun," he said.

"It was getting dark, so it was hard to tell for sure."

"He pointed it at us, so we had no choice. I fired a warning shot, and they ran off. We didn't know I'd hit anybody or we'd've called it in."

"Yeah. Damn right."

Gandy thought about it for a minute. The fabrication seemed bulletproof. The word of two upstanding U.S. citizens against the word of three illegals.

"Maybe you should talk to Brent Nielsen, just in case," Clayton added.

Gandy thought about that, too. Nielsen was one of the family attorneys. Local guy. "Maybe so."

"What should I do with this?" Clayton asked, meaning the backpack.

Gandy made a pass-it-here gesture. Clayton handed it over, and Gandy placed it on his desk, careful to avoid touching the blood, and unzipped it. Started pulling out the contents: four pint-sized bottles of water, some moldy tortillas wrapped in foil, a bag of peanuts, a package of beef jerky, a tightly rolled pair of faded jeans, a green T-shirt featuring the logo of a Mexican radio station, a flashlight, a cell phone.

Gandy opened the phone and scrolled through the menu. It was a prepaid phone on the T-Mobile network. Minutes left: five hundred. Calls placed: none. Calls received: none. Contacts stored in memory: just one. *Ricky.*

Gandy left the phone on his desk, but started stuffing the rest of the items into the backpack. "Go back to the blind and collect the casings. Then take all this shit and throw it in the river."

THREE

Wayne Skaggs had a fish mounted on the wall behind his desk. It looked like a trophy bass on a wooden plaque, but Ricky had heard about it from some of the other workers and knew it was really a toy—a birthday gift that Wayne's wife had given him a few months earlier. Push a button and the fish sings silly songs. Ricky couldn't imagine that Wayne ever pushed the button. On another wall were three stuffed deer heads, all of them with humongous antlers. Very lifelike, except for the eyes, which looked glassy.

Skaggs, too, had glassy eyes, and he smelled like liquor. He was probably fifty years old—a big man, at least six feet tall. Thick all over, with a big belly and muscles that were beginning to go soft. Like he used to perform hard physical labor when he was younger, but now he was in the middle of a slow decline. Some of the men said Wayne had been a prison guard many years ago, and that he had killed an inmate with his bare hands, but Ricky didn't know if that was true. Probably a rumor Wayne had started himself just so people would fear him.

He had invited Ricky into his office, told him to sit down, and closed the door. That wasn't a good omen. Whatever Wayne was going to say, apparently he didn't want Carmen to hear it. Ricky sat in a metal-framed chair, and Wayne was in the leather swivel chair behind his desk. The fluorescent lights overhead were buzzing. Now Ricky was feeling hot again. The fever. His stomach was not behaving well.

"You a troublemaker, José?" Wayne asked. He was sometimes hard to understand because his Texas accent was so thick. Calling Ricky *José* was not a mistake. He called all the workers *José*.

Ricky was puzzled by the question. "No, sir."

"Hell if you ain't. I can tell by looking at you. Goddamn troublemaker through and through. Right now, you're causing a couple of problems, and problems piss me off. I like everything running smoothly, and when somebody like you gums up the works, Christ, it really irritates me. *¿Comprende?*"

"Yes, but—"

"I got a ulcer the size of a goddamn silver dollar. My cholesterol count looks like Lance Berkman's batting average. Last thing I need is for you to create a bunch of headaches. Whatever you do on your own time, I don't give a shit. But here at Kountry Fresh, you toe the line. You follow what I'm sayin'?"

Ricky wasn't certain, but he nodded his head anyway. "What problems?"

Wayne opened a manila envelope, removed a single sheet of paper, and placed it on the desk in front of Ricky. "You care to explain this big turd?"

Ricky looked at it. Across the top it had an official seal from the Social Security Administration. Before Ricky could begin to read it, Wayne said, "Goddamn no-match letter. You know what that means?"

Ricky had heard other workers complaining about no-match letters on occasion, but he hadn't listened closely. "No, sir."

"According to the feds, the number you been using belongs to somebody else. You know anything about that? You give us a fake Social when you filled out your application?"

This was horrible news. The kind of thing that got a man deported. Ricky saw no other option but to lie. "No, sir."

"Well, it's a fucked-up god-awful pain in the ass, that's what it is. You realize the plant could be fined ten thousand bucks if we don't get this shit straightened out?"

"I don't want any problems," Ricky said. "I just want to work."

Wayne shook his head again and let out a long sigh. He seemed a little less angry now. "I understand that, but shit, I just don't know. This puts my ass on the line, too, and I want you to know I don't appreciate it. Listen, frankly, I don't care if you're in this country illegal or not, and I don't wanna know if you are, 'cause you're a damn good worker and I'd hate to lose you. But I think the best thing for me to do is to call the cops and let them sort this thing out. I hate to do it, I really do."

Ricky was starting to sweat. He didn't want to be sent home. There was little for him there. And every day it was getting harder to make it back into the United States. Immense fences were being built, with lights and cameras and motion sensors. More agents were patrolling the border than ever before. He'd even heard radio commercials that were intended to recruit more agents. *We protect America. Are you up for the challenge?* Ricky didn't know what to say, so he sat silently. His belly was churning.

Then Wayne said, "Before I do that, there might be one thing we can try."

Ricky waited.

Wayne pulled a pack of Pall Mall cigarettes from his shirt pocket and lit one up, even though it was a health code violation to smoke anywhere in the building. He stared at Ricky for several seconds, as if deciding whether he truly wanted to pursue this other alternative or not. Finally, he said, "I got a friend who works at the Social Security office in Laredo. He's helped me out with a couple of these letters in the past. Know what I mean? See, what he can do is get you a brand new number. The real deal. Give you a fresh start. You interested in an arrangement like that?"

"Yes, very much."

Wayne took a long pull on his cigarette and blew the smoke toward the ceiling. "Only thing is, it costs eight hundred dollars."

Mierda. Eight hundred dollars. That was a lot of money. Ricky had about six hundred dollars saved up, but he'd been hoping to buy an old Nissan truck that Howard had gotten at a county auction. They'd agreed on a price of nine hundred dollars. Now that money would be gone, and more. It was disappointing, but Ricky knew that nothing could be done about it. Setbacks like this were to be expected. You had to plan for them.

"Can I pay you a little at a time?" he asked.

"No can do. It's gotta be a cash deal, all up front. That's the way my friend likes it."

"Can I give it to you on Friday?"

"The sooner the better."

Ricky would be paid on Friday morning. He'd cash his check at lunchtime and get the money to Wayne afterward. "I'll have it on Friday afternoon."

Ricky began to stand, but Wayne said, "Not so fast, amigo." Ricky sat back down. "Problem number two. You're not supposed to get personal calls at work. That ain't just a suggestion, it's a rule. No personal calls. Ever. No exceptions. You wanna make a call, you do it from the phone in the break room. You clear on that?"

How could his wife have seen that singing fish and thought, *Oh, here's the perfect gift for Wayne?*

"But I haven't received any calls," Ricky said.

"You did this morning. Carmen took it, and she ain't got time to be your personal secretary." Wayne picked up a pink telephone message slip off his desk. "You know someone named Tomás?"

"Yes. He's my brother." Ricky had mailed Tomás a cell phone, with the number at the plant already programmed in. But he'd instructed Tomás not to use it unless it was an emergency.

Wayne said, "Well, I'm not sure how accurate this is, because Carmen said she couldn't hear him real good, and the call disconnected in the middle, but the long and short of it is that your brother had a little trouble last night."

Ricky was feeling lightheaded. "What kind of trouble?" *La migra,* no doubt. Tomás had been caught. Wouldn't they have taken his phone?

Wayne shrugged. "Carmen's not a hundred percent, but he mighta said something about getting shot."

Ricky couldn't seem to get enough air. His heart was pounding. He opened his mouth to ask another question—*Is Tomás okay?*—but he instead vomited on the linoleum floor of Wayne's office.

"Jesus fucking Christ," Wayne said. "Carmen! We're gonna need a mop in here!"

At three in the afternoon, Beth Ann Couch looked up from the romance novel she was reading when she heard the tinkling of the bell on the front door of the drugstore. It had been slow since lunch, but now she finally had a customer. A young Hispanic man. Filthy from head to toe, and she knew what that meant. A laborer on a lunch break, or a newly arrived immigrant, but illegal either way.

She gave the man a warm smile. He nodded in reply, glanced around the store, and proceeded to aisle four. The first aid section.

Frankly, Beth Ann didn't understand what all the fuss was about. So what if people from other countries wanted to come to the United States? Who could blame them? Besides, wasn't that how everybody had gotten here? Well, unless you were a native American Indian. They were already living here, wearing deerskin moccasins and hunting buffalo. Heck, back then, if the Indians had had the same attitude as most of the people in Rugoso, plus a little more fire-power, we wouldn't even *own* this country. But you start talking that way in a town of three thousand people—pointing out the irony—and boy could things get ugly fast. People calling you un-American. Calling you unpatriotic. Hypocrites is what they were, complaining about the illegals, then hiring them on a regular basis for the jobs the locals didn't want.

Beth Ann had never had an occasion to hire any of the illegals herself. Not much they could help with in a drugstore. That was probably for the best, be-cause, well, even though Beth Ann was totally open-minded—she really was—everybody knew that Mexicans sometimes stole things. Sad, but true. Not that white people didn't steal things, too. She always tried to keep that in mind, that one race wasn't any more trustworthy than the other. Heck, the Theriot boy had come in just the other day and tried to swipe a *Cosmopolitan* from the magazine rack. Stuck it under his jacket, like Beth Ann didn't know exactly what the little perv was up to. But she nailed his little butt and gave him a stern talking-to. Sent him packing.

No, she figured it was best to keep an eye on everybody—white, brown, black, or green—even if one color might be a little more inclined toward crimi-nal conduct than another, especially if they'd already proven themselves capable of breaking the law by sneaking over the border. So Beth Ann made her way over to aisle four, thinking it might be a good opportunity to protect her inven-tory while simultaneously using the small amount of Spanish she'd learned dur-ing her freshman year at Rugoso High School.

"*Hola*," she said in a very friendly manner, forgetting that the "H" was si-lent, but proving that she was not the least bit judgmental or resentful about his presence.

"Buenas tardes," the man replied.

In Spanish, Beth Ann attempted to say, "Is there something I can help you with?" What she really said was, "May I assist with yourself?"

The man rattled something back at her, too fast for her to catch most of it, but she recognized the word *gasa.* Gauze.

She said, "Yes, the gauze is right over here," though it came out as, "Yes, gauze is in the proper location."

She pointed at several types of gauze, both rolls and pads, feeling very proud of herself. See, it really wasn't that difficult for all of us to coexist. Communication was the key.

He selected a roll of gauze, then said something else. Again, she didn't understand, except for the word *antibiótico.* That was easy enough.

"Do you mean you need an ointment?" she tried to ask, instead saying, "Can you intend to own any ugly salve?"

He smiled. *"Antibiótico,"* he repeated, then rubbed a finger on the back of his other hand, as if he were applying a cream.

"Neosporin?" she said, which, in fact, came out as "Neosporin?"

"Sí. Yes. Neosporin."

Now they were getting somewhere.

She showed him the Neosporin, then he grabbed a bottle of Advil without any assistance at all, then they trooped together to the front counter, where she rang the items up.

Still speaking Spanish, she said, "Are you enjoying your stay in Rugoso?" ("Is this rugged pleasure for you?")

He laughed, which seemed an odd response. *"Sí.* Very much."

He pulled a worn leather wallet from his hip pocket, handed her several crumpled bills, and she gave him some change back.

She didn't know what else to say, so she stuck the items in a plastic sack and he said, *"Gracias."*

"De nada."

As he exited through the door, she could see that he had two friends waiting outside—both about his age, both equally sweaty and dirty. Truthfully, she was glad they'd chosen not to enter the store. Three Mexicans at once would've been a tad overwhelming. She'd shown herself to be a fair-minded and non-judgmental representative of her nation, but there was only so much biculturalism she could handle in one day.

FOUR

SOMETIMES, WHEN HERSCHEL GANDY spoke to his father, he wished the miserable old man would just die already. Sure would make life easier. Like right now, Sam Gandy was calling from his home in Houston, saying, "Walter Sevier is giving me hell about those scouting cameras. Wants to know why you're being so damn stubborn."

Always talking too loud, because he was going deaf. Herschel Gandy could hold the phone two feet away from his ear and still make out every word.

"He *called* you?" Herschel replied. He hated it when one of the longtime hunters went over his head. The newer ones never did that. They'd never met Sam Gandy.

"What?"

"He shouldn't have bothered you."

"I've known Walter Sevier for thirty years. He can call me whenever he damn well pleases."

"He's a pushy son of a bitch."

"What?"

"He's pushy."

"What's the story with the cameras?"

Getting senile, too. Christ, they'd gone over this three times already. Most scouting cameras worked like this: When an animal visits a feeder, the camera senses the body heat and snaps a photo. Simple. But all cameras weren't created equal. Sevier wanted the deluxe models, the ones that took the highest-quality photos possible and also shot short video clips. They had a built-in viewing screen, too, so you could sort through the photos and clips without hooking the camera up to your computer. Pricy, and not a good idea, for obvious reasons.

"Dad, it's a waste of money. The cameras he wants cost about a thousand apiece, and we'd be lucky if they lasted a full season out there."

"What's the problem?"

"Wetbacks, Dad."

"What?"

"The wetbacks."

"Jesus, son, haven't you run them off yet?"

Sam Gandy had never lived on the ranch, and he hadn't even visited it in ten years, so he simply didn't understand the situation. To him, from the time he'd bought the place in the late seventies, it had been nothing more than a refuge from the workaday world in Houston, a place to unwind with his oil industry buddies, drink some whiskey, entertain some women, and maybe even shoot a deer. Until seven years ago, he'd had a resident foreman who'd handled everything—the cattle, the deer hunters, and the problems with trespassing immigrants. But the foreman had retired, and Herschel had offered to run the ranch himself. Some days he regretted it.

"You don't just run 'em off, Dad. They're not squatters. It's different ones every day. Hell, every hour. You wouldn't believe how many there are. They steal everything they can. Dad, they eat the corn out of the feeders. Can you believe that?"

"Well, call the sheriff. Me and him go way back. I contributed to his reelection fund."

"There's nothing he can do. I've talked to the chief deputy, and he says it's the Border Patrol's problem."

"Then call *them*."

"I have, a thousand times, along with everybody else in the county. You don't know what's going on down here. Hell, I tell 'em exactly where the wetbacks are crossing, but they don't listen. I call it in, and an hour later I see 'em screwing around on some other part of the ranch. They don't go where I tell them to."

"I just don't understand why they'd steal those cameras."

"Why do they steal anything?"

"What?"

Herschel Gandy heard a strange noise. A buzzing. No, more of a humming.

"So they can sell them," Herschel shouted. When he lost his patience, he could shout. Made no difference. Sam Gandy thought his son was simply trying to be heard.

"Can't you chain 'em down?"

"Which, the cameras or the Mexicans?" Herschel couldn't help but smile. That was a good one.

"What?"

The humming again. Then he realized what it was. The phone in his desk drawer. The wetback's cell phone.

"Dad, I have to go. I'll talk to you later."

"Brent Nielsen says you called him. What's that—"

Gandy hung up and took a deep breath. Lord, it took patience sometimes. Then he opened the drawer. The phone was lying there like a rattlesnake ready to strike. It hummed again. It was set to vibrate. Well, sure. That made sense. If the wetback had it set to ring, and it happened to go off when he was hiding in the brush from the Border Patrol, wouldn't that be a story for the grandkids some day? Talk about a stupid way to get caught.

Gandy picked up the phone and checked the viewer display on the outside. *Ricky.*

∽

Ricky had never been angry while doing his job, but he found that it made him tremendously efficient. He was hanging chickens more quickly than ever before, bird after bird, crate after crate, to the point that there were brief moments—sometimes a full minute—when there were no chickens to hang. The two other hangers in the room were watching him out of the corners of their eyes, wondering what had gotten into their coworker, working harder than he had to.

Wayne Skaggs was such a fool. Why would he tell Ricky about Tomás *after* telling him about the problem with his Social Security number? Ricky did not value his job more than his own flesh and blood, but he could see that Wayne did.

And Carmen! When she had taken the call, why hadn't she asked for details? Was Tomás in a hospital? Which one? Who had shot him? When? Where? Why? All valid questions, but she hadn't asked any of them. The only thing she could tell Ricky was that Tomás hadn't made the call himself; she had spoken to a man named Vicente. Tomás didn't have any friends named Vicente.

Ricky had gone to the phone in the break room and called Tomás's cell phone number, but nobody had answered. Perhaps *la migra* had taken his phone away. When you are arrested in the United States, you are allowed one phone call, but did that rule apply to illegal immigrants? Would Tomás have a chance to call again? The question Ricky didn't want to ask himself: Was Tomás dead? It was a possibility.

He continued working, trying not to think about it. By the time he clocked out at six, he'd sent more than twenty thousand chickens to their deaths that morning and afternoon, plump birds that would end up on the tables of men like Wayne Skaggs. Ricky's arms were weary from the sheer combined weight of the poultry he'd hoisted. His hair was matted with sweat and urine. The feces had begun to dry on his forearms, forming a crusty shield over his skin.

He cleaned up as best he could, then went outside, unlocked his bicycle, and began the ride across town.

Past the hardware store. Past the Super S. Past the police department, whose deputies never asked your immigration status, because, as Howard said, they were too busy to be in "the deportation business." Past the strip of rental storage units, where Trino had once stolen an air compressor.

It would be a long night. He wished there were a phone at the trailer, in case Tomás tried to call. He considered calling Tomás's wife in Oaxaca—perhaps she'd heard something—but why frighten her if she hadn't?

Past the liquor store that had the best price on Coors Light, the barbecue restaurant, the auto shop, the small motel that employed maids who had no papers.

He was so tired. He had to shake this flu.

Past the pizza shop, the video rental store that was always crowded, the bookstore that was never crowded, the side street that he sometimes followed to Howard's house.

He turned on the dirt road that led behind the trees to the row of trailers, all owned by the poultry plant, all inhabited by workers who paid rent in the amount of one hundred and fifty dollars a month. Six to each trailer, one bathroom, no air conditioning unless you bought and installed your own window unit.

Up ahead, between Ricky's trailer and the neighboring one, were several large picnic tables where some of the residents would gather after a long day of work. Sometimes they would barbecue on a propane grill that Ruben had taken from the back porch of an empty house that had a FOR SALE sign in front, or they would simply sit and talk and drink beer late into the night. This evening, there was a larger crowd than usual. Ten or twelve men—half of them sitting, half standing—and there in the center, waving a bandaged hand as he told a story that had them all wide-eyed, was Tomás.

***

Herschel Gandy entered the Alegria Bistro and Wine Bar in Laredo at twenty after six and spotted Brent Nielsen seated at an isolated table in the back. Nielsen was an easy man to spot. Nice looking guy, about Gandy's age, but very tall and slender, and exceedingly fair-skinned. Scandinavian roots. See him walking down the street among the Mexicans and he looked like some sort of freak. You'd never guess he could speak Spanish as well as, or better than, anybody in the restaurant. It came from his dad being some sort of ambassador to Mexico when Nielsen was a kid, living in Mexico City. The lawyer rose as Gandy approached. They shook hands, and both of them sat.

"You're looking good, Herschel," Nielsen said. "Living on the ranch agrees with you." He was proper that way. Always knew the right thing to say. Not a suck-up, just smooth. Probably a big hit at Rotary Club luncheons.

"What're you drinking?" Gandy asked.

"Bohemia."

A waiter was suddenly at Gandy's elbow. "Same thing," Gandy said, nodding at Nielsen's mug.

They made small talk for a few minutes—Nielsen asking about the upcoming deer season, because he was an occasional hunter himself—then Gandy got right to it.

"Look, anything we discuss—it's privileged, right?"

Nielsen kept a poker face. "That depends on what it is. In general, yes.

What's up?"

"There was an incident at the ranch."

"What sort of incident?"

The waiter brought Gandy's beer and he took a long drink. Set the mug down and said, "It's probably nothing, but I wanted to cover my ass, just in case."

Nielsen waited.

Gandy said, "There were some illegals coming in. You know how that goes. It's a daily occurrence out there. So me and Clayton—lately, we've been doing something about it."

Still no expression on Nielsen's face. "Doing what, exactly?"

Gandy took another gulp of his beer. "This has to stay between you and me. I don't want my dad involved."

After a moment, Nielsen nodded.

"Okay, what we do is scare 'em a little, that's all. We fire a couple of shots in their general direction."

Now Nielsen showed some emotion. "You *shoot* at them?" As if he couldn't quite believe what he was hearing.

"Christ, keep it down. Not *at* them. *Near* them."

"Why on earth would you do something like that?"

"It's not a big deal. They run away, and that's that. Only thing that works."

Nielsen was shaking his head. "You know how dumb that is? You put yourself, and your dad, in a position of extreme liability. There was an outfit called Ranch Rescue that—"

The waiter appeared again, ready to take their dinner order. Grilled mahi-mahi for Nielsen, steak churrasco and another beer for Gandy.

When the waiter left, Gandy said, "Look, I don't need a lecture, okay?"

"Well, it wouldn't do any good now anyway. What's done is done. You'd better walk me through it. The 'incident.'"

So Gandy did. Told him about the three wetbacks, the warning shots, the blood on the backpack. Didn't say anything about the cell phone, or the call from someone named Ricky. This Ricky had left a voicemail, but Gandy didn't know the password to get to it.

Nielsen had that expression on his face again—judgmental—so Gandy said, "Look, I'm not sure I even hit the guy, okay? But even if I did, it wasn't on purpose. Now I just need to know if my ass is in a bind or not."

"When did this happen?"

"Last night, just before dark."

"And nothing since then? No police?"

"Nope. See, I figure he wasn't hurt too bad or the cops would've been in touch by now."

"Not necessarily. Maybe he hasn't spoken to them yet."

"If he was going to, why would he wait?"

"This might surprise you, but illegal aliens tend to be fearful of policemen." Gandy didn't care for the attorney's tone. Sarcastic.

"You're not making me feel any better about this."

"Is that what you want? For me to say you did the right thing?"

"You're saying it was wrong? That I should just let them take over my land?"

"Don't put words in my mouth," Nielsen snapped.

"You hear what happened in San Ygnacio?"

Of course he had. Everybody had heard about it. Eight days earlier, drug mules had crossed the river, invaded a woman's home, raped her repeatedly, then left her duct-taped to a chair. She was found five days later, dehydrated and near death.

"You can't use that as an excuse to be a vigilante," Nielsen hissed.

"Keep it down. And lose the attitude."

"You're incredible."

More than anything, Gandy wanted to punch him in the face. But that would only make things worse. He might need this guy later. "Okay," Gandy said. "I get it. It was a stupid thing to do. I'll admit that. But now what? What's gonna happen if this guy makes trouble?"

"Honestly, I have no idea. I'm not a criminal attorney. You know that."

Criminal. How could anyone think that word applied here? Gandy said, "I've been trying to put myself in his shoes. What would I do in this situation? Well, if it was me—if it was just a flesh wound—shit, that's easy. I'd get on down the road and forget about the whole thing. Otherwise, if I made trouble, I'd get deported, right?"

"Not necessarily."

"Would you quit saying that?"

Nielsen scoffed. "You want me to lie to you?"

The waiter brought Gandy's second beer. He quickly drank half of it. "What happens if he goes to a hospital?" Gandy asked. "Will they treat him?"

"Of course they will. Ever heard of EMTALA?"

Gandy shook his head. "Some sort of Mexican pastry?" Another good one. The beer was already loosening him up some.

No smile from Nielsen. "The Emergency Medical Treatment and Active Labor Act. It was signed into law in 1985. It's an unfunded federal mandate that says emergency rooms can't turn anyone away, even if they're uninsured, even if they're here illegally, and even if they can't pay."

"That's insane," Gandy said, and for once, Nielsen didn't disagree.

"It's causing a lot of problems, especially in the past few years," Nielsen said. "Bankrupting hospitals. Really screwing up Medicaid and SSI."

"If he goes in for treatment, what then?"

"What are you asking?"

"Will they deport him or not?"

"The hospital's not going to deport anybody. What you mean is, will they contact Immigrations, and I'd say that's doubtful. Most hospitals deal with dozens of undocumented immigrants every day. But I can tell you this for sure: any person who comes in with a gunshot wound—illegal alien or not—the medical staff is obligated to report it to the police."

Not good.

FIVE

W ARREN COLEMAN'S WIFE ELLEN was throwing together a casserole, since it was her night to cook and his night to do dishes. Canned chicken breast, with noodles and mushrooms and diced green peppers. The old standby. Nothing fancy, because she had papers to grade later. She taught English to a bunch of eighth graders at a private school. Warren would sooner juggle chainsaws blindfolded.

He was still in uniform, drinking a can of beer, perched on a stool on the other side of the pass-through serving bar. He said, "Last week—Thursday— me and Danny were—"

Ellen made a clucking sound.

"Danny and I," he said, "were eating lunch in Rugoso and this man comes up to our table. He said he'd found eight thousand dollars in cash in his son's bedroom, and he was worried that the kid was working with drug runners. Said the kid's been skipping school, putting a lot of miles on his truck. The man had been to the sheriff's office, but they brushed him off. Said they'd talk to the kid, but they never did. So he saw us sitting there and decided to ask us what to do. Stupid me, I agreed to talk to the boy. Andrew. We went to the school, but Andrew wasn't there, so we called his cell number, and he agreed to meet us in the parking lot of the Dairy Queen."

"You want a salad with this?" Ellen asked as she rinsed a paring knife. She'd heard a thousand stories like this one.

"Don't go to a lot of trouble."

"Yes or no?"

"No."

"What did you have for lunch?"

"Enchiladas."

"We should have a salad."

"Either way is fine with me."

She opened the refrigerator. "Crap, we don't have any tomatoes. We don't even have any lettuce until I can shop this weekend. How about a can of peaches instead?"

"That's fine."

She proceeded to the pantry and started moving some cans around.

"Anyway," he said, "we talk to this Andrew—we tell him what his dad said—and he says no, he's not dealing drugs. Nothing like that. So where did all the cash come from? He didn't want to tell us at first, but we kept after him, and he finally admits he's been selling hamburgers to the wets."

She often rebuked him when he used that term—"wets"—but not tonight. Instead she said, "No peaches either. Pears okay?"

Warren wasn't particularly fond of pears. "Yeah, whatever," he said. "See, what Andrew would do is buy a hundred burgers at a time off the dollar menu at McDonald's, then he'd meet the *coyotes* and their groups and sell the burgers for two bucks apiece. Seven days a week he's been doing this, sometimes several trips a day, so he's been pulling in some pretty good cash."

Ellen was opening the can of pears, and now she dumped them into a bowl for them to share. Fewer dishes to wash that way. The pears looked a little brown. She raised the bowl to sniff them. They seemed to pass inspection.

"Nothing illegal about it," Warren said, "unless he doesn't pay income taxes. Hell, the kid's building his own college fund. Dad should be proud, right?"

She went back to the fridge to weigh their beverage options. "Iced tea?" She came out with a blue pitcher.

"I've got a beer," he said.

She took two large glasses from a cabinet, opened the freezer door, and began to fill the glasses with ice.

"I have to get up early tomorrow," Warren said. "Eddie wants me in his office at seven."

"Tomorrow?"

"Yeah, tomorrow morning."

"What for?"

"He didn't say."

Ellen tipped the pitcher and filled both glasses with tea. Then she opened the oven, removed the casserole, and placed it on one of the stovetop burners.

Warren said, "I don't even know what I'm doing anymore. Today I saw three of them crossing Eighty-Three and I just let 'em go. It looked like one had injured his hand pretty bad, and I could've gotten him some medical attention at least, but I didn't do anything at all."

Ellen was digging at the casserole with a metal spatula, plopping steaming portions onto two plates. "You're gonna have to let this dish soak," she said.

◦

Ricky hugged Tomás, of course—even right there in front of the other men—because he was so relieved and happy to see his younger brother. Now Ricky felt foolish for having let his imagination run wild. Tomás was fine. He was standing right here, not lying in a morgue. His hand was injured, but he was fine.

"I got your message at the plant," Ricky said in Spanish. "What happened to you?"

"I was in the middle of my story with these guys," Tomás said. He was grinning. He had a beer in his right hand, the one that wasn't wrapped in gauze. "It was crazy."

"Tell me."

Tomás tipped his beer can and drained the contents. Oscar, standing nearby, quickly popped the top on another can—Tomás obviously couldn't do it himself—and passed the fresh can to him. Tomás took a drink and paused for a moment. He had always been a dramatic storyteller.

"We got across without any problems," he said.

"Who were you with? A group?" Ricky asked.

"Me and two other men I had never met before. They're already on their way to San Antonio."

Ricky studied Tomás's face as he spoke. He had changed in the two years since Ricky had last seen him. Tomás wasn't such a boy anymore.

"They said they knew a good place to enter, and they were right about that. We were on a large ranch, following a *sendero* that would take us to the highway. From there we were to cross another ranch that would take us to another highway—the one that leads to Rugoso. One of the men, Luis, said he knew where we could get water, or even food if we were desperate."

Ricky understood what that meant. There were seasonal homes and hunting cabins. When Ricky had crossed three years earlier, his group had broken into several empty homes and stolen all sorts of things.

Tomás said, "Less than thirty minutes after wading the river, we came over a small hill and saw a hunting blind—a tower high off the ground. The other guys wondered if it was deer season, and I told them it wasn't, but I thought I saw something moving inside the blind. I tried to tell them we should go around it, but Luis didn't want to leave the *sendero*. It was beginning to get dark, and there was no moon, and they were worried that we would get lost in the brush. One of the men was scared of javelinas, but I told him that was silly. We all had flashlights, but we couldn't risk using them. So I said we should go back a little ways and wait until morning, but they didn't want to do that either. They wanted to make it to the first highway before midnight."

Tomás was enjoying himself—drawing the tale out—but Ricky was getting impatient. "So what happened?"

"We pushed forward, planning to run if anybody began to climb down from the blind. We hadn't seen a vehicle anywhere nearby, and we figured we could outrun any fat *americano*."

Everyone laughed.

"We took each step slowly, and again I thought I saw something moving, but one of the other men said it could be birds living inside the deer blind. That made sense to me at first, and then I realized how wrong he was. See, the blind had little windows on every side of it, for the hunter to see out. And the windows in the front were *open*. That made no sense. Wouldn't the hunters *close* the windows at the end of the season? To keep birds and insects out? To keep rain out?"

The men were totally absorbed by Tomás's story. Several men nodded in agreement, but nobody said anything.

Tomás said, "I was just about to point out this fact—to ask them why the windows were open—when ... BLAM!"

Tomás slapped the top of the picnic table with his good hand. Several men jumped, then giggled nervously.

"There was a shot!" Tomás said. "And I felt a burning pain in my hand, as if it had been stung by a hornet."

"What did you do?" Trino asked.

"What do you think we did? We ran! Back the way we'd come, but there were more shots. BLAM! BLAM! BLAM!"

"How many?"

"I wasn't counting, but at least seven or eight. Maybe more. I could hear each shot flying over our heads. He was trying to kill us! He kept shooting until we made it over the hill. It was the scariest thing I've ever experienced."

Tomás took a long drink of beer, satisfied that he had told his story well.

"There must have been two men shooting," Trino said. "Most deer rifles don't hold that many bullets."

"What do you know about hunting rifles?" Oscar said to him.

"I used to hunt when I was young. Most rifles hold five or six bullets. Not a dozen."

Victor said, "Maybe it was a military weapon. They're easy to get here."

"Where did you go after the shooting?" Oscar asked.

Tomás said, "We found a narrow trail into the brush, and we followed it for about a hundred meters. That's where we slept for the night. The next morning, just as we were getting ready to leave, we heard a vehicle. We moved closer for a better look, and we saw a truck pass by with one man in it. He went over the hill, back to the deer blind, and we heard him stop. A few minutes later, we heard the engine again, and the truck passed by in the other direction. We waited for an hour, until we thought it was safe, then we continued on the *sendero*, past the deer blind." Tomás grinned. "This time, the windows were closed."

"You lost your pack?" Ricky asked.

"I did, including the phone you sent me."

"What happened to the men you were with?" someone asked.

"They stayed with me until they were sure I was okay. They bandaged my hand in Rugoso."

Ricky studied Tomás's hand. The gauze was dirty, and blood had seeped to the outermost layer. "How badly is it injured?" Ricky asked.

"Bad," Tomás said. "It throbs constantly, because the medicine is wearing off."

"What medicine?"

"One of the men gave me some pills."

"What kind of pills?"

"I don't know. Codeine, I think. They're all gone now. I took some Advil a little while ago, but it isn't helping much."

Ricky didn't like the idea that Tomás had taken pills without knowing exactly what they were. "Do you need a doctor?"

"Perhaps."

"We'd better take a look. You need a fresh bandage anyway."

Tomás set his beer down and began to unwrap the gauze slowly from his left hand. It was obvious that he was in a lot of pain. All of the men watched quietly. With each layer of gauze that Tomás unwound, the layer underneath was more and more bloody.

"I warn you that this isn't pretty," Tomás said. "It could ruin your dinner."

Some of the men laughed. Nobody looked away.

Tomás continued unwrapping, until he was down to the final layer of gauze. He pulled it away, wincing as he did so, and Ricky was horrified by what he saw.

Tomás no longer had a thumb on his left hand.

jueves

SIX

Howard Iczkowski was eighty-four years old and couldn't remember the last time he'd slept past five in the morning. That wouldn't be so bad, except he could never fall asleep before one o'clock the following morning. Make sense of that. A tiring cycle: sleepy all day, but he'd never developed the ability to nap. Then wide awake at night, watching that tall redheaded talk show host, or that silly Scottish man. Jay Leno was okay—more of an old-school host like Carson, his predecessor. A true legend. Good old Johnny, long gone.

Now Howard's clock read 4:38 AM, and he was lying in bed, knowing there'd be no more sleep. He could hear a familiar sound—*ploink!*—coming from the kitchen. Every minute or so, *ploink!*

Wasn't like he had much to get up for, but he didn't mean that in a defeatist way. You live a good life, work hard, then you retire, and what? Your wife of fifty-one years dies and your only child moves to Dallas. You're on your own now.

Well, you kept busy the best you could. Harder during the week, because the world was working. Very few garage sales on weekdays. Sometimes on Fridays. Sertoma meetings once a month, but he didn't know many of the members anymore. What're you gonna do? Become a greeter at Wal-Mart and deal with people who'd just as soon run you over with their carts? Play chess at the park?

Howard swung his legs sideways and dropped his feet to the carpet. He looked for Roscoe in his own bed on the floor. Then he remembered. Roscoe died last year. Howard had thought about getting another dog, another rescue from the shelter, but he was too old for that.

He simply sat for a few minutes, letting his blood circulate. Get up too quickly and he'd be lightheaded.

Ploink!

Johnny used to have some fantastic guests. Frank Sinatra. Dean Martin. Jimmy Stewart. Judy Garland. Ray Charles. George Carlin. All of them gone now. Real entertainers. Not like the guests Leno had to put up with. Actors Howard had never heard of, hawking their latest piece-of-crap movie. Explosions and special effects. Fighting terrorists or psychotic serial killers. Where was Spencer Tracy when you needed him? What happened to genuine drama? Authentic human emotion?

Howard rose slowly and padded in his socks to the kitchen to put some coffee on. *If you're having insomnia,* his doctor had said, *you need to cut back on your coffee, or switch to decaf.* You kidding me, doc?

While it was brewing, he flipped the switch for the light over the carport and peered out the window, past his hulking Buick, to the end of the short driveway. Wishful thinking. The newspaper rarely arrived before five thirty, and it would be even later today, because it had begun to drizzle overnight. The newspaper was part of his regular routine. Howard would read every word, not counting the ads, which would keep him busy until Regis came on. Howard liked to stay up on current events, even though most of the articles were depressing. The planet had turned bitter and ugly. For kids, though, it was the status quo. Hatred. Fear. Vengefulness. Paranoia. Don't trust anyone who isn't just like you.

He went to the bathroom, patiently took a leak, then went back into the kitchen and checked the saucepan resting on the vinyl floor. Directly overhead was a yellow stain in the ceiling. The pan had two inches of rainwater in it. He dumped the water into the sink and put the pan back into its spot, with a folded paper towel in the bottom to soften the sound. Then he poured a cup of coffee and took it to the small dinette table. He kept a small black-and-white TV on the table, and he turned it on. Some guy with a loud voice was selling a can't-miss real estate system. Make ten or twenty thousand a month. Sure. Piece of cake. Just buy these CDs for four easy payments of $59.95. Howard sat there watching, wondering how anyone could fall for such a crock.

∞

He was reading the weather report—clearing this morning, but rain returning in the next day or two—when somebody knocked lightly on his front door. It was still dark outside. Twenty minutes after six. Howard kept a shotgun behind the door for situations just like this. The neighborhood had gone downhill in the past twenty years. All the old-timers had died and a new class of people had moved in.

Howard made his way through the living room, past chest-high stacks of boxes and other assorted piles, to the front door. It went without saying that he wouldn't open the door if he didn't know who it was. The shotgun was right there if he needed it.

Three small windows ran diagonally across the upper third of the door. He peeked through the lowest one. Ricky was standing there, fairly wet from the drizzle. Good kid, this Ricky. Always smiling, happy, but right now he wasn't.

Howard opened the door, and Ricky said, "I'm sorry to bother you this early, Howard, but I need to ask a favor. If you say no, I'll understand."

Eddie Bustamante, fifty years old, silver-haired, sitting behind his metal government-issue desk, said, "It's a goddamn sieve, really. That's what the border is like. A sieve. Or maybe a colander. I always get those two mixed up. Which is the one with the larger holes? More of a perforated bowl than a mesh screen?"

"I'm not really sure," Warren Coleman said. Eddie had been Warren's boss for several years.

"I think it's a colander, and *that's* what the border is like. We plug those holes up and we've done our jobs. Stop the flow through the holes. Of course, we can't plug every hole completely—a noodle or two, or sometimes a big group of noodles, will still slip through—but we can sure as hell catch a bunch of noodles. That's why this"—he opened a green folder on his desk, shaking his head—"this just doesn't make any sense. Christ, Coleman, your noodle count is way down. I just don't understand it."

He spread the contents of the folder on his desktop. Graphs. Pie charts. Complicated tables with columns representing a range of variables. Warren's work—his successes and failures—were reduced to ratios and percentages.

Eddie said, "See, right here—this spring, you were all over the place, rounding 'em up left and right. Setting goddamn records. You were one of my top performers. Then summer came, and you did okay, but not great. After that, in the last two months, you've had a steady decline, week after week. You're down about thirty percent. Got any explanation for it?"

Warren shifted uneasily in his chair. He didn't like the colander analogy. His own analogy—catching raindrops with a thimble—was more accurate. "No, sir," he said.

"I know the traffic hasn't slowed, because numbers are up throughout the sector. Way up. I'm bringing in new agents every day and we still can't keep up with it all. But your numbers are down. The odd thing is, your contraband seizures have remained level. You're finding the drugs, but not the people." Eddie flipped the folder shut and leaned back in his chair. "Let me ask you this: Are you burned out? Sick of it all?"

"No, I—"

"Believe me, it happens. It's a helluva grueling job. Everybody knows that. Day in, day out, fighting a battle that seems ... hopeless. It was bad enough in my day, but now, Jesus, I can't even imagine. I bet there are times when you want to say fuck it, I give up." Eddie was eyeing him closely now.

"That's not the case." *Sort of, but not exactly*, Warren thought.

"You start to wonder if you're making any difference at all. You wonder if you're really serving your country's best interests. Let me tell you personally: you are. You might not realize it, but you're making a hell of a difference." He waved a dismissive hand over the folder. "Well, not as much of a difference lately, but still ... "

Warren waited.

"The other problem—I've only seen this a couple of times—is when you start to go soft. You start to *feel* for these people, and who can blame you? All they want is a better life, right? And, Jesus, look at what they'll go through to get it. I was still working the Tucson sector when we launched Operation Safeguard, which, let's be honest, didn't accomplish much at all. Pushed their crossing points out into the desert, into all that heat, and no water anywhere. Deaths skyrocketed, but we screwed up their economy so bad with NAFTA, they had no choice but to keep on coming. Stubborn people. So, yeah, I've been there. I ever tell you about the time I found a skeleton in a watering tank? I'm talking a kid-size skeleton, maybe eight, nine years old. Man, I know what something like that can do to your head. If that what's happening here, you can tell me. There's no shame in it."

Was it a trap? Warren wanted to open up and admit what he was feeling. He really did, but he also wanted to keep his job. "No, sir," he said.

Eddie took a deep breath, steepled his hands, and said, "There's one other possibility. I hate to even bring this up, but ... some people would look at these numbers and wonder if you were, well ... earning a little extra cash on the side. You know how it works. You agree to turn a blind eye, and for that you—"

"Absolutely not," Warren said. "No way. I would never do that. Frankly, it pisses me off that you'd even—"

Eddie held his hands up. "Okay, okay. Simmer down. I wasn't making any accusations, believe me, but it's been known to happen. I'm just trying to understand the situation. Forget I even said it."

Warren waited some more. Eddie was tapping his fingers on the desktop, thinking.

"You got problems at home?"

"No, sir. No more than—"

"Stress? Anxiety? Depression? Insomnia?"

"No, sir."

"Health concerns? Something wrong with your vision?"

"No, sir."

"You've been working with Olguin a lot lately. Is he dragging you down?"

"Pardon?"

"He's still fairly new. You can tell me if he's not up to snuff."

"Danny does a great job."

"This new wave of recruits ... well, don't even get me started. Even the good ones, some of these rookies start out strong, like they've got the magic touch, then"—he snapped his fingers—"just like that, they lose it. Or they say to themselves, hey, it's a government job, so why am I busting my ass? I'm not a bounty hunter. I'm not paid by the head. So they start to slack off. That sort of attitude can spread like a goddamn virus."

"Danny doesn't think that way. He's as committed as I am." *Maybe that's not the highest compliment right now,* Warren thought.

Eddie's phone began to ring. He checked the caller I.D., let out a heavy sigh, and said, "Okay, let's just agree that you're having a slump. A dry spell. But I need you to snap out of it. Real soon. Camp out on the riverbank if you have to. Bring your numbers up, and I mean pronto."

He put a hand on the telephone receiver, preparing to answer.

"Yes, sir," Warren said.

Eddie gave him a solemn we're-all-in-this-together look. "You get back out there, Coleman, and you *catch those noodles.*"

"Yes, sir. I will, sir. You can count on me."

છ

Tomás didn't ask for help opening the small bottle of Advil; rather, he clenched the childproof cap in his teeth and twisted the bottle open with his right hand. He then let the cap fall into his lap.

He'll face much tougher challenges than a bottle of Advil, Ricky thought. Perhaps it had not occurred to Tomás what lay ahead. This was not a broken finger or a sprained wrist. The anger Ricky had felt yesterday—directed at Wayne Skaggs and Carmen—was nothing compared to how he felt now. And frustration, too, because the person at whom he was angry had no face and no name.

"How many of those have you taken?" Ricky asked.

"Not enough," Tomás said.

"You took four at midnight and four an hour ago. You shouldn't take any more. They can damage your liver. Especially since we don't know what those other pills were. Some medicines don't go well together."

Tomás sighed and placed the opened bottle on the dashboard of the Nissan truck. The drizzle from earlier had disappeared.

"It's hurting?" Ricky asked.

"The worst yet. Like I smashed it with a hammer."

Howard had been kind enough to lend them the vehicle, and now they were waiting outside the clinic in the gray light before sunrise. Seven twenty. The sign in the window said the clinic opened at eight o'clock. Another sign, in both English and Spanish, said: THIS IS NOT AN EMERGENCY CLINIC. IF YOU ARE EXPERIENCING AN EMERGENCY, CALL 911. WE HAVE NO NARCOTICS ON THE PREMISES.

It had been a long night. Ricky and Tomás had talked for hours, catching up, and as the night wore on, Tomás's hand had given him more and more trouble. Tomás had been apprehensive about seeing a doctor—he was afraid of being reported to *la migra*—but by five o'clock, he had agreed that there was no other alternative. The pain was too much to bear. There was no hospital in Rugoso, so Ricky had decided that the clinic was the place to go. If they could not treat Tomás here, then they would make the drive to the hospital. That's where things might get difficult. If they turned Tomás in, he would have to cross again later, if he could. The problem was, the more times they caught you crossing, the more severe the punishment. They were actually putting people in jail now.

Headlights swept the interior of the truck as another vehicle, a Honda, pulled into the lot. It parked far away from the entrance to the clinic. Perhaps another patient arriving early. First come, first served. But after a moment, the driver stepped from the car and walked toward the front door. She had her purse strap over her left shoulder, a paper coffee cup in her right hand.

"Wait here," Ricky said.

Tomás nodded, his eyes closed.

Ricky climbed out, closed the door, and waited beside the truck. He didn't want to scare her in the dim light. When she got closer, he said, "Cris?"

She hadn't seen him, and she stopped suddenly. "Yes?"

"It's Ricky. From two days ago. The man with the flu."

She came closer. "Yes, how are you doing?"

"I'm okay, but I'm here about my brother. He injured his hand."

"Injured it how?"

"He was working on his car and got his thumb caught in the fan belt." He hated lying to her.

She took a step closer. "How bad is it?"

"His thumb is gone."

"It stripped all the flesh from the bone?"

"No, there is no bone. It's all gone."

She showed no reaction. She must see all sorts of injuries. "When did this happen?"

"Yesterday."

"And he's just now seeking treatment?"

There was no lie to explain this. "He was afraid."

Cris didn't answer right away. She understood what Ricky was saying. "Dr. King doesn't come in until eight thirty, but there's nothing he can do anyway. Your brother needs treatment at an emergency room."

"Will you take a look?"

She hesitated.

"Please," he said. "I'm afraid, too. I know they'll ask a lot of questions."
Still nothing. He was putting her in a tough spot. Time to tell the truth.
"It wasn't a fan belt," he said. "He was shot in the hand when he was crossing. If they know that's what happened ... "
She was shaking her head. "Dr. King can't treat that type of injury."
"He just needs something for the pain."
"He's going to need a lot more than that if his thumb was shot off."
"Stitches?"
"Look, I can't stand here and diagnose his condition. You need to take him to the hospital."
Ricky had learned from friends—also here illegally—that a trip to the emergency room was not, in itself, a cause for concern. Tomás wouldn't need proof of citizenship or insurance to receive treatment. But if the doctors learned that Tomás had been shot, they would alert the police. Ricky was worried that the doctors would take one look at Tomás's hand and know exactly what had happened. Then the police would investigate, and Tomás would be deported.
"Please," he said again. "Take a look. I need to know what to tell them. I can't tell them what really happened." He felt ashamed to ask such a favor.
Maybe she herself would call the police. Maybe she would turn them in to *la migra*. But, instead, she walked over to the truck. Ricky opened the passenger-side door. "This is Tomás," he said.
Neither Tomás nor Cris said anything. Ricky turned on the dome light to give Cris a better look. Tomás raised his injured hand and Ricky unwrapped the fresh gauze he had dressed it with that morning.
It looked even worse. His hand and remaining fingers were swollen and discolored.
"He's going to need surgery. Did this really happen yesterday?"
"The night before that," Ricky admitted.
"He should've gone to a hospital immediately. It was very foolish to wait."
Ricky didn't say anything.
"I'm sorry you're in pain," she said to Tomás, "but I can't give you anything for it. They'll take care of you at the hospital."
Tomás nodded. "Thank you."
Then, to Ricky, she said, "Tell them it was a lawn mower accident. A fan belt wouldn't create an injury like this."
"Thank you," Ricky said.
"Go to the hospital. Right now." Then she turned and walked to the clinic door without looking back.

SEVEN

Herschel Gandy sat in his truck, drinking coffee, gazing west across the Rio Grande to Mexico. The clouds had cleared and the sun was cresting a ridge behind him, ready to heat the day. But for now, early, the air was crisp and cool.

Sometimes he drove up and down the bank of the river for hours at a time, patrolling. Other times he'd just park on a hill, where his white Chevy was easily visible. Every thirty minutes or so he'd stick his .45 out the window and fire a few rounds into the dirt. A warning. Letting the *mojados* know they'd have to cross at their own peril. Armed response, boys. That was the message he was sending. Better keep your asses off my land.

Some people might call him fanatical, but he didn't give a shit. There was too much at stake. The foreigners—mostly Mexicans, so he called them all Mexicans—were slowly taking over the country. But the change was happening so slowly as to be almost unnoticeable. Half a million new illegals every year. In a country of three hundred million, yeah, it wasn't much—but it was half a million *every* year, year after year, and it was starting to add up. Plus, when they got here, they'd squeeze out six or eight babies, compared to one or two for your average white couple. The result? A major transformation in the cultural make-up of America. Compare today with twenty years ago and anyone could see that things had changed drastically. Back then, for example, if you scrolled through the radio dial, you might find one or two Spanish-language stations, and *those* were broadcasting from the Mexican side. But today, Christ, there were more Spanish stations than English-speaking stations. Gandy had seen bumper stickers for a station calling itself *La Invasora*. The Invasion. Pretty obvious what that meant. Gandy would listen to some of those stations occasionally, because it was like having a spy in the enemy's camp. His Spanish was pretty crappy, but he could pick up the basics. What he learned was that a lot of Mexicans thought the whole situation was pretty funny. They often bragged that they didn't need guns to take over a country—just time, patience, and an American population that didn't seem to care what happened. He'd heard one ad, for a car dealer in Laredo, that said, "English is also spoken here." Making a joke, but it wasn't funny at all. That same dealer ran newspaper ads featuring a Mexican flag. Gandy had complained to his state congressman, but nothing came from it, of course. What do you expect from a politician named Hernandez?

Gandy raised his binoculars and studied the Mexican countryside. Some mornings, he could see movement. Goats. Cattle. Deer. Brown-faced people. Right now, he saw nothing. Funny how the land over there looked exactly like the land over here. *They've got everything we've got, more or less.* Plenty of natural resources. Enough to be a wealthy country. If the poor don't get their share of the pie, they need to do something about it, rather than relying on the United States. Show some goddamn gumption.

His cell phone rang. He answered, and Clayton said, "Bad news."

"What's up?"

"I came down here for another look, just in case, and Sherlock found something."

Gandy placed his coffee mug in the cup holder. "No details. Not on the phone." Gandy knew it was possible that border agents monitored cellular calls. The Patriot Act and all that. Fighting terrorism. Gandy had no problem with it, but it meant they had to be careful what they said. "Where are you?"

"Same place we saw 'em the other night. You need to take a look at this, Herschel."

As Gandy turned the key in the ignition, he noticed that his palms were beginning to sweat. "On my way."

෫෮

Ricky knew something about *la migra*. The law granted them more power if they were within twenty-five miles of the border. Within that zone, they could enter anyone's land, at any time, without a warrant. Ricky didn't know all the rules they had to follow for stopping vehicles. He knew they couldn't pull you over without a reason—unless they were operating a checkpoint and stopping all vehicles on that route. There were permanent checkpoints—everybody knew where those were—and there were temporary checkpoints, which caused the most concern. You never knew when and where they'd appear.

The nearest hospital was in Laredo, and getting there, driving *toward* the border, wouldn't be a problem. But what about coming back home? It would be risky.

The alternative was to drive to the hospital in Carrizo Springs, which would add an extra hour both ways. But they'd never be closer than twenty-five miles to the border. They'd be much less likely to encounter *la migra*. Ricky left it up to Tomás. Laredo or Carrizo Springs?

"Don't be stupid," Tomás said. "Carrizo Springs."

"But if you're in pain ... "

"It can wait. I didn't come this far to get caught now."

Ricky said to hell with it and chose Laredo.

"The fortune cookie—according to this—was invented right here in America," Danny Olguin said. "Is that some crazy shit or what?"

Traffic check again. Warren driving, Danny in the passenger seat.

Catch those noodles.

"Really?"

"It's right here."

Warren said, "That's interesting, but what I'm wondering is, how do you know that book is accurate?"

"What do you mean?"

"Well, who's to know if they got their facts right? If they're talking about all these topics that nobody knows anything about, why couldn't they just make stuff up? Who'd know?"

Danny was shaking his head slowly. "Man, you can't just make shit up in a book. Unless it's fiction. This isn't fiction."

"All I'm saying is, you never know. Remember that guy who wrote his life story a few years ago and it turned out to be a total crock? He said he'd gone to jail and been homeless and a bunch of stuff like that. None of it was true."

Danny stared at him for several moments. "For real? I don't remember that."

"He confessed on Oprah. She bawled him out pretty good."

"Damn." Danny looked at his book again, studying the back cover. Searching for some sign that what he'd been reading was packed with falsehoods. Then his head popped up again. "Oh, I talked to Darrell Simmons this morning. You know Darrell? Big tall guy at the Carrizo Springs station? He and I were in the same class?"

"Yeah, I've met him."

"Okay, so he picked up a couple of guys yesterday afternoon, and he's hauling them in, and they start whining about what a violent country this is and they can't wait to get back home, because—get this—they say someone took a potshot at 'em before they'd even been in the country ten minutes. They said they were with a third guy, and *that* guy got hit in the hand. Blew his thumb clean off."

Warren had a flashback. Three men crossing the highway—one with a bandaged hand. Could it be? "Where did this happen?"

"Well, that's why Darrell called, because it supposedly happened right here in our sector. They said they crossed the river south of Laredo."

"How far south?"

"Ten or fifteen miles."

"Did Darrell file a report?"

"See, that's the thing. When he pushed them on it—saying he'd have to hold them in custody while we investigated it—they changed their minds. Said they'd made the whole thing up and just wanted to go home."

A mile passed in silence.

"But Darrell wanted us to know about it anyway," Danny said. "Just in case we've got an idiot on the loose."

₭)

The call came in at 9:22 AM.

Wayne Skaggs should've expected it. Everything was running smoothly at the plant, which meant that something was bound to come along and fuck it up. Something always did. He knew that from experience. Just when things were going well, a critical piece of machinery would break down, or a key employee would quit without notice, or the plant would fail a health code inspection. There was always something that prevented the Rugoso plant from being the top performer in the Kountry Fresh family. There was always some hurdle, some roadblock, some clusterfuck that kept Skaggs from being promoted to regional manager.

There was, for instance, his former secretary, a gal named Gloria. Sure, he'd flirted with her some, touched her inappropriately on a couple of occasions, and maybe even pressured her to perform a few tasks that weren't in her job description. Nothing outrageous, mind you. Just a quick hand job at lunchtime. Was that so much to ask? It wasn't like he threatened to fire her if she didn't comply. Next thing he knows, she's filing a complaint with Human Resources. Then she's threatening to sue. Skaggs vehemently denied every last word of her accusation, and there was certainly no proof, so the Kountry Fresh attorneys offered her fifty grand to be on her merry way. She took it, and that was the end of that nasty chapter. It was also the main reason Skaggs kept his mitts off the new girl, Carmen, even though she made Gloria look like the "before" shot from one of those makeover shows his wife was always watching. No, Carmen was off limits. He didn't want more headaches, because there were always plenty of headaches to go around.

Still, he didn't expect the call at 9:22 AM. It came to his cell phone, not his office line. He checked the caller I.D. screen, then picked up on the second ring.

"Doc," he said, by way of a greeting.

"Can you talk?"

"Yeah, what's up?"

"This employee of yours named Ricky Delgado? He came to see me Tuesday. Classic flu symptoms, except for a few red flags. So I drew some blood, and the results just came back. It's not good."

Skaggs closed his eyes for a moment. Then he said, "Hold on a sec." He rose from his desk and closed his office door. Then he picked up the phone and said, "Okay, what's he got?"

ಲ

As soon as he and Tomás walked through the front door of the emergency room, Ricky's worries evaporated. The waiting room was a sea of people just like him. No gringos, no Asians, no blacks. Many of them—maybe all of them—were likely illegal. Tomás would blend right in.

"A lawn mower?" the admitting nurse asked. She didn't appear convinced. Because she thought Ricky was lying? Because she was amazed at Tomás's bad luck? Because it was such a stupid way to injure yourself? Or was her skepticism in Ricky's imagination?

"Yes," he said firmly. "A riding mower. He fell off." Ricky had decided that a riding mower was more believable than a push mower.

She asked Tomás to unwrap the gauze so she could have a look. Didn't even flinch when she saw the wound. Then she took his name and told him to have a seat. They'd be with him as soon as possible. To Ricky, Tomás's injury was gruesome and substantial, but to this nurse, it seemed to have no more significance than an infected mosquito bite.

"Can he have something for the pain?" Ricky asked.

"We'll get to him as fast as we can."

They found two empty seats even though the waiting room was nearly full. A man cradled his wrist as if it were broken. A woman had apparently been bitten on the leg by a dog. A little girl had a large gash on her forehead, which her mother repeatedly blotted with a tattered bath towel. Other people sat quietly with no obvious injuries. Several people were slumped in their seats, sleeping. Occasionally someone coughed or sniffed. Spanish was spoken, but no English.

Fifteen minutes later, Ricky heard the faint whine of a siren in the distance. In a matter of seconds, it grew much louder. A moment later, two swinging doors slammed open—causing several people in the waiting room to jump—and a cluster of medical personnel rapidly wheeled a patient on a gurney down a glass hallway. A separate entrance for more serious cases. The admitting nurse didn't even glance up.

It occurred to Ricky that he should call Carmen and let her know he'd be missing work today. He would say it was because of health reasons, which was true.

ಲ

Gandy kicked at the object in the dirt with the toe of his boot. There was no mistaking what it was. The better part of a thumb. Nail on one end, jagged flesh on the other.

"Had to wrestle the damn thing out of Sherlock's mouth," Clayton said. "He saw it before I did and picked it up. Stupid dog was gonna swallow it. You got any of that hand sanitizer in your truck?" Sherlock was straining at the end of a leash, hoping for another shot at this intriguing morsel. "Who knows what the hell kinda germs I might've picked up from that thing."

Gandy bent down for a closer look. Just a nasty-looking thumb. That wasn't so bad. A white shard of bone was protruding from the end of it. Small price to pay. "Where'd you find it?"

"About right there where it is. Wasn't like we played fetch with it."

Gandy stood up straight and looked southwest along the *sendero*, toward the rise where he'd last seen the three wetbacks. Had they gone back to Mexico? Decided that the U.S. wasn't the land of opportunity after all? He hoped so.

Gandy said, "You said 'bad news' earlier, but this is good."

"How so?"

"We have our answer now."

"Answer to what?"

"How bad he was hurt. He lost a thumb. He should be grateful it wasn't worse."

"I guess we all should."

Gandy looked at him. "You think I was concerned? I guarantee, I wasn't."

"I'm just saying, it woulda been a bitch to bury him. Better this way."

Gandy stood there a moment, staring at the thumb. "I was aiming for the center of his backpack. Guess my shot floated high. Might need to check my scope."

"Either that or you flinched."

"I don't flinch."

"Hell, I've seen you flinch."

"Well, I didn't flinch this time, okay?"

Clayton didn't say anything.

Gandy toed the thumb again, then kicked it. It tumbled along the ground and skittered into the brush. Sherlock emitted a high whine, clearly disappointed.

"So you think that kid's okay?" Clayton asked.

"Well, sure. Won't be picking melons anytime soon, but it's not like he's gonna die. He'll be all right."

Again, there was that doubtful expression on Clayton's face. Same as yesterday morning.

"What?" Gandy asked.

"Might be other problems."

"Like what?"

"Could get infected. When I was ten, my cousin shot me in the foot with a twenty-two. My daddy cleaned it up real good, but it still got infected."

Shit. Gandy hadn't thought about an infection. An open wound like that would be a prime breeding ground for germs. He glared at Clayton. "Why do you always have to be so damn negative?"

EIGHT

A<small>FTER TWO HOURS, THEY CALLED</small> Tomás's name, and Ricky went with him to a large room separated into smaller rooms with curtains. There, in one of those rooms, they waited again; Tomás in a bed, Ricky in a chair. Ricky could hear somebody moaning. In the room next door, a man and a woman argued about the car accident they'd had that morning.

"You shouldn't have been talking on your cell phone."

"How many times are you going to say that?"

Tomás had just fallen asleep when a woman—not a nurse, because she wasn't in scrubs—wheeled a cart with a computer on it into the room. She asked, in Spanish, for Tomás's full name, his date of birth, his next of kin, any known allergies. As Tomás answered, she typed. She didn't seem surprised that he had no employer, no Social Security number, no insurance.

She asked what he was here for. What was his medical complaint?

Didn't we already go through all this? Ricky wondered.

Tomás said he'd cut off his thumb with a lawn mower. "It hurts a lot. Can I get something for the—"

"A nurse will be right with you." And she was gone.

Tomás sat quietly, miserable, waiting his turn. He'd be okay. He was tough. He made no sound.

The man next door: "What was I supposed to do? Hang up on my boss?"

"You could've pulled over."

Ricky tried to take Tomás's mind off the pain. "I know these two guys, José and Carlos, who panhandle at the same intersection. José always collects a lot more money than Carlos. Almost every driver that passes by gives money to José. One day, Carlos asked José how he does so well. José said, 'Look at your sign. It says you have a wife and six kids to support.' And Carlos says, 'So? What's wrong with that?' And José says, 'Well, look at my sign. It says I need just ten more dollars to move back to Mexico.'"

℘

Ricky thought about all the things Tomás wouldn't be able to do with one hand. He couldn't wash dishes or paint houses or lay brick. Couldn't use a shovel or a chainsaw. Couldn't hang chickens. When a man pulled up in a truck looking for laborers, he wouldn't want a worker with a disfigured hand. There would be very little work available to Tomás. He might be able to push a lawn mower. That was ironic.

"The ranch where this happened," Ricky said quietly. "Can you find your way back to it?"

Tomás had been resting with his good arm over his eyes, blocking the light. He lifted it and looked at Ricky, puzzled. "I think so. Why?"

Right then, the nurse finally came. A short Hispanic woman. Maybe sixty years old. She took Tomás's temperature, blood pressure, heart rate, respiratory rate. Left, then came back and drew some blood. Left again, then came back and started an IV.

Another long wait, then another person, a young white man in scrubs of a different color, came with a gurney and said he was taking Tomás for surgery.

"Where should I go?" Ricky asked.

"Follow us. There's a waiting room near the O.R."

ಸಿ

Ricky chose an open chair in a corner of the room away from the television. It was a different sort of crowd here. More white people. Less chaotic. Most of them hadn't come to the hospital at a moment's notice; they'd brought a loved one for a scheduled surgery. Now they were waiting for the results. Nobody was crying or moaning. They were reading magazines or paperback novels, listening to iPods.

Ricky was trying to decide whether he should call Tomás's wife or wait and let Tomás call her himself. That would probably be best. Sarafina would freak out if Ricky told her what had happened. She might not believe that Tomás was okay. She might think Ricky was making it sound less serious than it was.

It brought back memories.

Ricky was eleven when his favorite uncle, Raúl, set out for Arizona to work as a carpenter. Before he left, he told Ricky he would write him a letter once a week. He'd send pictures of his adventures in the United States. "Then, when you're older, you can come see me," he said. "We can live together and work side by side."

Several weeks passed. No letters. Ricky began to worry—everybody knew that the trip to the United States was dangerous—but his parents said they were sure that Raúl was fine.

Ricky came home from school one day and his mother said that he'd just missed a call from Tío Raúl. Everything is okay, she said. He is enjoying his new life. A few weeks later, the same thing. Raúl seemed to have a knack for calling when Ricky wasn't home. Ricky began to suspect that his parents weren't telling him everything. Something must have gone wrong. Perhaps Raúl hadn't made it across the desert. There was little talk of Raúl for a year, and when Ricky would suggest calling him, his parents said that Raúl had no phone. Ricky wanted to send a letter, but his parents didn't know the proper address.

When Ricky was fourteen, they said he was old enough to know the truth, that Raúl was dead. His first week in *el Norte*, he'd been shot while burglarizing a home in Tucson.

ℇↄ

Warren was lost in thought, still thinking about Darrell Simmons's story, paying little attention to his driving, when Danny Olguin looked up from his book again and said, "Ooh, good eye."

"Huh?"

Danny gestured toward the vehicle fifty yards in front of their SUV. Warren realized that, without thinking, he'd fallen in behind a Ford Econoline. A white cargo van. Windows in the rear doors, but none on the sides. Mexican plates. Heading east on Highway 359 toward Mirando City. Tooling along at five miles below the speed limit. Nobody in the passenger seat.

"I like the looks of that one," Danny said. "What is that, an early nineties model?"

"Late eighties."

You had to be careful who you stopped or they'd say you were profiling. You couldn't just go with your gut. The foreign plates weren't nearly enough. This far in, you had to have reasonable suspicion, and that was a murky area nowadays. You had to put the facts together in a way that justified the stop.

You studied the driver closely. Was he nervous? Avoiding eye contact and staring straight ahead? Or acknowledging you with a wave or a nod of the head? Did he wave too vigorously? Did he slow down when he first saw you, as most drivers did when they spotted any sort of law enforcement vehicle, or did he speed up?

What type of vehicle was it? New or old? Vans were always of interest, as were trucks and large sedans. Tinted windows raised an eyebrow, of course. Was the vehicle dirty? Was it within twenty-five miles of the border? Was it operating in a rural area where smuggling and illegal immigration were common? Was it riding low on its springs? This particular van certainly was.

"He's loaded to the gills," Danny said. Eager. Looking for reasons to make the stop.

"Could be bad shocks," Warren replied.

Rationalizing, even though he'd vowed to start the day with a renewed sense of purpose. He'd tried to recall how he felt when he was a rookie, when he'd approached the job with no ambivalence at all. But, just this morning, Warren had heard a news report about an illegal immigrant named Jesús Manuel Cordova. Cordova was crossing the desert in southern Arizona when he came across a nine-year-old boy wandering alone, disoriented, looking for help. There'd been an accident. The boy led Cordova to an SUV that had plunged deep into a canyon—and the boy's mother was still pinned inside the wreckage. Cordova tried to extract her, but couldn't, and she died shortly thereafter. Cordova could've said, "Hey, good luck, kid," and taken off. But he stayed and comforted the boy. Night came and the temperature dropped. Cordova gave the boy his jacket, then built a fire. Kept telling him everything would be okay. The next morning, some hunters passed by and called for help. Cordova could've left then with a clear conscience. He'd saved the boy, who likely would've gotten lost and perished in the desert. But still, Cordova stayed. Right up until the time agents from the Tucson sector arrived. Cordova was being processed for deportation. People were calling him an angel.

Was there a Jesús Cordova in the van Warren was trailing? Danny wanted to run the plates, so they did, and it came back clean. Registered to a company called South Texas Imports, which might account for the load. Could be carrying a ton, literally, of pottery.

They followed the van for a couple of miles, both of them watching through the rear windows, waiting to see silhouettes of heads bobbing up and down nervously. Nothing. Didn't mean anything. Illegals had learned to stay low and out of sight. They'd ride for hundreds of miles like so many sardines packed in a can. *Jorge, meet Pablo. You'll be riding in his lap to Fort Worth.*

"Let's take a look at the driver," Danny said.

Warren switched to the left-hand lane and began to ease up alongside the van. He'd once detained an Econoline carrying twenty-two illegals, a sector record for a two-axle passenger vehicle. All of the rear seats had been removed to allow more people to fit inside. They kept pouring out of the open doors like clowns from a circus car. They'd come from a small Mexican village where the economy had gotten so poor, the mayor had committed suicide. The passengers in the van had been using a mop bucket for a commode.

Was this van similarly loaded? Warren pulled even with it and held his speed steady.

"Latino male," Danny said. "Mid-thirties. He's looking this way."

Warren snuck a peek and saw the driver make eye contact and give a small nod.

"Looks nervous," Danny said.

"You think so? I didn't get that." Which was the truth. To Warren, the driver appeared quite calm. Nothing out of the ordinary.

"See how he won't look over again?"

"He already looked once."

"Yeah, and now he's starting to sweat."

"You can actually see him sweating?"

"No, man, I didn't mean literally. Look how stiff his arms are. See how he's gripping the wheel?"

Warren took another look. The man was simply driving. Then he did glance over at them again. Was there fear in his eyes? Maybe. What must it be like to be an illegal alien and suddenly have *la migra* pull up beside you? Studying you. Preparing to yank all your dreams away.

"He's a live one," Danny said.

"You're stretching it."

"Oh, come on. We're good to go."

There was an off-ramp coming up. Would the van leave the highway? A sudden turn was considered a solid platform on which to build reasonable suspicion.

"If he takes the next exit, we'll pull him over," Warren said.

"Deal."

Warren lowered his speed and fell behind the van again. Three hundred yards to the exit.

Keep on going. Don't be stupid.

Two hundred yards.

Warren slowed even more, so the van driver would feel less pressured.

One hundred yards.

Don't turn, don't turn, don't turn ...

The van's turn signal flashed and Danny let out a whoop.

∽

That afternoon, Clayton called Herschel about a downed cow in the eastern pasture, so he drove out to see. The animal was bedded under some mesquite trees.

"I noticed her last week," Clayton said, leaning against the fender of his truck. "Looks even worse now."

The cow was in horrible shape. Skin and bones. Eyes drooping, head hung low.

"Grass tetany?" Gandy asked.

"Too early in the year. Besides, she ain't lactating."

"Broke mouth?"

Clayton shook his head. "Too young."

"What, then?"

"Same as last time, I imagine."

"Well, shit."

In late summer, one of Gandy's best bulls had died from gangrene. The wetbacks often left behind plastic tortilla bags, and the cattle were attracted to the smell. They'd swallow the bags, which would strangle their intestines. Slow death.

Herschel stepped behind the cow, careful not to spook her, and pushed on her haunches. She made no effort to rise. "You got any cubes?"

Clayton went to the bed of his truck and opened a fifty-pound bag of range cubes—large, compressed pellets of protein-rich cottonseed meal. The cows loved them. He tossed a few where the cow could reach them, if she was interested. She didn't react at all.

"She's too far gone," Clayton said. "Can't even take her to the sale barn."

Gandy shook his head, frustrated. *This* was why he had no more patience. *This* was why they should seal the border as tight as a goddamn prison yard.

"Go ahead and do it," he said.

Clayton returned to his truck for his 30-30. He walked to within five yards of the cow, jacked a shell into the chamber, and shot her in the head.

ॐ

While Danny approached the driver's-side window, Warren took a quick glance through the dusty rear windows into the cargo area. No Jesús Cordova in there. Nobody at all, just cardboard boxes. Each box was a cubic foot in size, stacked three high. Forty or fifty boxes total. Each had a customs sticker on the side.

Ceramic tile. Warren had seen enough of these boxes over the years to know what was inside. All this trouble to check a load of tile.

He placed a hand on one of the rear doors—leaving a print—then moved along the passenger side and stopped at the trailing edge of the front door. Good view from here. Warren's job, as back-up, was simply to observe. Danny would conduct the interview, which he began by greeting the driver in both Spanish and English ("*Buenas tardes*. How are you today?") and asking for identification.

The man—neatly groomed, dressed in jeans and a plain T-shirt—answered in Spanish, then presented a passport and a B-1 visa. The B-1 gave him temporary admission to the States for commercial purposes.

Danny studied the documents. "Your address in Nuevo Laredo is still correct, Mr. Herrera?"

"Yes, sir."

"Where are you headed today?"

"Falfurrias."

Warren studied the man's hands. Rough. Calloused. Of course they were.

He handled tile all day.

"Going there on business?" Danny asked.

"Yes, delivering Saltillo to a homebuilder. His name is Armando Mendes." Calm. Collected. "I make the trip every month. He's my best customer."

Danny used the mic clipped to his shirt to request a check on Herrera's visa. It would take less than a minute to see if it was valid. Herrera glanced over at Warren, then turned his attention back to Danny.

"That's what's in the boxes?" Danny said. "Tile?"

"Yes, sir. They already inspected them at the bridge."

"Mind if we take a look?"

A moment's hesitation. The man checked his wristwatch. "It wouldn't be a problem, but I'm running late. I have to be there by five or Armando will leave."

"Why the rush?"

The man smiled. "His son has a high school baseball game. Armando said he'd wait for me until five."

Warren had been studying the interior of the truck, looking for anything out of place—seeing nothing—but now his heart jumped and his eyes went back to the driver.

Danny grinned back at the man, no indication that he'd caught the lie. "We'll make it quick, I promise."

Warren unsnapped the holster holding his .40 automatic. He had a nephew who played baseball. He knew the season was in the spring, not now, in the fall.

"I really need to get going," the man said.

"I understand that, sir, so the sooner we get started, the sooner you can get back on the road."

Danny took a step backward, using body language to encourage the man to exit the vehicle. That's when the gun appeared. Warren had no idea where it came from—maybe the space between the driver's seat and the door—but suddenly the driver had a black revolver in his left hand and he was raising it toward the window.

NINE

THIS WAITING ROOM ALSO HAD MAGAZINES, mostly written for American women. One article revealed the secret to deeper, more satisfying orgasms. Another proclaimed that it could help you get rid of cellulite forever.

It was nearly four o'clock when a nurse appeared in the doorway to the waiting room and called Ricky's name. She told him that the surgery had gone well and Tomás was in a recovery room. Shortly, he would be taken to a room on the third floor. He might be released tomorrow afternoon, but more likely the day after that.

At a quarter to five, the nurse returned and gave Ricky a room number. He took the stairs, followed the numbered placards beside each door, and found Tomás in a semi-private room divided with a curtain. Ricky could not see the patient on the other side of the curtain, but he could hear snoring.

Tomás, too, was asleep. His hand was heavily bandaged. An IV tube led to his good arm. He looked good, considering. Ricky sat in a chair and waited. Once again, he wasn't feeling well. He had forgotten to take his medicine and he felt as if his fever was back. The flu continued to linger.

❧

You train for something just like this, but those exercises can't replicate the real thing. Not even close. You panic. Your vision narrows. You feel as if your mind is fumbling. Betraying you. You can't possibly move quickly enough.

Warren wasn't sure what he yelled, but he yelled something. Maybe it was "Gun!" or "Danny!" or just some guttural nonsense. Didn't matter. Whatever it was, the sound was just leaving Warren's lips as Herrera's gun rose to window height.

Danny was simply standing there, expressionless, then just beginning to understand, starting to cringe, when Herrera pulled the trigger.

Christ, it was incredibly loud. Like lightning striking five feet away.

Warren had his own gun in his hand. Didn't remember pulling it, but there it was. He extended his right arm, braced it with his left.

Where was Danny? Couldn't risk a crossfire, but Danny was gone. On the ground? Running?

Herrera was wheeling around with the revolver when Warren fired the first shot into his torso. Followed by several more. Three? Four? He lost count.

The revolver fell.

Herrera writhed briefly, restrained by the seatbelt, then all movement stopped. Over and done with in a matter of two or three seconds.

This can't possibly be happening. I knew it wasn't baseball season.

"Danny?"

Warren's ears were ringing. If Danny was responding, Warren couldn't hear it. He jerked the passenger door open, keeping his gun trained on Herrera. He felt like such a fraud. Like he hadn't done anything correctly, and all of this could've been avoided. He had no business being an agent.

"Danny!"

No answer.

He leaned into the van, one knee on the passenger seat, and retrieved the revolver. Tossed it behind him, onto the grassy shoulder.

Herrera was dead. No question. Eyes unmoving, staring through the windshield. Blood oozing from his mouth.

Warren scrambled from the van. Heard a transmission from the radio handset on his belt. The dispatcher responding to Danny's twenty-seven request. Negative. No wants or warrants.

He ran around the rear of the vehicle, coming to the driver's side. There was Danny, limp on the pavement, blood on his brow. Oh, Jesus, shot in the head. His shirt was torn.

Warren couldn't breathe. Thumbed his mic, but he could hardly get the words out. Shots fired. An agent down. Need an ambulance. God, please hurry. His voice was shaky. His hands were trembling.

He was aware that a vehicle was parking behind the Tahoe. An old Chevy truck pulling a livestock trailer. A civilian.

Warren knelt beside Danny and checked the pressure point on his wrist. Yes. A heartbeat. A strong one. There was blood, but not as much as Warren expected from a shot to the head. Something about the wound wasn't right. Not a round hole, but a furrow right at the hairline.

"You need some help?" the driver of the truck called, keeping his distance. An older bearded man.

The torn shirt. How did that happen? What did it mean? Warren ripped the shirt open and suddenly he understood everything. *Oh, sweet Jesus. Oh, thank you, Jesus.* A dent in the protective plate in the center of Danny's Kevlar vest. It had done its job. Protected the vitals.

Herrera had only fired once, which left only one explanation. The bullet had ricocheted, causing the head wound.

The civilian was standing behind Warren now. "He gonna be all right?"

Just to be certain, Warren raised Danny's head gently and felt the back of his skull. No blood. No brain matter. No exit wound. Unconscious from the impact. Warren was beginning to weep silently.

The civilian, now standing beside the Econoline, looking inside, said, "You got a dead Mexican in here."

༃

At ten minutes past seven, Tomás stirred, and Ricky rose from his chair and stood beside the bed. A flicker of eyelids, then Tomás opened his eyes a little. Glassy.

"How are you feeling?"

Tomás looked past Ricky, at his surroundings, remembering where he was. "Not too bad." His voice was raspy.

"Any pain?"

"Not right now. I can't feel my hand. Everything is numb."

Ricky figured that would change when the anesthesia wore off.

"I'm thirsty," Tomás said. "Is there any water?"

"All I can give you is ice chips. That's what the nurse said. You want ice chips?"

"Yes, please."

Ricky didn't know where to find ice chips, so he went out into the hallway and asked a nurse at the nurses' station. She said she'd bring a cup of ice chips to the room. When Ricky went back inside, Tomás's eyes had closed again.

"Tomás?" Ricky whispered.

"Yeah?" Eyes still closed.

"You go ahead and sleep. I'll be back tomorrow after work."

No reply.

"You hear me?"

"Yes, tomorrow."

༃

"You should burn his house down," Trino said. Trino was a big talker, especially when he was drunk, as he was now. Even sober, he wasn't a pleasant man. Old and grumpy. Oscar said the civil war in El Salvador had turned him bitter. Trino carried a lot of anger with him.

Ricky had followed smaller county roads back from Laredo without any problems. No sign of *la migra*. Now, most of the same men from the night before were gathered around the picnic tables again, drinking beer—always drinking beer—and barbecuing some chicken legs. You never ran low on chicken when you worked in a poultry plant. Chickens, both dead and alive, had a way of disappearing out the back door.

The men had asked how Tomás was doing, and Ricky had told them of the day's events. Told them how he had lied to the nurses at the hospital. Talk had led to the man who had shot Tomás, and everyone had an opinion.

"Kill his cattle."

"Poison his well."

"Cut every fence on the place."

"Just tell the police. Let them take care of it. They'll send you home, but you can always come back."

"It's harder than ever to get across."

"How's he supposed to prove the guy shot Tomás on purpose? Ricky would need evidence."

"What're you, a lawyer now?"

"Do you even know who shot him?"

Ricky was too tired to think about it. Besides, it was crazy talk. Wasn't it? Shouldn't he just let it go? Tomás was here now, and that was the main thing. Nothing could bring back his thumb.

"Whoever it was, the son of a bitch should pay for what he did," Trino insisted. He was one to talk. Trino sometimes stole things and bragged about it.

"You feeling okay, Ricky? You don't look so good."

"Hey, Carmen was asking about you today," Ignacio said.

"But I called in sick," Ricky said. "I left her a message."

"Yeah, she got it. She was wondering how you were doing. She seemed very concerned. She asked me to give you this." Ignacio pulled something out of his pocket and handed it to Ricky. A sealed envelope.

Everybody was grinning. Teasing him. For Carmen to inquire about anyone's welfare was an unusual thing.

"Must be a love note," one of the men said.

"Perhaps she has her eye on the world-renowned chicken hanger, the man with such fast hands."

"Move quick, little Ricky, before she loses interest. Women like Carmen are fickle."

"If I could spend just one evening with her," Oscar said, "she'd never be the same."

"You're right about that," Victor said. "She'd become a lesbian."

There was a lot of laughter after that remark. Somebody cracked open another beer.

"Hey, aren't you going to open the envelope?" Ignacio asked.

"Not in front of all you jerks," Ricky said.

They complained as he went inside, but he didn't care. He took his shoes off, laid down on his bed, and tore open the envelope. Inside was a small slip of paper. A prescription slip from Dr. King's office. Tetracycline. That was an antibiotic.

Carmen had attached a note.

Ricky, Dr. King wants you to take this medicine.
    —C

Strange. An antibiotic for the flu? Ricky had had an infection once from stepping on a nail. He remembered the doctor saying that antibiotics worked well on bacterial infections. But the doctor also said that antibiotics did nothing for viruses, such as the flu.

℘

"What I oughta do is track that son of a bitch down and make him pay market price for one head of Red Brangus," Herschel Gandy said. Making a joke, Clayton Dupree figured.

Clayton knew that Herschel wanted him to agree, even though it was a bullshit proposition, so he sat silently instead, sipping from a glass of Crown Royal over shaved ice. They were on the back deck of the ranch house, boots up, enjoying the peace and quiet. Clayton could hear a covey of bobwhite quail somewhere in the distance. When the wind was blowing strong from the east, it carried the sound of traffic on Highway 83.

"Haul that thumbless bastard back here," Gandy continued, "and make him work off his debt. Him and his two buddies. Sort of a tariff for crossing my ranch."

Clayton was used to Herschel's blowing off steam when he'd had some whiskey. You could practically gauge his consumption by his level of righteous indignation. One glass—mildly peeved. Two glasses—increasingly intolerant. Three glasses or more—downright hostile.

Of course, Clayton usually enjoyed a drink or three himself, which often caused him to stop thinking of Herschel Gandy as his lifelong best friend and to see him for what he really was: a spoiled brat. A rich punk. The kind of guy who'd insist that you perform a half-ass autopsy on a cow—just as Clayton had done late that afternoon—to prove that the wetbacks *were* responsible for the cow's demise.

"Doubt it was him specifically that left that bag behind," Clayton said. He knew he should keep his mouth shut, but sometimes he just couldn't help it.

"Yeah, I *know* that, but all of 'em together is responsible for it, so they all owe me."

Clayton could more or less understand that point of view. The wetbacks were collectively guilty. Made sense. "How would you find him?" he asked, knowing it was just drunk talk. Hell, they were lucky they hadn't gotten arrested. Herschel was smart enough to know he'd been lucky this time around.

"I've got his cell phone, remember? Somebody named Ricky called it yesterday. Ricky. What sort of name is that for a Mexican?"

"Probably short for 'Ricardo.'"

"Whatever. I should call him. Betcha I could get him to tell me who his friend is."

"You serious? You're not really thinking about collecting for that cow?"

Herschel didn't say anything for half a minute. "Naw, he wouldn't have the money. But at least I could tell him to spread the word about the Gandy Ranch. Cross here and you're fucked."

"Why stir things up?"

"You think I won't call Ricky?"

"No, I know you would, but why would you?"

Herschel was already putting his drink down, rising from his chair. "Hold on."

Going inside for the Mexican's phone. What an idiot. A minute later, Herschel came back outside with the phone open in his hand. "Shit. Battery's low." But now he was scrolling through the menu, finding the incoming number, and calling it back. Grinning and holding a finger up, like *Watch this.*

After a few seconds, Herschel said, "I'm sorry, who is this?" Then he abruptly closed the phone. "The chicken plant in Rugoso," he said, obviously proud of himself. "That's where this guy Ricky works. See how easy that was?"

Clayton was relieved that Ricky hadn't answered. He'd just as soon they put this entire fiasco behind them. Be grateful Ricky's wetback friend hadn't gone to the authorities.

Herschel settled back into his chair, looking pleased with himself. Took a drink. "I'm surprised he even has a job."

&

Warren Coleman lay in the dark and wondered if he would ever sleep again. Hard to keep still. Too much adrenaline still flowing. Nearly three in the morning and he couldn't stop replaying the traffic stop in his head. Revising it. Editing it. Creating new outcomes in which he hadn't had to kill a man.

On the other hand, it could've been much worse.

Danny was in the hospital with a fractured sternum and a mild concussion. Many people think of a Kevlar vest as a magic shield that prevents all harm. Not true. Danny was lucky to be alive.

The majority of the boxes in Herrera's van had indeed contained Saltillo tile. The rest had held cocaine. More than three hundred pounds of it, with a street value of nearly ten million dollars. A major bust that would've been worthy of national headlines even if it hadn't involved a shootout. Herrera, of course, wasn't alive to tell where he'd gotten it, so the trail would probably end there. He had no previous record, so, most likely, he was simply a carrier, known as a "mule," enticed or coerced into service by one of the brutal Mexican cartels. They had their ways. Promise a sizable amount of cash, or threaten to kill a loved one. And when the cartels made a threat, they followed through. Nuevo Laredo, in recent years, had become a hotbed of drug-related kidnappings and killings. Like a war zone in some overseas country.

Most of the news networks, including CNN and MSNBC, were reporting the incident in a fairly straightforward manner. A commentator on FOX News had called Warren and Danny heroes. He used the incident as an excuse to rant about national security, saying we shouldn't allow commercial drivers—even those with proper permits—to cross the border. *Do we really need people like Mr. Herrera in our country, folks?* he'd asked. *As we've seen time and time again, anybody who wasn't born here represents a threat to U.S. sovereignty.*

Warren felt movement, then Ellen's hand on his chest. "Can't sleep?" she asked.

"No. Am I keeping you awake? Want me to sleep in the guest room?"

"Of course not. I don't want you going anywhere." She moved closer, placing her head in the fold of his shoulder. When he'd finally gotten home, after telling his story three times to investigators, he'd been surprised by how tightly she'd clung to him. Surprised, then ashamed for feeling that way, because of course she loved him. When had he begun to doubt that? Had he become that cynical?

He placed a hand on her bare back. It had probably been ten years since they'd lain together, in the middle of the night, simply holding each other. They used to talk for hours about every topic under the sun, until day-to-day life had drummed them into a routine.

"I don't know if I can do it anymore," he said suddenly, without thinking. It felt good to say it out loud.

After a pause, Ellen said, "The job?"

"Yeah."

"Then don't." She had a matter-of-fact tone to her voice.

"What?"

"Quit. Give notice tomorrow. Do something else."

"Like what?"

"You could be a cop again."

"Where? Laredo? I don't want that."

"I don't either."

"Then where?"

"Anywhere. We could go back to Hebbronville. Heck, we could move to Montana, or Florida, or anywhere we want."

Again, she was surprising him. "What about *your* job?"

"I'd get another one."

"Simple as that?"

"Why not?"

"It sounds like you've already thought this through."

"Of course I have. Don't you think I know how unhappy you've been for the past few years?"

"No, actually, I didn't."

"Well, then, that's my fault. I get too wrapped up in my own problems—we both do—and we don't talk like we used to."

He laughed. "That's what I was just thinking."

"We're talking now, though. Better late than never. I worry about you, you know. For nine years, I've been afraid something would happen, and today it did. And all I can wonder is, when will it happen again?"

"Didn't you worry when I was a patrolman?"

"Yeah, but not as much. Not in Hebbronville. It's so quiet. I sort of miss it."

He laughed again. "Nobody has ever missed Hebbronville."

They didn't speak for several minutes. Then Warren said, "I've never been to Montana."

viernes

TEN

Ricky had unpleasant dreams, and in the morning, his temperature was one hundred and three—the highest it had been yet. He was achy all over, and he found himself needing to cough frequently. His head was pounding, and he could feel a large ulcer forming on his tongue. He took three aspirin and the antiviral medication the doctor had given him two days earlier. Only two days, yet it seemed like two weeks. So much had happened.

He slid the thermometer back into its case and thought of Cris. Beautiful Cris. Ricky had dreamed that one day he'd hold a better job and be worthy of a woman like her. Be able to buy a home and start a family. It was a dream, all right.

He wanted desperately to remain in bed, but he couldn't miss work again. Too many sick days and they'd likely fire him. Also, if he didn't work, he didn't get paid, and he needed money. Especially now, with Tomás to take care of, and with Wayne Skaggs expecting eight hundred dollars this afternoon for a new Social Security number.

Seven o'clock. Just enough time to drive over to Howard's and ask if he could use the Nissan for one more day. It was a lot to ask, and Ricky hated to put Howard to any trouble. If Howard said no, as he expected, Ricky would ride his bicycle to the plant and come up with some other way to bring Tomás home from Laredo. But how? He had no idea.

♫

The Today Show.

That was another good example of a broadcast that had been much better in its prime, four or five decades ago, back when Dave Garroway was the host, and you could expect some real entertainment or actual news with your coffee. That whole J. Fred Muggs mascot thing was silly in hindsight, but back then, it was groundbreaking television. They managed to keep the quality at a steady level with John Chancellor, Hugh Downs, Barbara Walters, Jane Pauley, Tom Brokaw. Then came Bryant Gumbel. Why not just flush the franchise down the toilet while you're at it? Obnoxious jerk. Prima donna. Well, things change, don't they? Sometimes for the better, sometimes not. Howard wasn't particularly fond of Matt Lauer and Ann Curry. Both of them seemed stiff, like every word out of their mouths was scripted, or they were afraid of offending one group or another, or they were behaving the way they thought a host was *supposed* to behave, rather than just being themselves. Al Roker was no Willard Scott, but was that a positive or a negative? And don't even mention Kathie Lee Gifford. Howard couldn't stand the woman, even though she filled out her dress nicely.

His doorbell rang.

That'd be Ricky, returning the truck, just like he had said he would. Howard had been thinking about the boy and this brother of his, Tomás, who'd injured his hand somehow. Ricky hadn't given any details yesterday morning, but Howard could tell that Ricky was quite upset. Not just upset. Angry. But he was a private sort, not inclined to share his troubles. Howard decided he'd have to press him a little. Maybe he could help the kid out somehow.

∞

"Come on in and have some coffee," Howard said, holding the door open.

Ricky didn't want to be rude, but he was worried about spreading his illness to a man as old as Howard. Plus, he had to get to the plant on time, and if he had to ride his bicycle, he'd need to be on his way soon. "I'd better not. I have the flu. I might be contagious."

"And you're going to work?"

"I feel pretty good," he lied.

"I had a flu shot last month. I'll be fine. Come on in for a minute."

Ricky hesitated.

"One cup of coffee, son," Howard said. "Then you can be on your way."

Ricky stepped inside, intending to keep the visit short. Sit down with Howard for a few minutes, ask to use the truck for one more day, then go to work. Instead, he ended up telling the old man everything.

∞

Danny looked pretty good. His forehead was bandaged, but he had color in his face and a smile on his lips when he saw Warren walk through the doorway of the private hospital room. The TV was tuned to CNN, the sound turned low.

"Hey, man," Warren said. "How ya doing?" He was starting to grin, too. He didn't know why. Probably a shared silent acknowledgment of the drama they'd experienced yesterday. *That was some wild shit, huh? You bet your ass.*

"You just missed Tony Valencio," Danny said. He was speaking softly and carefully, not moving his head much, like he had a scorpion sleeping on his chest and was afraid of waking it.

"Tony came by?"

"Left five minutes ago. I worked nights with him when I first signed on."

"Tony's a good guy," Warren said, though he didn't know Valencio that well.

"Hey, have a seat."

There was only the one chair—a big, faux-leather recliner, designed to accommodate a loved one during an overnight stay. Warren sat.

This was weird. He had no idea what to say. Fortunately, Danny spoke again.

"First things first, man. You saved my ass. Thank you."

"Your vest saved your ass."

Danny was shaking his head. "If I'd been out there alone, he probably would've popped me again. No witnesses that way. You're a fuckin' hero, man. Accept it."

There was that word again. *Hero*. Warren knew it was a lie, or, at best, simply inaccurate. He hadn't *tried* to save Danny's life. Warren had simply shot Herrera because it was what he had to do. At the time, he'd had no idea whether Danny was dead or alive. He was saving himself, that's all.

Warren let the moment pass without saying anything.

"You're wearing civvies," Danny said, "so ... "

"Yeah, administrative leave. Until they rule the shooting good."

"Oh, it was good. I'm here to tell you, it was good."

"Do you remember it?"

"Nope. Last thing—I was talking you into pulling him over. Guess that was a mistake."

On CNN, a reporter was saying something about turmoil in the Middle East. What else was new? Looking back, it was obvious how dramatically Warren's job had changed over the years. The result of ever-increasing panic. *We must secure our borders!* The boss had changed their mission statement to emphasize the war on terrorism. Yeah, good luck. All it would take is one vehicle slipping in uninspected. One vehicle among the millions that crossed yearly. Needle in a haystack. How was Warren—or anybody—supposed to prevent that?

"How's your chest?" he asked.

"Not as bad as you'd think, as long as I don't cough or sneeze. But then again, I'm on some pretty good meds. It's bruised like a son of a bitch. I'm getting out this afternoon, after the doctor checks me over again."

"Your forehead?"

"Stitches. Did you know the upper forehead is the hardest part of your skull?"

Danny and his trivia. Which reminded Warren of the plastic bag in his hand. He opened it and removed a book by Paul Harvey. *The Rest of the Story.*

Short anecdotes with surprise endings. Like the 1950s presidential candidate who killed a teenage girl. And the American founding father who kept his wife locked in the cellar. Warren wondered which founding father had done that, but he hadn't taken the time to look in the book. He handed the slim paperback to Danny, saying, "Figured you'd have some time on your hands."

Danny studied the cover. "Cool. Thanks a lot." He opened the book and flipped through the first few pages. "Hey, write something in here for me, will you?"

"Like what?"

"You know, sort of commemorate the event. An inscription."

"Really?"

"It would mean a lot to me. Something I can show my grandkids someday, when I'm telling them about the man who saved my life."

"Danny, I didn't—"

"Please?"

How could he say no? "I don't have a pen."

"There's one in that drawer."

Warren rose reluctantly and retrieved the pen. Then he opened the book and wrote:

> *Danny—*
> *Paul Harvey is right. Things are not always as they seem. Get well soon. We need men like you on the line.*
> *Warren*

∞

He walked down the hallway toward the elevator, suddenly overcome by emotion, but unable to identify exactly what had a hold of him. Anger? Guilt? Sadness? Did it even matter? Time to go back to Hebbronville. Right?

The frustrating thing was, he'd keep this job—hell, he'd approach each day with gusto—if he could concentrate solely on drug smugglers. But if you fish for tuna you're bound to catch a few dolphins in your net.

He was passing the nurses' station, turning his head to avoid eye contact with the two women there, and he looked into a patient room and froze. Stopped dead in his tracks. Through that doorway was a patient lying upright in bed. A young Hispanic man with a bandaged left hand. Warren had seen his face before.

Through a pair of binoculars.

∞

When Ricky clocked in at the plant that morning, he saw a new face working in the hanging room. Not unusual, because hangers came and went with regularity. Few lasted longer than three or four months on the job. Some lasted just a few weeks. Ricky remembered one kid from Veracruz who walked out after a single hour, without telling anyone he was quitting. Ricky, with eight months experience hanging chickens, was an old hand. He rarely got to know his fellow hangers well. It was difficult to hold a conversation while wearing protective gear, including earplugs, and hanging chickens at a furious pace.

It was a horrible job, but it was steady—unaffected by the economy or bad weather. If you were a construction worker, a recession or rising interest rates could bring homebuilding to a halt. If you were a busboy or dishwasher, people could stop going out for meals. If you picked crops, an unexpected freeze or drought could ruin the season.

But chicken ... everybody ate chicken, even when times were tough, maybe *especially* when times were tough, because chicken was inexpensive. Plus, it was healthier than red meat, and people were taking that into consideration more and more lately. As a result, the plant never rested. It continued to crank out chicken, twenty-four hours a day, just as fast as Ricky and his coworkers could send the birds down the line.

There was another positive aspect about being a hanger—it kept Ricky's hands busy, but his mind was free to wander. Right now—despite the noise, the overwhelming stench, and the flailing of the doomed chickens—Ricky was thinking about his conversation with Howard in the old man's kitchen. It had felt good to share his troubles with somebody.

He had begun by telling Howard about his problem with Wayne Skaggs—the Social Security "no-match" letter, and his fear of being fired.

The old man started shaking his head and said, "That's horseshit."

"What do you mean?"

"He's ripping you off. It's a scam."

"Are you saying the letter is a fake?"

"Well, maybe so or maybe not. But even if it's legit, your boss is using it to blackmail you. Those letters make a point of saying a company can't fire an employee just because his Social comes back wrong. Hell, half the time it's a mistake anyway, because the government records are so screwed up."

Ricky hadn't considered the possibility that Wayne Skaggs was lying to him. "How do you know all this?"

"Son, you remember what I used to do for a living?"

"You said you were an electrician."

"Not just an electrician. I owned my own company. Small, but I usually had at least three or four men on the payroll, sometimes up to a dozen. I hired all kinds of people, and I got no-match letters for some of them. I know how those things work. I remember being relieved because, yeah, I mighta hired some illegals, and back then, everybody knew you could just ignore the letters. And it said right there on the letter that I wasn't supposed to fire anybody. In fact, if I *did* fire anybody, and it turned out they were legal, I coulda gotten sued."

"Maybe things have changed since then. Maybe the government is using these letters to find undocumented workers."

Howard took a moment to think about it. "Well, you could be right about that, but if your boss is offering to get you a new Social, that's the part that makes my alarm bells go off. How much does he want for it?"

"Eight hundred dollars."

Howard let out a snort. "Greedy son of a bitch. If he suckers ten or twenty people a year, that's some nice extra income, don't you think? Tax free, too."

"He has to split it with his friend in San Antonio."

Howard was shaking his head again. "Don't you see? There ain't no friend in San Antonio."

Ricky felt foolish. How could he have fallen for a trick like that? He should have known better than to trust a man with a singing fish.

Howard said, "Did he give you a copy of the letter?"

"No."

"See, that makes me wonder if the whole deal is a crock. Wouldn't take much to phony up one of those letters on a computer. If you start asking around at the plant, I bet you'll find a bunch of fellas who've fallen for this scheme."

Ricky didn't know what to think. Even if Wayne Skaggs was taking advantage of him, what could he do about it? "I should just pay him," Ricky said. "I'll have enough money once I get paid today."

"I wouldn't give that jerk a dime. Besides, I thought you were saving up to buy the Nissan."

"I was," Ricky said. "That's why I came here today. I was wondering if I could borrow it for one more day."

"I'll make you a deal. You just keep the truck and pay me a hundred bucks a month."

Ricky was excited by the idea. "That would be very helpful. For how many months?"

"Nine. Just like we agreed. Nine hundred bucks."

"That's a loan with no interest."

Howard waved his hand. "Why make it complicated?"

"I should pay interest. It isn't fair to you."

"Don't worry about it. You're doing me a favor by taking it off my hands. My neighbors already complain about all the junk I have around here. I don't need that old truck sitting in my driveway."

"You are very kind."

Howard didn't say anything.

Ricky took out his wallet and removed five twenties. "My first payment." He was smiling broadly. It felt good to be buying a vehicle. He'd owned a small sedan back home, but it was broken down more often than not.

Howard took the money, walked over to the countertop, and opened a Folgers coffee can. "Petty cash," he said, sticking the money inside. He sat back down. "So ... you want to tell me what happened to your brother?"

ELEVEN

WARREN STEPPED INTO THE HOSPITAL ROOM. Looked around. Had no idea what to say. The TV was on, with the volume turned low. A Mexican soccer game. The young patient was looking at Warren—not fearful, but curious, or maybe confused. Probably thinking: *This white guy ... not a doctor ... why is he here?*

"*Hola*," Warren said.

"*Hola*."

"You speak English?"

The man shook his head.

So Warren continued in Spanish. "Mind if I sit down?"

"Okay." Tentative.

Warren sat. Took his time. Looked around some more. It was a two-patient room, but Warren couldn't see the other patient because of a curtained divider. He heard snoring.

What to say? Or should he say nothing? Get up and leave? He nodded at the TV. "Who's winning?"

"Santos, two to one."

"Who are they playing?"

"Morelia."

The team names meant nothing. Warren couldn't even name an American soccer team, much less a Mexican one.

What now?

"What's your name?" he asked.

"Tomás Delgado." Tomás had a slight smile on his face. He seemed to know that something odd was happening, but he didn't know what.

"How did you hurt your hand?"

"Accident with a lawn mower."

"Really? What happened?"

"I cut my thumb off."

"Ouch. That had to hurt. Completely cut it off?"

"Yes."

"A push mower?"

"No, a riding one."

"Did you fall off?"

"Yes. I fell off." Still smiling. *Silly me. Fell off a lawn mower.*

"Was it a newer model?"

"Yes."

Warren had researched riding mowers the previous summer, but had decided against buying one. Too pricy. But he'd learned about all sorts of safety features, including something called 'operator presence control.' You fall off the seat, the blade quits spinning. Sure, a determined idiot could still maim himself with a modern mower, but it was a lot more difficult than it used to be.

"You aren't telling the truth," Warren said, "but I don't blame you for that."

Tomás's smile slowly faded. "Why are you here? You work for the hospital?"

"No."

"Who, then?"

A deep breath, then: "Border Patrol."

Tomás's only reaction was to avert his gaze to the television. Suddenly interested in the game again.

"I'm not here to create problems for you," Warren said. "Nobody knows I'm here."

Tomás said nothing. A soccer player in a yellow shirt was rolling around on the ground, holding his leg. Apparently, he'd been kicked in the shin, and it was the gravest injury he'd ever suffered. His face was contorted with pain. The poor man was in agony. Then the ball was kicked downfield, and the player sprang up and sprinted after it, as if he'd never been healthier.

"Your two friends were caught yesterday in Carrizo Springs," Warren said. "They've already been sent home. But before they left, they told us what really happened to your hand. They said you were shot. Is that true?"

Tomás looked at Warren again. "I don't want to cause trouble," he said softly.

"I can understand that. Let me repeat: nobody knows I'm here."

"What do you mean by that?"

What *did* he mean? He wasn't sure. He was making this up as he went along. "I'm not going to arrest you. I want to help you. If someone shot you on purpose, I need to know about it. Otherwise, the person who did it might do it again. Someone could get hurt even worse than you did. Someone could get killed."

"If the two other men already told you what happened, why do you need to hear it from me?"

Tomás, like many illegal aliens, was distrustful of anyone who worked for the government. Warren had no choice but to tell the truth. "They wouldn't go on record. They didn't give any details. Then they changed their story and decided the shooting hadn't happened after all."

"And now they are home?"

"Yes."

"Where would they be now if they'd agreed to be witnesses?"

Smart kid. "They'd probably be held in custody while the shooting was being investigated."

"In other words, they'd be in jail."

"Not jail. Not exactly."

"But they couldn't leave. And they couldn't work. Then, when it was all over, they'd be sent home. Right?"

"Yes."

"Then a man would be an idiot to come forward."

"What about punishing the man who shot you?"

Tomás made a derisive sound. "I know how things work here. People don't want us around. There would be no punishment for the guy who did it."

"You're wrong about that," Warren said, though he knew he didn't sound convincing.

Tomás looked at the TV again. "I have nothing more to say."

೫

Ricky suspected that Wayne would send for him after lunch, before the end of the day, and that's exactly what happened. During Ricky's mid-afternoon break, while he was in the coffee room, Carmen appeared and told him to come to Wayne's office. No, she said, he didn't need to clean up first, though she wrinkled her nose in disgust.

It was Friday, the day when the employees in the front office dressed more casually, and Carmen was wearing a short denim skirt and a tight black blouse. High heels, too, of course. It was a genuine pleasure to follow her through the narrow hallways. Her perfume was extraordinary. He could detect it even above the stench of poultry that clung to his skin and clothing.

"Thanks for sending that prescription from Dr. King," Ricky said. "I heard that you were very concerned about my condition."

He was merely teasing her to see what she would say. He knew—despite the remarks the other men had made last night—that Carmen had no personal interest in him. More likely, Wayne had wondered when his most productive chicken hanger would return to his post. The hangers, after all, set the pace for the rest of the plant. If the hangers fell behind, all of the other departments felt the effect. That meant fewer chickens were processed, and as far as Wayne was concerned, that was a catastrophe.

Carmen didn't respond to Ricky's remark. She acted as if she hadn't heard him, but Ricky knew better. Carmen would never lower herself to make small talk with a filthy chicken hanger.

They came to her work area and she led Ricky past her desk to Wayne's door, which was closed. She tapped lightly with the ends of her fiery-red fingernails.

"Come in."

She swung the door open and allowed Ricky to pass, then closed the door behind him. Wayne was too busy with some paperwork on his desk to greet his visitor. Ricky stood and waited. The singing fish watched him with one dull eye. Ricky thought about the money in his wallet. His savings, combined with the paycheck he'd cashed at lunchtime, amounted to a little more than nine hundred dollars. Most of that would soon be gone. Unless he followed Howard's advice. Maybe the old man was nutty. Or confused.

Ricky waited some more. Finally, Wayne closed a manila folder and looked up.

"Have a seat."

Ricky sat.

Wayne said, "Regarding the problem with your Social Security number, I've got everything ironed out. My friend came through with no problems at all. That just leaves your part of the deal. Did you take care of things?"

"You mean the money?"

"Yes, the money."

"I have it. All eight hundred dollars."

"In cash?"

"Yes."

Ricky didn't move. Wayne stared at him. "Well?"

"I think I'd like to see the letter myself. I'd like to have a copy of it."

Ricky could tell by the pained expression on Wayne's face that he was not pleased with that request. "You want a copy of the letter?"

"Yes, please."

"You mind telling me what for?"

"For my files." That was a joke on Ricky's part. As if he had files.

Wayne remained silent for several seconds. Then he said, "Listen, I'm doing you a big favor here, you understand? And, frankly, you're not in a position to be asking for anything. You follow me?"

"I do, yes, and I appreciate your help. But I'd still like a copy of the letter."

Wayne laughed, but there was nothing mirthful about it. "Goddamn. I knew it." Now he was shaking his head. "I knew you were a fuckin' trouble-maker. Didn't I say that the other day? You sat right there and told me you weren't, but here you are, causing trouble. Well, shit. What I want to know is, what possible use could you have for that letter? What's a guy like you gonna do with a letter from the Social Security Administration? Don't you know it's best to be as far off the government's radar as possible?"

"I understand, but the letter is about me. So I feel I should have a copy."

Wayne was beginning to raise his voice. "You're wrong, José. That letter is about your job here at this plant, and it's addressed to me, not you. ¿*Comprende?*"

"Wouldn't you want a copy if the letter was about you?"

"That's hard to answer, because a letter like that would never *be* about me."

Ricky was starting to feel his own temper rising. "Why wouldn't you want me to have a copy?"

Wayne looked uncertain of himself. He opened his mouth, then closed it. Then he seemed to have an idea. "Because that letter is part of the confidential files we keep here at the plant. Nobody—and I mean nobody—gets a copy. If you were careless with it, someone could find it and make the assumption that we were hiring illegal aliens. I'm protecting the reputation of this plant."

An obvious lie. Ricky knew that Howard was right. The letter was a fake. Wayne had made the whole thing up to take Ricky's money.

Ricky had one final test. "I won't give you the money unless you give me a copy of the letter," he said.

"You know what? Screw the letter, because you're fucking fired. As of this very minute, you no longer work here. I want you to get your shit out of your locker and get out."

Ricky hadn't been expecting that. But surprisingly, he felt a sense of relief. He was tired of Wayne. Tired of hanging chickens. Tired of everything. He could do better than this, couldn't he? There were plenty of jobs available for those willing to work hard.

"Right now," Wayne said. "Get out of this plant."

"You are a thief," Ricky said.

Wayne's face turned bright red. He pointed at Ricky. "You'd better watch your mouth."

"You hire people who are vulnerable and you take advantage of them. You should be in jail."

"In about five seconds, I'm gonna come around this desk and remove you from the premises myself. And believe me, it'll be the highlight of my day."

It was tempting to stay seated. Let Wayne attempt to throw him out. Yes, Wayne might have been a tough prison guard at one point, but now he was thick and slow. Ricky would punch him so hard the singing fish would close his eyes in horror. But then the police would come. Ricky would be arrested, and they'd learn he was a *mojado*, and they'd soon know there were many more just like him working at the plant. Dozens of people would lose their jobs and have to return home. It would all be his fault. Yes, he could tell the authorities about Wayne's Social Security scam, but would they even care? Besides, Ricky couldn't prove any of it. Not without a copy of the letter.

He rose slowly, with dignity. "I'm going to spread the word about your trick," he said. "Nobody will fall for it anymore."

Wayne grinned. "That's right, keep talking. Here's what happens. The plant owns the trailer you live in, remember? I want you out of there by tomorrow morning. I'm gonna send somebody over there to make sure you're gone. Hell, I might even do it myself."

Ricky was pretty sure there were laws that prevented this kind of treatment, but again, what could he do? He yanked the door open and walked out without another word. For one brief moment, he caught Carmen looking at him, her fingers poised above her keyboard, and Ricky knew she'd been straining to hear the conversation in her boss's office.

Suddenly, he had a wonderful idea. He'd walk over to her, say something dramatic and suave, then plant a kiss on her lips that she'd never forget. Like something out of a movie. Make her realize that her attitude toward Ricky was wrong. That she didn't know what she was missing. Leave her breathless and wanting more. Change her haughty attitude.

He left quietly instead.

∞

The patient's name was Rocendo Ochoa. Twenty-four years old. Normal vital signs. Overall, a young, healthy individual. Well muscled. Handsome, too. Except for several large, ugly lesions on his upper lip and across his cheek. These were hardened purple lumps called erythema nodosum. A few measured as large as an inch across. Not ulcerated. Warm to the touch.

"How long have they been there?" Cris asked in Spanish.

"Three days."

"Ever had anything like this before?"

"No."

"Been sick lately? Strep throat, mono, anything like that?"

"Not really."

"What do you mean, 'Not really?'"

"I had a little fever last week. You're very pretty, you know that?"

"Did you have a cough? Any respiratory problems?"

"Yeah, a little. But it's gone now."

"As far as you know, you don't have tuberculosis or hepatitis?"

"No. Do you like to go dancing? I know a great club out near Aguilares."

"Leukemia?"

"I sure hope not."

"Syphilis?"

Rocendo Ochoa grinned. "I don't think so."

"When was the last time you had unprotected sex?"

"Why, are you offering?"

Cris didn't smile. "When was the last time?"

"Way too long."

"How long?"

"Maybe three months."

Cris recited her standard speech. "You should always use a condom, unless you are in a monogamous relationship and you know your partner's health status."

"That sounds complicated. Will you show me how to use one?"

She stopped writing in his chart and stared at him for a few seconds. "Do you honestly think that kind of talk is interesting to a woman?"

"Aw, I'm just trying to ask you out."

She went back to the chart.

"We could have a good time together," he said. "I could take you to some nice places."

"Are you on any medications?"

"Nothing."

"No penicillin for anything?"

"No."

"Do you have any allergies?"

"I don't think so."

There could be literally dozens of underlying causes for erythema nodosum—everything from sarcoidosis to inflammatory bowel disease to the Epstein-Barr virus—but in half the cases, you never knew why an outbreak occurred. The nodules themselves weren't particularly dangerous, just somewhat painful, and in this case, unsightly. She doubted he would have even sought treatment if the lesions were located on his shins or lower legs, where they typically occurred, rather than on his face.

"You don't have any cats, do you?"

"No, of course not. Why would I have cats?"

"Where do you work?"

"The chicken plant."

TWELVE

THE WETBACK'S PHONE RANG WHILE Herschel and Clayton were repairing holes in the eight-foot deer-proof fence on the southern property line.

The high fences surrounding Gandy's ranch were designed to keep his superior deer on the ranch while keeping inferior deer *off* the ranch. It was the only way you could properly manage the genetics of a deer herd. When you had total control of the population, you could cull the lesser deer and let the big bucks breed like bunnies. After several generations, you ended up with some nice trophies.

The problem was, some assholes didn't like high fences—either because they thought deer should be allowed to roam freely, which was a load of shit, or because they wanted a shot at the deer behind those fences. Gandy's neighbor to the south was one of those people, and Gandy knew it, because the southern fence always had a lot more holes than the others.

The neighbor always blamed it on the wetbacks, but Gandy knew better. The Rio Grande ran north to south past the ranch. Which meant the wetbacks traveled from west to east. So they cut the fences on the west side of the ranch, near the river, and on the east side, near Highway 83. They had no reason to cut the southern fence.

Gandy had complained to the game warden about his neighbor's actions, but the warden had said, "Can you prove it's him doing the cutting?"

"No."

"Call me when you can."

Worthless jerk.

Repairing the fence wasn't a major task—you simply cut a new piece of wire mesh fabric and spliced it over the hole—but Gandy was getting tired of having to patrol the fence line like a guard in a Nazi prison camp.

Clayton had just cut a splice for the third hole they'd found within a quarter-mile stretch when the phone in Gandy's pocket rang. He wasn't sure why he was still carrying the damn thing around, but he hadn't tossed it yet. He'd even switched the settings from vibrate to ring. Somehow, holding that phone in his hands gave him an odd sense of success, a minor victory, over all the anonymous wetbacks who crossed his land on a daily basis. Like he'd finally taken something from them, rather than the other way around.

The phone rang again. Nothing fancy, just an off-the-shelf ringtone. Gandy checked the caller I.D., thinking he'd probably see the name "Ricky" again. Instead, it said unknown number. He noticed that the battery was nearly dead.

Gandy answered with a simple but cheerful, *"Hola."* Nobody responded, so Gandy said, *"Buenos días."*

A woman said, "Tomás?" Sounding unsure of herself. Wondering who this man was, because it sure wasn't Tomás.

Gandy said, *"¿Quién es éste?"*

"Sarafina."

Clayton had stopped working and was watching him. Gandy said, "Do you speak English, Sarafina?"

No answer.

"I said, *¿Habla inglés?"*

"No. ¿Dónde está Tomás?"

"You're going to have bear with me, Sarafina, because my Spanish is pretty shitty. You understand? I've forgotten most everything I learned in high school."

She didn't say anything.

"You're looking for Tomás?"

"Sí, Tomás."

Obviously she understood a little English. "Does he have a friend named Ricky?"

No answer. Too complicated for her. He heard a beep. The phone was warning him that the battery was almost dead.

Gandy said, *"¿Usted conoce Ricky?"*

"Sí, Tomás se supone que está con Ricky. ¿Dónde están?"

Gandy didn't catch any of that. She spoke much too quickly. If she spoke English, he could have some fun, but she didn't, so his options were limited. *"¿Es Tomás su esposo?"*

"Sí."

Okay, then. This was Tomás's wife. "I'm afraid I have some bad news for you, Mrs. Tomás. *Bad noticias. No bueno."*

"¿Qué ha sucedido?"

"It turns out ol' Tomás ain't much of a swimmer. I'm afraid he drowned crossing the Rio Grande."

"No le entiendo."

"It's sad, really, the poor guy. He's laying down there with the buzzards picking at him."

"Christ, Herschel, give her a break," Clayton said, shaking his head. "That's really cold."

Gandy couldn't help but grin.

Sarafina said something, but it was obvious she still didn't understand what Gandy was telling her.

"Okay, I'll put this as gently as I can. Tomás is dead, you got me? He's an ex-wetback. *Muerto. Tomás es muerto.*"

The phone finally died, but not before Gandy heard a wailing shriek from the woman on the other end of the line.

&

When Ricky entered Tomás's room, there was somebody in there with him. A young, pretty white woman. She was sitting in a chair and had a clipboard in her hands, so Ricky knew she was an employee of the hospital.

"Here's my brother now," Tomás said, in Spanish, so Ricky assumed that this woman must also speak Spanish. "I wasn't expecting you until later." Tomás looked good. Sitting up in bed, smiling, plenty of color in his face.

The woman rose and extended her hand. "You're Ricky?" Hardly a trace of an accent. She had a firm grip.

"Yes, ma'am."

"I'm Sally Moreno. I'm a financial counselor here at the hospital."

"Pleased to meet you."

"Tomás is ready to check out, so I was just going over the bill with him. He told me I should discuss it with you. Is that okay?"

"Yes, fine."

"I understand that Tomás isn't covered by an insurance plan."

"No, ma'am."

"How about worker's comp?"

"I don't think so."

"Where did the accident with the lawn mower occur?" She was at least the sixth hospital employee to ask that question. Didn't they share information?

"At home," Ricky said.

"So he'll be paying the bill himself?"

Ricky didn't know what to say. How did things work here in the United States? He had never been a patient in a hospital himself. Finally, he said, "I guess so."

"Good, then I assume he'll want to set up some sort of payment plan. We can do that right now, before he leaves." She seemed very eager.

"How much is the bill?" Ricky asked.

Sally Moreno consulted her clipboard. She flipped through several pages until she came to the one she was looking for. "Eighteen thousand, six hundred and seven dollars and thirty-four cents. That doesn't include any follow-up care that he might require."

&

"So what do you think?" Cris said. Dr. King had just exited the examination room and was walking toward the area everybody called the bullpen.

"About what?"

Cris followed behind him. "Mr. Ochoa's condition."

"Could be a number of things."

"Any theories?"

"Most likely strep."

"Want me to do a swab?"

He stopped in the hallway and turned to face her. "I wasn't planning on it, no. His nodules are already regressing."

"What then?"

"Send him home with some naproxen and that should do it. If it comes back, we'll take a closer look."

He started to walk away.

"He works at the plant, you know."

He turned again. "So?"

She realized she was being pushy. "Well, one of the things that can cause EN is psittacosis."

He came closer and spoke in a low voice. "I know very well what the causes are. I have no reason to think that's the case here. In all my career, I have never seen a single case of psittacosis."

"I think we should do a culture or draw some blood."

"I totally disagree."

"I'm starting to wonder about that other patient ... Ricky Delgado?"

"What about him?"

"He's the one who came in with the flu. He works at the plant, too."

"I remember him."

"Psittacosis can mimic the flu."

He sighed. "Let me ask you something."

"Okay."

"Are you a doctor?"

She'd gone too far. "No."

"That's right, you're not. Try to remember that."

଼

"Eighteen thousand dollars," Tomás said. He gave a whistle. "That's crazy."

"And six hundred and seven dollars and thirty-four cents," Ricky added.

They were in the truck—*his* truck—pulling out from the hospital parking lot.

"I'll never be able to pay it," Tomás said.

"I don't think they expect you to."

"What will happen if I don't?"

"As far as I can tell, not much. You'll have bad credit. That will make it harder to buy a house."

They both thought that was amusing. What did Tomás care about ruined credit? Tomás was as likely to buy a house as he was to fly to the moon. Newly arrived *mojados* didn't go out and buy houses. Ridiculous.

"Even so," Tomás said, "I can't believe you gave her your real address. Now they can find us."

"Not for long," Ricky said.

Tomás looked over at him. "What's up?"

Ricky took a breath, then told him the full story. The no-match letter. Howard's opinion that it was a lie. The meeting in Wayne's office that afternoon. Ricky's refusal to pay. Getting fired. Getting evicted.

"So that's why you were early to the hospital," Tomás said.

Ricky went east on Chihuahua Street, which took him to Highway 359. He was in a legal vehicle. There was no reason for anyone to pull him over. He'd make sure to obey the speed limit. He was tired of driving on the back roads.

"What now?" Tomás asked.

"I don't know."

"This sucks."

"No argument from me."

There was plenty of traffic until they reached the city limits. Then it thinned out, and Ricky began to feel conspicuous. He became nervous. He fell in behind a semi-trailer and let it lead the way.

"You seem like you feel pretty good," he said.

"My hand still throbs, but not like before."

"I'm glad. I was worried."

"The weird thing is, it feels like my thumb is still there. I try to move it, then remember it's gone. The doctor said I'd get used to it."

They rode several miles in silence, then Tomás said, "Something strange happened this morning."

"What?"

"A guy came to see me in the hospital."

Now it was Tomás's turn to tell a story.

∞

"It looks like we might have another one."

"You shittin' me?" Wayne Skaggs said, holding the phone tight to his ear. He was already in a pissy mood. His lower back was killing him, an injury from years ago, when he did actual work for a living, instead of sitting behind a desk.

"Afraid not," Dr. King said.

"But you don't know for sure?"

"His symptoms are very minor. Could be something else entirely. But I thought you should know."

"Who is it?"

"His name's Rocendo Ochoa."

"Yeah, okay. I know him. Works in the kill room."

"Is that, uh, messy?"

"What do *you* think?"

"My point is, that kind of environment would be ideal for the spreading of bacteria."

"I imagine it would. Lot of blood and shit flying around."

"Then you'd better disinfect that place from top to bottom before things get out of hand."

ഔ

If you were talking about seventies-era washing machines, it was hard to beat a Kenmore. Durable. Reliable. A real workhorse. Not a lot of bells and whistles compared to today's models, but an all-around solid piece of machinery.

Howard had one sitting on his front porch for seven weeks now and it didn't look like it was going anywhere anytime soon. It was avocado green, which didn't help, but the main problem was a noisy belt. Every now and then, some bargain hunter would ask about it, but when Howard plugged her in and let her spin, the squeal turned the customer off right quick. Howard would try telling them a belt could make a racket like that for years, didn't mean it was going to break down. Stick it in the garage and you won't even hear it. They'd shake their heads and move on.

That's why Howard was on his knees behind the old Kenmore, preparing to pull the back panel off and see if he could quiet that belt down. Sometimes you could tighten the nut on the spin tube and that'd do the trick. Sometimes not. But one way or another, he wanted to get the thing sold and make his forty dollars back, and maybe a little extra.

He'd just pulled his flathead screwdriver out from his toolbox when he heard a vehicle parking at the curb. He recognized the sound of the engine, and sure enough, it was Ricky in the Nissan. With someone in the passenger seat.

Howard struggled to his feet and waited. Kind of early for Ricky to be off work. Not yet six o'clock. Ricky stepped from the truck and waved, and the kid in the passenger seat climbed out, too. His left hand was bandaged, which meant it was Ricky's brother, out of the hospital already.

As they got nearer, Howard nodded toward the Nissan and said, "She handle the trip all right?"

"No problems at all," Ricky said, and he stepped up on the porch to shake Howard's hand. Then he said, "Howard, this is my brother Tomás."

Tomás stayed on the grass. "*Buenas tardes.*"

"Good to meet you, Tomás."

Tomás nodded.

"He doesn't speak English very well," Ricky said. "Hardly any at all."

"How'd you learn and he didn't?"

"I had a teacher who said it was a good idea to speak English, so I took some lessons and watched a lot of American television. Tomás didn't."

"Well, he'll pick it up if he wants to. How's his hand?"

"He says he feels much better."

"Good to hear it. You talk to your boss?"

Ricky laughed. "Yes, I talked to him. I asked him for a copy of the letter."

"Attaboy."

"He fired me."

"He did, huh?"

"Yes."

"Sorry about that."

"It wasn't your fault. Proves you were right, that he was trying to cheat me. Thank you."

"Hell, you lost your job. Don't thank me."

"I'll find another job."

"I know you will. Plenty of people can use a man like you."

Ricky reached for his wallet. "Since I didn't give him any money, I can pay you the full amount for the truck."

"Hell, you don't have to do that. We have a deal. You pay once a month."

Ricky pulled a bunch of twenties and a few hundreds from his wallet. "No, I want to pay now."

"What're you gonna do about living quarters?"

Ricky hesitated, still holding the money out. "I don't know yet."

"Okay, how's this? I'll take that money, and y'all can stay here with me for a while, until you figure something out."

Ricky didn't react the way Howard expected him to. He looked down at the porch and didn't say anything. When he finally raised his head, his eyes were shiny. "You are very kind to me."

Howard waved his hand like it was nothing. Really, it *was* nothing. Who wouldn't open his home to a hardworking man who was down on his luck? If Ricky was the type to sit back and ride the American gravy train, Howard wouldn't tolerate having him around. But Ricky didn't expect to have things given to him. He contributed.

Ricky pushed the money at Howard. "This is the remaining eight hundred."

Howard took the bills and stuck them in his pocket. More cash for the coffee can.

Ricky turned to his brother and spoke for a moment in Spanish. Telling him about the new living arrangements, from what Howard could pick up. He heard the word *'casa'* in there. When Ricky finished talking, Tomás looked at Howard and said, *"Muchos gracias, señor. Seremos buenos compañeros de cuarto, se lo prometo."*

Ricky said, "He promises that we will be good roommates."

"Yeah, I know you will. We'll need to move some stuff out of that back bedroom. I got a lot of junk in there."

Ricky laughed. "Somehow that doesn't surprise me. Just tell me what you want us to do and we'll do it."

"You got all your stuff in the truck?"

"No, I need to get it from the trailer. It won't be much."

"Well, whenever you're ready. I'll give you a key so you can come and go as you please."

"Thank you, Howard."

"De nada. Here's something else. I've been thinking about this situation with your brother and that rancher. I have an idea."

Ricky listened, and what Howard suggested was so outrageous, so unexpected—so *American*—Ricky at first thought he was joking.

THIRTEEN

W ARREN COLEMAN WAS PARKED on the shoulder roughly one mile north of where he and Danny had set up on Wednesday morning. The difference this time? He was in his own vehicle, a blue Chevy truck, and he could see the open gate to the ranch Tomás Delgado and his fellow travelers had crossed two days earlier.

Warren had done his research. The ranch was a fairly large one, filling the strip from the highway all the way to the Rio Grande. That told him something: namely, the shooting had almost certainly taken place on that ranch. Warren had been on the property several times in the course of duty, and he had met the owner on a couple of occasions. Well, the owner's son, to be precise. Guy named Herschel Gandy. Sort of a jerk. Used to call the Laredo field office and complain about the increasing number of illegals crossing his land, then he'd raise hell if he didn't think the response was quick enough. The type who thought government employees were at his disposal, that he could tell them where to go and when to get there. But would he shoot at a trespasser? Hard to say. Didn't seem like a stretch, put it that way.

There was a man who worked for Gandy ... Clayton something. Tall and taciturn. Not a loudmouth like his boss. Someone more inclined to communicate with action, not words, in Warren's estimation. Maybe this Clayton had gotten tired of patching fences and decided to take things into his own hands. Could be that Gandy didn't even know about the shooting.

Then there were the hunters on Gandy's ranch. Deer season hadn't started officially yet, but Warren knew there were various permits a landowner could get that extended the season. Perhaps a hunter had taken a potshot at a trespasser for the sheer amusement of it. A beer or six before the hunt could ruin your judgment, not to mention your aim.

Lots of possibilities. So Warren was simply watching, wanting to see who came and went. The sun was sinking, painting cirrus clouds an amazing purple, when his cell phone rang. Calls had been coming in all day from friends and family members. Now and then an unfamiliar number would pop up, and every time Warren took a chance and answered one of those calls, it was a member of the media. Persistent sons of bitches. Warren had no comment. How the hell had they gotten this number? But this time it was Raymond Ortega, the chief of police in Hebbronville. The first thing he said was, "Heard you had some excitement down your way." He'd always been a man of understatement.

"You might say that."

"I was worried at first. Glad you walked away from it. How's your partner?" Ortega's voice was rough from the cigarettes he'd smoked for forty years. He'd quit this past spring. That was the last time Warren had talked to him.

"He'll be fine," Warren said.

"Good to hear. They gonna clear you on this thing?"

"Absolutely."

"Between you and me, you're damn lucky your partner's a Latino. More or less takes the racism thing out of it. If he was white, you'd have all the bleeding hearts screaming for your head *and* his. They'd shout brutality and oppression and all that bullshit. Forget the fact that the lowlife was about to make your wife a widow. So you dodged a bullet on that one, no pun intended."

"You might be right."

Warren saw movement. A white Ford truck was coming down the ranch's gravel road toward the open gate.

"You need anything from me, you let me know, you hear? I mean it."

"I appreciate that, Ray."

"Well, all right, then. I just wanted to make sure you were still in one piece. The reports said you were fine, but I *know* I can't believe everything I see on the news, because they're calling you a hero. The way they tell it on FOX, you should be wearing a cape."

Ortega, lightening the mood with a little levity.

"Actually, there is something," Warren said.

"Name it."

The Ford drove over the cattle guard and pulled onto the highway. Warren turned the key in the Chevy's ignition.

"I'm thinking of making a change," he said.

"What sort of change?"

"You need an extra patrolman?"

Ortega laughed. "You kidding me?"

∞

On the way to the trailer to pick up Ricky's things, Tomás said, "I like him."

"I knew you would. He's a good man."

"Where is his family?"

"His wife died last year. His son lives in Dallas."

They had reached downtown Rugoso, which wasn't much of a downtown. There were only seven stoplights in the entire city. Ricky realized that driving wasn't making him as nervous as it had yesterday. He wasn't checking the rearview mirror every mile, expecting to see police or *la migra* on his tail. But he had to be careful not to become complacent, because that would cause him to get caught. Always buckle the seatbelt. Always use turn signals. Don't speed. "This idea of his ..." Tomás said.

Ricky waited, but Tomás didn't continue. "You don't like it?" Ricky said.

"Seems crazy."

"Maybe, but it's how they handle things like this."

"To be honest, it scares me. I think it might be better to forget the whole thing."

"Just let the guy who shot you get away with it?"

"I don't want to get in trouble. I just got here. I don't want to leave already. It was a tough trip, and I don't know if I'd be willing to repeat it."

"You won't have to leave."

"How do we know that? How can we be sure Howard is right?"

Ricky didn't know the answer to that, but he trusted Howard. He was an old man, but he was wise. "Just think about it, okay?"

Tomás was studying the buildings and businesses they were passing. Wal-Mart. Home Depot. The library. The courthouse. Dairy Queen. Ricky wondered how the town looked through Tomás's eyes. Did he see hope and opportunity? Potential? Deliverance? The truth was, Rugoso wasn't a very pretty town. Some of the businesses were boarded up. Weeds grew tall in the medians. If the chicken plant ever closed its doors, Rugoso would dry up and blow away.

"Can we find a pay phone somewhere?" Tomás said. "I need to let Sarafina know what's going on."

"You haven't called her yet?"

"When have I had a chance? Besides, I told her I didn't know how long it would take to get here. I said I'd call her this weekend at the latest. Today is Friday, right?"

Ricky pulled over at a convenience store and parked on the side of the building. He removed a long-distance calling card from his wallet. "Use this. The instructions are on the back. Can you dial okay?"

"I'll be fine," Tomás said as he opened the door.

Ricky waited in the truck and listened to music. The little Nissan had a decent stereo, complete with a cassette player. Ricky didn't have any cassettes, so, for now, he tuned it to Z93, broadcasting out of Laredo. "Esperando Su Llamada" came on, one of Ricky's old favorites. Great song. Meanwhile, Tomás was having an animated conversation with Sarafina. Shaking his head repeatedly. Gesturing with his good hand. Now he was crossing himself. Ricky wondered what that was about.

He'd also been wondering about the story Tomás had told him, about a member of *la migra* coming to his hospital room. It was very puzzling. How did the man know where to find Tomás? How did he know Tomás was in the hospital? Ricky could come up with only one explanation: Since Tomás's traveling companions—Luis and Vicente—had provided details of the shooting, *la migra* must have assumed Tomás would seek medical care. But why hadn't the man arrested Tomás? Neither Ricky nor Tomás could come up with a reasonable answer to that question.

Customers came and went from the busy store, but Tomás kept talking, using up many precious minutes on Ricky's calling card. Finally, after five more songs and a commercial break, Tomás hung up and returned to the truck. He wasn't smiling. Something was wrong.

"What?" Ricky asked.

"The man who shot me is a dog," he said.

"Yes, I know. Why do you say that now?"

"Sarafina called my cell phone this morning, and the man who answered told her I was dead. Son of a whore. She's been crying all day, and telling our friends I was dead. She even went to see a priest. You should have heard the shriek when I first said hello."

Ricky turned the radio off. "Good thing you called," he said. "She might've started planning your funeral. Is she okay now?"

"She's fine."

"You miss her?"

"Very much. She said I have to call every day from now on."

"I can't blame her. She's worried, considering what happened to your hand." Tomás remained oddly quiet.

"You *did* tell her about your hand, didn't you?"

"How could I? It was hard enough just convincing her that I was still alive."

Ricky couldn't help laughing again. "You need to tell her."

"I will. Tomorrow. I promise. One more thing. I've changed my mind."

"About what?"

"Howard's idea. Let's do it. Let's sue the son of a bitch who shot me."

&

Warren followed the Ford into Rugoso, where it pulled into the Home Depot parking lot. Not many customers this time of day, near dark, so Warren parked a couple of rows over and waited.

It was the man named Clayton who stepped from the Ford. Warren still couldn't remember his last name. Clayton walked inside and Warren followed a minute later.

He had no plan. No strategy, no tactics. He was winging it. And why? Why was he doing this? He didn't have a clue. Everything else—his job, his future—

was pretty much settled in his head. Move back to Hebbronville. Ride patrol for another decade, then retire with a decent pension. Forget about the border and the turmoil surrounding it. Forget about immigrants whose thumbs had been blown off. What a relief that would be.

He went inside. Strolled through hardware, plumbing, electrical, lawn and garden. Finally, he spotted the man in the fencing aisle.

∽

Clayton had a secret—something everyone except Herschel Gandy would find very funny. No, ol' Herschel wouldn't see the humor in it at all.

The truth was, wetbacks weren't responsible for every hole in every fence on the ranch. Some of the holes, sure, but sometimes, when Clayton was filling feeders or checking cattle, he'd stop and do a little cutting himself. Part of it had to do with his job—there really wasn't that much work to keep him busy, and he didn't want Herschel or the old man wondering why they were keeping him on the payroll—and part of it was simply because he liked to see Herschel get all worked up. Man could go into a fit at the thought of a few beaners crossing his property. Nothing much he could do about it, really, short of hiring a full team of security guards. And why bother? That would cost a lot more than fixing the damage.

Herschel would say, yeah, well, what about all the things they steal? What about the scouting cameras that are always going missing? Clayton would love to spill the beans. Funny you bring that up, boss, 'cause I'm getting upwards of seventy bucks a pop for those units on the Internet. That's right. Yeah, I know they cost three hundred brand new, but once they've been used, even a little, you have to come way down on the price. Then he'd tell Herschel to use his fucking head. What good is a scouting camera to a wetback? It's not like they can eat it, ride it, or fuck it. Clayton had dealt with enough pawn brokers to know they shied away from illegal aliens. So why would the Mexicans steal them? Where would they sell them? Come on, Herschel, you think there's some vast underground network of shady hunters buying cameras directly from wetbacks? Some sort of black market in hunting-related accessories?

It always tickled Clayton to come in here with the ranch credit card and buy a roll or two of goat fence, then stop off at the sporting goods store to replace the cameras those thieving illegals had run off with.

Today, though, something was making him uneasy. He couldn't figure out what it was until he turned his head and saw a man studying him from over by the T-posts. Clayton caught the guy staring, but the man didn't look away. In fact, he smiled and nodded, as if they were old buds. Tall guy. White. Clean shaven, with short hair. Did they know each other?

"How ya doing?" the guy said, still with that loopy grin on his face.

Clayton nodded at him, then grabbed a roll of fourteen-gauge field fence and placed it on his rolling cart. A few seconds later, Clayton could sense the guy behind him.

"You're Clayton, right?"

Clayton turned, "I know you?"

"Warren Coleman. Border Patrol."

Of course. Now Clayton recognized him. One of the feds. "I didn't place you right away without the uniform. How you been doing?"

"Just fine. And you?"

"Well, I could complain, but who'd listen?"

Coleman nodded, agreeable as hell, like, *I know how that goes,* and they stood there uncomfortably for a few seconds, all alone in the aisle. Then Clayton remembered something. "I heard on the radio about a shootout yesterday. Out there on Highway Three Fifty-Nine? Was that any of your boys?"

Coleman simply stared at him. Like he was puzzled by the question. Strange. Then he finally said, "Yeah, it was."

"Everybody okay?"

Another pause. "I guess you don't watch much TV."

"No, sir."

Coleman was looking at the items on Clayton's cart. The roll of fencing. A spool of baling wire. A can of patching tar for a water trough that was starting to pit. "Yeah, everybody's fine."

Clayton didn't like the way this was going. It was something about Coleman's behavior, with all the short answers. Friendly, but not really. "Well, that's good to hear. They said something about it being drug related, which don't surprise me a bit. I know y'all are busting your asses, but it seems like the problem's only getting worse every day. I mean, you want my opinion, a fence is the way to go. Twenty feet high. And electrify the damn thing if we have to. Then put an armed guard about every half mile or so. Shoot first, ask questions later. Give y'all a little more leeway as far as taking care of business. That's the way I see it."

Clayton expected Coleman to say thanks for the support, and it's good to know the citizens are behind us. Something along those lines. Instead, he said, "That's an interesting point of view. You ever thought about shooting at 'em yourself?"

FOURTEEN

CRIS MISSED THE TURN AT FIRST, because the road was unmarked and she passed it by. *That can't be it,* she thought. *That's just a gravel road.* She double-checked her Yahoo map, decided it *was* the right road, then ventured down it, her Honda bouncing over deep potholes in the dark.

Fifty yards later, she came around a line of trees, and sure enough, a trailer park came into view. Six dilapidated mobile homes sat on either side, their noses toward the road. The light was weak back here—just bare bulbs weakly illuminating front porches. There were only a few cars, and they appeared inoperable, but there was plenty of junk: piles of rotting garbage, scrap metal and lumber, a torn sofa without cushions, a dirty mattress, a group of rusty oil drums. The ground was covered with downy pillow stuffing. But no residents at all. Kind of spooky. Where was everybody? She didn't feel particularly safe.

She wanted to turn around, but couldn't find a place to do it. So she kept creeping forward, trying to spot numbers on the trailers, and she finally saw a large group of men—perhaps thirty of them—clustered in the space between two trailers, some standing, some sitting at picnic tables. Shadows danced as a fire burned in an open pit. Chicken was on tonight's menu, judging by the aromas wafting through Cris's dashboard vents. Made sense. These were all poultry plant employees. Then it occurred to her that the material on the ground wasn't pillow stuffing; it was feathers from plucked birds.

The socializing came to a complete halt as every man in the group turned to see who had just driven up. Cris was tempted to simply put it in reverse and get out of there. Pretend she had taken a wrong turn. But that was silly. She had nothing to fear. *Don't be such a wimp.* She killed the engine, and stepped from the Honda, trying to appear confident. *Norteño* music was playing from a boombox, until somebody reached over and snapped it off. Now the only sound was from dry mesquite crackling in the flames.

"*Hola,*" Cris said. No sense in even trying English.

Somebody—one lone man—answered back without much enthusiasm. Many of the men were shirtless, and all were drinking beer. Blowing off steam on a Friday night. And staring at her. She gathered that the trailer park didn't get many female visitors.

"I'm looking for Ricky Delgado," she said. She was still wearing her scrubs and felt awkward. She'd been hoping she'd see at least one person she knew, a patient from the clinic, but none of the faces were familiar.

One young man took a few steps forward and said, "Pardon me, but … who are you?"

"My name is Cris Ruiz. I'm a nurse at Dr. King's office. It's important that I speak to Ricky."

A large mixed-breed dog emerged from the crowd and decided to give her legs a good sniff. She put a hand on its head to keep him from getting too personal.

"You just missed him," the man said. "He and his brother left about fifteen minutes ago."

"Do you know when he's coming back?"

"He's not."

The dog decided Cris was okay, and he wandered off to pee on her front tire.

"He's not coming back tonight?"

"Not ever. He doesn't live here anymore. He took all his stuff with him."

The music came back on. Most of the men had started going about their business again—drinking, eating, talking. She was no longer the object of curiosity, and she was glad for it.

The young man was still watching her from twenty feet away. "Ricky told me about a pretty nurse at the doctor's office. He must've been talking about you."

She smiled. He wasn't being coarse or lewd. There was respect in his voice. Harmless flirting. "What's your name?"

He came closer still. "Ignacio. Ricky was my roommate."

"Good to meet you, Ignacio. Do you know where Ricky went? Where is he living now?"

"I don't know, exactly. With some old man named Howard. That's all I know. Howard has garage sales."

"When is Ricky's next shift at the plant?"

"Oh, he was fired. That's why he doesn't live here anymore. These homes are only for employees. Is Ricky very sick?"

"Dr. King thinks it's the flu."

He lifted a bottle of beer and took a long drink, eyeing her the whole time. Then he said, "That's why you came out here on a Friday night? Because of the flu?"

Smart kid. "Did Ricky leave a phone number?"

Ignacio shrugged. "Sometimes he has a cell phone, but not right now. I don't know how to reach him. Hey, you want a beer? Maybe some chicken?"

"Thank you, but no. I have to go."

"Maybe you could come back sometime when it's quieter. I could make you a nice dinner."

"That's very kind, but I have a fiancé. He wouldn't understand."

"You're getting married?"

"Yes," she lied.

"Well, he's a lucky man. I hope he takes good care of you."

Under other circumstances, Cris might've said, *I don't need a man to take care of me.* Tonight, she simply said, "Thank you." Then, "Will you do me a favor, Ignacio?"

"For you, Cris, of course."

"If you see Ricky, will you ask him to call me?"

🔊

Herschel Gandy was writing an e-mail to Walter Sevier—firmly but politely saying sorry, I'm not buying thousand-dollar scouting cameras only to have them ripped off by wetbacks, and if I did, I'd only have to raise the lease fees—when he heard the front door open and close. Clayton coming back from his errands. Nearly eleven o'clock, which meant Clayton had stopped off for a few. He tended to do that on a Friday night, or they'd both go into town together and chase tail in the honky tonks until closing time. Not tonight, though, because opening day was coming up fast, and there was still a lot to do. They needed to clear brush all day tomorrow and move some blinds around. The hunters were always wanting the blinds in new locations.

Herschel continued typing, wording it just right, and pretty soon he sensed Clayton standing in the office doorway. He heard ice cubes rattling in a glass of whiskey.

"What time we starting in the morning?" Clayton asked.

"First light. I wanna get it all done tomorrow."

"That's a lot of brush for one day. Plus the weather forecast says a chance of rain."

"What, are you gonna melt?" Herschel said. He wrote: *If you intend to purchase the cameras yourself, please keep in mind that my insurance policy won't cover it if they're stolen.* Then he went back and deleted the word *please.* Sevier would probably gripe to Herschel's dad again, but screw it. This was a business, not a charity.

Clayton said, "You hear about that shootout on Three Fifty-Nine? Wetback got killed?"

"What about it?"

"That border agent—you know him?"

"He's been out here a few times. Why?"

Again the tinkle of ice cubes.

"Take it easy on that Crown Royal," Herschel said. "I don't want you draggin' ass tomorrow."

Clayton didn't give a smart-ass reply. Instead, after a pause, he said, "I'm hitting the hay. See you in the morning."

sábado

FIFTEEN

Howard's friend, the lawyer named Peter Wynn, had a very nice office. The waiting room featured a leather couch beneath an oil painting of a deer with many antlers. There were two matching chairs on the other side of a glass-topped coffee table. All of the furniture rested on a rug that appeared to have come from Asia.

Peter Wynn's assistant, Maureen, who was maybe fifty years old, sat at a desk across the room, typing on a computer keyboard. She seemed like a nice woman. She'd offered coffee when they first arrived, and Ricky could tell it wasn't an empty gesture. She also didn't seem upset that she'd had to come in on short notice on a Saturday morning. Or maybe they—she and Peter Wynn—typically worked on Saturdays anyway.

Now Tomás was sitting on the couch, with his legs crossed, sipping carefully from a ceramic mug. He looked good—though oddly out of place—in freshly laundered khaki pants, a striped golf shirt, and black loafers. His belt even matched. Ricky was similarly dressed, except his pants were more of a stone color, and his shoes had laces. They'd put the outfits together last night, sorting through mountains of used clothing in Howard's spare bedroom.

"Got that shirt for fifty cents," Howard had said at one point. "Still has the tags on it. Got those shoes for a dollar. This sport coat—well, it won't fit either of you, but it cost me two bucks. I'm gonna give it to my son next time he comes down. Good as new, except for a small tear in one of the pockets. His wife can sew that up."

Now they waited, and Ricky didn't mind, although he was a bit on edge. Howard had said Peter Wynn was a friend from the Sertoma Club, a good man, and smart, too. He'd know what to do. Ricky had asked what the Sertoma Club was, and Howard said it was a volunteer organization. *Service to mankind.* That's what Sertoma stood for. Howard had been a member for more than forty years. Not as active as he used to be, but still attending meetings once a month.

Ricky was about to ask Maureen if there was a bathroom he could use when the door to Peter Wynn's office opened and two men came out, still in the middle of a conversation.

" ... the deposition on Thursday," one man was saying. He was in his forties, with thick black hair and rimless eyeglasses. Tall and handsome, wearing a dark suit that made him look like a politician. "Once we get that out of the way, it should be smooth sailing. I imagine they'll be ready to settle at that point."

And the second man—much older, maybe seventy, dressed in a crisp white shirt with a blue bowtie and suspenders—said, "Thanks, Tom. I'll keep you posted."

That meant the older man was Peter Wynn. Ricky had been hoping he was the younger man. But Howard had said it was a good omen to hire an attorney named Wynn. The two men shook hands, and the one named Tom left, giving a quick wave to Maureen on his way out.

Then Peter Wynn turned to Howard, gave him a big smile, and said, "There you are, you old goat. Come on in here, and bring your friends."

ॐ

He spoke nearly flawless Spanish, this Peter Wynn. After Howard had introduced everybody, Mr. Wynn turned to Tomás and asked him to tell the full story, starting with his arrival in Nuevo Laredo.

Tomás recounted it all in less than fifteen minutes. He hadn't known how or where to cross, so he began asking around. Many people were willing to speak freely, but most referred him to a *coyote*, or guide. Tomás couldn't afford to pay a *coyote*; the going rate was two to three thousand dollars. Perhaps he'd have to try it on his own. Later, Tomás was in a nightclub when the bartender directed him to two inebriated men named Luis and Vicente. They had plans to cross the next evening at a secluded point some miles south of town, where Luis had entered once before. The men agreed to let Tomás tag along for the fee of one thousand pesos. If he slowed them down, Luis warned, they would leave him behind. It would be a hard trip with many miles of hiking across rough terrain. Tomás assured them he could handle the challenge.

Peter Wynn was taking notes as Tomás told his story.

Tomás said he bought a backpack and a small supply of food and bottled water the next day. Then he met Luis and Vicente in the mid-afternoon at a restaurant near the downtown market. They were drinking again—working up the courage to cross, they said. Tomás helped them finish a bottle of tequila. Shortly thereafter, a fourth man—Luis's cousin, a taxi driver—arrived and drove them south, well out of town, then east, where he dropped them off in the middle of nowhere. Tomás was required to tip the cousin three hundred pesos. It would be worth it if they managed to cross successfully.

But that's when they made a bad decision. The original plan was to cross after dark, less than an hour later, using flashlights sparingly, and only if they needed to. The river was shallow and wouldn't present any great difficulties. Luis, however, said there was no reason to wait until sunset, and he'd have an easier time spotting recognizable landmarks if they left now. Vicente agreed, and Tomás had little choice in the matter.

They waded across the river easily enough and quickly found a *sendero* to follow in a northeastern direction. Neither Luis nor Vicente had brought along a compass; they said *la migra* would accuse you of being a *coyote* if you carried a compass, and you would be treated more harshly, so it was best to navigate by the sun or stars.

"They weren't very organized," Tomás said. "They didn't have any sort of plan, really. But neither did I, so I couldn't complain. I just followed behind, which was easy, because they weren't in very good shape. Luis was a smoker and had a hard time catching his breath."

Tomás began to wonder if *he* would have to leave *them* behind, but he never had to make the decision. They had been on United States soil for less than twenty minutes when they spotted a deer blind—a tower—on the horizon.

"That's new," Luis said. "It wasn't here last time."

"Is it deer season?" Vicente asked.

"I don't know."

"No, it's not," Tomás said. He'd known to check on that before starting his journey.

"So the blind is empty," Luis said.

"I didn't say that," Tomás replied.

Nobody had binoculars. Why carry the extra weight?

"What do you want to do?" Vicente asked Luis. "Stay on the *sendero* or go around, through the brush?"

Go around, Tomás thought. *Why risk it?*

"I hate walking through this thorny shit," Luis said. "Let's get a better look."

The men edged forward slowly. Tomás thought he saw movement inside the blind, but he couldn't be sure.

"Should we wait until dark?" Vicente asked. He mentioned javelinas. He was scared of them. Tomás said that was silly. Then he saw movement again, and Luis said it was probably birds living inside the blind. Vicente agreed. Tomás began to wonder about the birds, and it occurred to him that the windows of the blind were *open*. Shouldn't they be closed? Why would the windows be open if there wasn't anybody inside the blind?

Tomás never got a chance to ask those questions, because that was when the first shot was fired.

                                               ᔓ

Peter Wynn asked questions at that point. "Did you ever see the person who fired the shot?"

"No. We ran."

"You didn't have any sort of confrontation or provoke him in any way? This is very important."

"No, absolutely not."

"How far were you from the deer blind?"

"Seventy or eighty meters."

"Earlier you said 'the first shot.' So there were more?"

"Yes, several."

"How many?"

At least ten or a dozen, Ricky thought. That's what Tomás had said when he told the story outside the trailers to all the men from the plant.

"Three more," Tomás said. He glanced at Ricky with a quick look that said, *Okay, I stretched it a little.*

Wynn said, "Do you think the person was trying to hit you? Or were they simply firing warning shots?"

Ricky knew what the lawyer was hoping Tomás would say. Apparently, so did Tomás. He said, "I don't know. I can't say that he *wasn't* trying to hit us. I would swear that I could hear the bullets passing right over my head."

"How did you react when the shot hit your hand? Did you scream out? Did you fall down?"

Tomás thought about it. "No, I just ran. I wasn't sure what had happened. I knew my hand was injured, that was all."

"Okay, please go on."

Tomás said the wound was painful, but Luis was able to stop the bleeding. The three men spent the night in the brush. They heard a truck the next morning, and saw it driving toward the blind. They didn't get a look at the driver because they were too busy hiding. The truck passed in the other direction not long afterwards. So they continued on their journey along the *sendero.* Tomás looked for his backpack, but couldn't find it. They hiked all morning and into the afternoon, crossing several county roads and highways, and they finally reached Rugoso at about two o'clock. They felt a great sense of relief, because now they were more than twenty-five miles from the border. It meant *la migra* couldn't stop them for questioning without a good reason. Luis went into a drugstore to buy some first-aid items for Tomás's hand, and not long after that, the men split up.

Peter Wynn had more questions. "When you first crossed the river onto the ranch, did you see any NO TRESPASSING signs?"

"Yes, a couple."

"Were they written in Spanish?"

"In both English and Spanish, I think."

"But definitely in Spanish?"

"Yes."

Wynn nodded, writing on his pad. "You never told the police about the incident?"

"No."

"If you went back to the ranch with the police, would you be able to show them where it happened?"

"Absolutely. There would probably be bloody rags where we spent the night."

"That would be excellent evidence. What about these other men, Luis and Vicente? Do you have a way to reach them? A cell phone number?"

"Sorry, no."

"Do you know where they were from?"

"Mexico City."

"Do you know their last names?"

Wynn obviously thought it would be important to find the men. They were witnesses who could back up Tomás's story. But Tomás shook his head at Wynn's last question.

"Do you know where they were going?"

"San Antonio at first, but I don't think they were planning to stay. Luis said they were thinking about California again. Lots of crops to pick out there. But I guess they never made it."

"How do you know that?" Wynn asked.

Tomás told him about the Border Patrol agent who'd visited his hospital room. According to *la migra*, Luis and Vicente had been picked up and eventually deported, but not before they told what had happened to Tomás. Then they changed their story and denied everything.

Peter Wynn appeared confused. "That's very interesting. This agent wasn't in uniform?"

"No."

"Did you get his name?"

"No."

"How did he know where to find you?"

"We've been wondering that, too. We don't know."

Wynn pondered it, made some more notes, then appeared to move on. "Okay, just a few more questions. This one might embarrass you, but I don't mean to cause you any discomfort. If you prefer, we can speak alone."

"No, please go ahead. Ask me anything."

Wynn said, "I need to know if you have any sort of criminal history in Mexico. Even a misdemeanor."

"No, nothing."

"You've never been arrested for anything at all? Never spent the night in jail?"

"No, sir. I've never even gotten a ticket."

Wynn smiled. "That's what I like to hear." He set his pad down and took a sip of coffee. He was carefully considering everything he had learned, and the other men waited patiently. He finally said, "Before we go too much further, let me ask another question: Have either of you ever heard of a group called Ranch Rescue?"

ର

Now it was Peter Wynn's turn to talk.

He told a story of two Salvadorans named Edwin and Fátima who were caught crossing a ranch in south Texas. The men who caught them were members of a volunteer paramilitary organization called Ranch Rescue, and their primary objective was to prevent illegal immigrants from entering the United States. Some people called them vigilantes, but spokesmen for the group claimed they were simply exercising their legal right to protect private property.

"These guys were a bunch of yahoos," Wynn said, "but they had all the right gear. Electronic surveillance equipment. Night vision goggles. All-terrain vehicles. Even trained attack dogs. But in this particular case, they crossed the line. They took the law into their own hands."

The two Salvadorans claimed that members of Ranch Rescue—dressed in camouflage—detained them at gunpoint, threatened them with death, and struck Edwin in the head with a pistol. The immigrants were eventually released, but they told their tale to authorities, and charges were filed against one member named Nethercott.

"To make a long story shorter," Wynn said, "the jury deadlocked on the assault charge, but Nethercott had a previous felony, so he got five years for possessing a handgun illegally. That charge really had nothing to do with the beating, so maybe he got off easy, I don't know. But the civil suit was a different story. Nethercott didn't answer the suit, so the judge ruled against him by default to the tune of eight hundred and fifty thousand dollars."

Ricky was doing the math in his head, to translate the sum into terms he could fully understand. $850,000. Roughly nine million pesos. ¡Dios mio! A fortune. He couldn't believe his ears. That much money for being struck in the head? How could that be? He looked at Tomás, who seemed to be in shock.

Wynn continued. "Of course, Nethercott didn't have that much money, but he did have a seventy-acre ranch in Arizona. So the court awarded ownership to the two Salvadorans. If I remember right, they sold it and wound up with a good bit of cash. Nowhere near the original judgment, but still a nice amount."

Ricky had questions. Lots of them. But before he could begin asking them, Wynn added, "And here's one more thing that might interest you. Do you know what a 'U-visa' is?"

Ricky and Tomás both shook their heads, still numb from what they were hearing.

"Well, I don't want to get your hopes up too much, but it's a special visa that is sometimes granted to illegal immigrants who are the victim of violent crime—providing you cooperate with the authorities."

"You—" Ricky said. "You are saying that Tomás would be allowed to stay in the United States?"

"If he was granted one of these visas, yes, for four years. And a visa holder who remains in the states continuously for three years can then apply for permanent residency."

"He could live here forever? Legally?"

"It's a possibility. In fact, I'd say there's a very good chance of that, *if* we can prove the crime occurred."

Tomás looked like a kid who'd just busted open a piñata filled with gold coins. Ricky began to laugh.

Howard, who spoke very little Spanish, had been sitting quietly during the entire conversation. "What?" he said, looking at Wynn, then at Ricky. "Is it good news?"

SIXTEEN

DUPREE.

That was the man's last name. Clayton Dupree. Warren had it now. He hadn't thought to ask last night, but now it came to him as he sat watching the Longhorns play Nebraska, because there was a cornerback with that name.

Warren couldn't remember the last time he'd watched a University of Texas game, because he'd always been out in the field on Saturdays. When he went back to Hebbronville, he'd have a more regular schedule. Weekends off. Nights, too, because that's what he'd told Ray Ortega. Not asked, *told*. No evening patrol. Ray had said yeah, no problem. When can you start? Once they clear me in the shooting, he'd told Ray, I'll give notice.

Now that Warren had made up his mind for sure, and given voice to his intentions, it was like having a three-inch splinter removed from his brain. He could think clearly. He could breathe. He'd slept like a baby last night, after he and Ellen had fooled around for the first time in six weeks, making that connection again, enjoying the closeness, the talking afterward, the giggling, like the early years. Wearing each other out, him on top first, then her. "Jesus, that was great, but what have you done with my husband?" she'd asked afterward, her face flushed, sweat beaded on her forehead.

It made him understand that life didn't have to be complicated. He didn't have to pick sides or decide what's right or wrong. All he had to do, when he got back home to Hebbronville, was bust speeders and assist accident victims and maybe keep the occasional stray cow off the highway. That was enough, wasn't it? He didn't have to save the country. Or choose not to save it.

But it was hard for Warren to quit thinking about Dupree.

Last night, the man wouldn't open up. Warren had said he was looking into the shooting of an illegal alien, and Dupree said, "I got no idea what you're talking about." Standing there in the aisles of Home Depot, lying his ass off. Warren could see his face tighten up, could hear the slight tremor in his voice.

"Who works the ranch nowadays?" Warren asked him. "Just you and Gandy?"

"Yes, sir."

"Any hunters out there this week? Getting ready for the season?"

There was a pause. Warren could almost hear the gears spinning. Dupree was wanting to say yeah, there were a bunch of hunters out there—but then he'd have to come up with a list of names. And phone numbers. And Warren would call them. So Dupree said, "No, but we get poachers sometimes. Check with the warden. He'll tell you."

Shifting the blame. Pointing the finger elsewhere. So typical.

"You hear any shots on Wednesday evening?"

"I hear shots almost every day, people shooting at coyotes or hogs or sighting in their rifles."

An attractive middle-aged woman in a velveteen jogging suit was coming down the aisle slowly with a cart, scanning the shelves.

"But did you hear any on Wednesday evening?"

"I can't remember. Maybe."

"Where were you?"

"When?"

Warren was starting to lose his temper. "We're talking about Wednesday evening, aren't we?"

Clayton Dupree had the air of a tough guy, an authentic cowboy, all weathered skin and wiry muscle, but he was plainly intimidated. "Okay, take it easy. You weren't clear. I guess I was hanging around the ranch, because this is my first time in town since last weekend."

"Where was Gandy?"

The woman had gotten closer with her cart, and she had one hand on a roll of chicken wire, but she was looking around for a sales associate.

Dupree started to say something, but seemed to change his mind. Then, in a lower voice, he said, "Look, I don't know where you're headed with this, but I can't help you. I don't know anything about it, and neither does Herschel."

"How do you know?"

"How do I know what?"

"Whether Herschel knows anything. Were you with him on Wednesday evening?"

Dupree shook his head slowly and let out an exasperated sigh, like, *The nerve of this guy.* "Man ... I got nothing else to say."

"Excuse me." It was the woman, suddenly at Warren's elbow, smiling. "Do either of you know anything about chicken wire?"

Clayton was obviously happy for the interruption. "Sure do. What would you like to know?"

"Well, an armadillo has been tearing up my garden ... "

"Those little boogers are pests, ain't they? You want to fence him out?"

"I'd like to, yes."

"Well, you're gonna need something a little stronger, like horse fence, or even stock panel. Here, let me show you."

And Warren had let him go. The guy wasn't going to talk. And what if he did? It wasn't even an official case, and if it were, it would be the sheriff's responsibility, not Warren's. Plus, if Warren learned anything about the shooting, he'd have to come forward and share it, which meant he'd eventually have to tell what he saw on Tuesday morning. *That's right. I saw some illegal aliens crossing the highway and I did absolutely nothing about it.*

No, the smart move was to let it go. Forget about it. All things considered, it wasn't that big of a deal, was it? It wasn't like ignoring a homicide or a major drug-smuggling ring.

So he cracked another beer and tried to focus on the game. Texas had just scored when Warren's cell phone rang. Eddie Bustamante, asking if Warren could come see him that afternoon. He had some news.

℘

It turned out to be a very bad day, and the label on Herschel Gandy's plastic bottle of non-dairy coffee creamer was at least partially to blame. It was written in both English and Spanish, and that pissed him off more than words in either language could express. He'd noticed it before, of course. How could you not? Walk down the aisles of a grocery store and you'd see that just about every label was bilingual nowadays.

But at the moment, as Herschel sat in his truck—supervising as Clayton mowed down brush with the Bobcat—the words on the bottle really began to eat at him. He'd just made himself a fresh cup of coffee, and he'd put the bottle on the dashboard, and his eyes kept straying to the words on the label.

CREMA SIN LACTOSA PARA CAFÉ
DATOS DE NUTRICIÓN
SIN COLESTEROL

Just words, right? Not hardly. They were symbols of the threat to America, and that was obvious to anyone who took two seconds to think about it. What those Spanish words said, between the lines, was, "Hey, you don't need to speak English to make it in America! Just come on up and keep speaking Spanish. You don't have to change. We'll go out of our way to accommodate you!"

What was that buzzword he heard all the time? *Assimilation.* Politicians used it to describe the blending of foreigners into American culture. Yeah, well, it was all bullshit. Mexicans weren't blending, they were bringing their own culture with them, creating their own communities—and *that* was the problem.

Think about it.

Who was it that turned this country into the one and only superpower on the globe? The answer was obvious, if you were honest. It was white people. White men, to be specific. Men like Washington and Jefferson. Patton and MacArthur. Ronald Reagan. Leaders with vision.

What would happen when men like that no longer held the reins of power in this country? What would happen when the Mexican population grew large enough to elect one of their own as president? Most people didn't have the guts to ask those questions, but Herschel knew they crossed a lot of people's minds. What would the future hold when the minorities took over? If Mexicans ran the country, wouldn't it end up just like Mexico? Why wouldn't it? Most important of all, why were we all sitting back and letting it happen?

The label on the creamer had a phone number on it. Herschel couldn't resist. He unfolded his cell phone and dialed. He was greeted by an automated voice—one that instructed him to *oprima el dos* if he wanted to continue in Spanish. He waited. After a moment, a pleasant young woman answered.

Herschel got right to it. "I'd like to talk to somebody about the label on your coffee creamer."

"Yes, how may I assist you?"

"What I'm wondering is, how come you repeat all the words in Spanish?"

"Pardon?"

"Why do you repeat everything in Spanish?"

"That's for the convenience of our Spanish-speaking customers."

"Well, duh, but where *are* those customers?"

"I'm sorry, I'm not sure I understand the question."

"Where are they located? Are your Spanish-speaking customers in Mexico?"

"No, they are chiefly in the United States."

"So they're here, where they should be speaking English, but they don't have to learn, because companies like yours are making it easy on them."

"Sir, I—"

"You're bending over backwards to make the Mexicans happy. Don't you think that's a crock of shit?"

"Uh, sir, I'm going to let you speak to my supervisor."

Herschel was getting worked up. "I think that's a dandy idea."

She put him on hold, and after a brief wait, another pleasant woman—this one older—came on the line. "This is Andrea Bates, how may I help you today?"

"Andrea, here's the situation. I don't think your company should be putting Spanish words on your product labels, because it means Mexicans don't have to learn English, and if you want to live here, you should learn how to speak it."

"I understand your concerns, sir."

"And?"

"And what?"

"What are you going to do about it?"

"I'll be happy to forward your complaint to our director of marketing."

"I got an idea. Why don't you just let me talk to him directly?"

"I'm afraid he's not at this location, he's at corporate headquarters. I can transfer you if you'd like."

"What are the odds I'll actually get to talk to him?"

Andrea Bates chuckled. "Honestly, sir, pretty slim. He's a busy man. But you can definitely speak to someone in his department."

"Okay, fine, go ahead and transfer me. What's this guy's name?"

"The director of marketing?"

"Yeah."

"Roberto Benavides."

"Jesus, you've got to be fucking kidding me."

He hung up on her.

♋

Early Saturday afternoon, Ricky and Tomás propped a ladder against the back of Howard's house and climbed up on the metal roof. Good thing the sunlight was blocked by the canopy of a large pecan tree or the sheet metal would be too hot to touch. Get up here in August, in direct sunlight, and it could raise blisters in seconds. But it was manageable right now.

Tomás had insisted on helping, even though his abilities were limited. He sat nearby with a coffee can full of roofing screws as Ricky searched for the source of the leak in Howard's kitchen.

They hadn't spoken much about the meeting that morning in Peter Wynn's office. The thought of what could happen—it was overwhelming. To talk about it too much might jinx it.

Now, though, Tomás said, "Hey, Ricky. Did you understand everything he said? The lawyer?"

"Mostly, I think, yeah."

"I think I did, too. Except maybe the part about the evidence."

Wynn had said that a civil case was different than a criminal case. Instead of proving something beyond a reasonable doubt, you simply needed a "preponderance" of the evidence. As an example, he said that was why the Goldman family had been able to sue O. J. Simpson successfully, even though he hadn't been convicted of a crime. Interesting. Wynn also said there was a high probability that the case would be settled, which meant there wouldn't even be a trial. Depending on the terms, he'd said, that might be best for Tomás. If they went to trial and won, they'd have to wait through various appeals, and the entire process could take years. Also, Tomás could very well lose. You just never knew what a jury was going to do, especially right now, when the immigration issue was causing emotions to run high.

Ricky was turning screw heads with a quarter-inch socket, and it was easy to see why the roof had been leaking. He'd encountered this problem before.

The constant expansion and contraction of the metal had slowly pulled many of the screws out of the underlying wood runners. That created a small gap between the metal roof and the rubber washer on the screw; a place for water to sneak in. Many of the screws could be retightened, but some of them couldn't get a good hold in the wood because it had softened from the moisture.

"I would like to have a car like his someday," Tomás said, grinning. "Maybe I'll buy one for you, too."

After the interview at Peter Wynn's office, all four of them had climbed into his Mercedes sedan and taken a drive. The attorney wanted Tomás to point out the ranch where the shooting had taken place. Tomás had found it easily enough.

"That's what you want?" Ricky said. "A fancy car?"

"Well, not just that. I want a truck first—for work—then a nice house for me and Sarafina. A place where we can raise some kids."

Ricky didn't want to ruin Tomás's daydreaming by repeating what Peter Wynn had said at the end of their meeting, so he concentrated on the task at hand. What he'd do is pull the screws that wouldn't retighten and patch those holes with silicone caulk. Then he'd drive a new screw a few inches away, in firm wood. Shouldn't take long. If he didn't finish today, he'd finish tomorrow morning. Then the roof would be as good as new. Howard would be pleased. Earlier, he had said that a roofing company had given him a repair estimate of seven hundred dollars. Howard told them they were crazy. The next salesman said Howard needed an entirely new roof, and that would run about eight thousand dollars. But Howard wasn't dumb enough to fall for it. He told the guy, "All that roof needs is ten cents' worth of caulk in the right place." He knew that water can't go through metal unless there's a hole, and if there's a hole, all you have to do is patch it. But Howard was too old to be climbing on a roof.

"The homes here are so large," Tomás said. "Why do they build them so big?"

Ricky didn't answer, because he was making a list in his head. He'd need to make a trip down the ladder for the caulk, a caulk gun, and a cordless drill. Howard had all of those things, of course. He seemed to have at least one of everything.

"Just two bedrooms," Tomás said. "Maybe three. That's all we'd need. I can always add on later."

Ricky sat down on the roof and took a break. "You shouldn't even be thinking about those things."

Tomás shrugged. "What does it hurt?"

"What if Peter Wynn is wrong? What if you don't get to stay here? And even if you do, what about Sarafina?"

Tomás fidgeted with screws in the coffee can. He didn't say anything.

"They might not let her into the country," Ricky said. "You should prepare yourself for that possibility. If they give you a visa, she won't be able to join you for at least three years. Probably more like four or five, or even longer. And you can't go back home to see her. That's what Peter Wynn said. You have to stay here for three years *continuously*."

Tomás still didn't say anything. He was picking up handfuls of screws and slowly letting them drop back into the can. Ricky's backside was getting warm from the metal. He should get on with the repair, but he needed to finish this conversation, because he knew exactly what Tomás was thinking.

"She can't come here illegally, Tomás. If she does, and they catch you with her, you'll both be sent back home. You understand that?"

Tomás finally looked up. "They won't catch her."

"That's a stupid thing to say. How can you know that?"

"We'll be careful. She'll stay home."

Ricky laughed. "You'll keep her in the house all the time like a prisoner? You really think Sarafina will go for that? It would drive you both crazy."

"Why wouldn't they let her in?"

"Weren't you paying attention to Peter Wynn?"

"Of course I was."

"Then you already know the answer. There's a waiting list, and not everybody on the list gets approved. Very few get approved."

"He said Sarafina would automatically get a visa if I earn citizenship. He said spouses don't have to wait."

Ricky stood and brushed the seat of his blue jeans. The clouds were getting darker. It might rain tonight. "Yes, but that will take years, if it happens at all. That's my point. Can the two of you be apart that long? Is it worth it? You have to be realistic."

Tomás grudgingly said, "Yeah, I know. You're right." Then his face brightened. "If I win enough in the lawsuit, there won't be any reason to stay here. I might as well take the money and go home."

SEVENTEEN

WHEN THEY BROKE FOR LUNCH and a cold beer, Herschel was still fuming about the coffee creamer. What was the point of speaking to a man named Benavides? As futile as talking to a congressman named Hernandez or a district attorney named Cortez. Waste of breath. And frustrating. Scary thing was, men like that were slipping into positions of power, then quietly changing the way things worked.

Herschel tried to push it from his mind, checking the sky, which was starting to cloud up. Rain coming.

"You need to pick up the pace," he said to Clayton, who was sitting on the tailgate of Herschel's truck, eating a ham sandwich.

Clayton didn't reply right away. He kept chewing, concentrating on his sandwich, then said, "Going as fast as I can."

"I want to get it done today."

Now Clayton looked up. "Yeah, I know, but what am I supposed to do?" Defensive as hell.

"Quit driving that rig like an old lady."

Clayton snorted. "You wanna drive it for a while?"

"That's *your* job."

"Then get off my ass."

They locked eyes for a few seconds, but Clayton finally looked away. Took another bite. Herschel didn't like being sassed, but he didn't have a quick reply, because he'd never bothered to learn how to operate the Bobcat. He finished his beer, tossed the empty over Clayton's head into the truck bed, and grabbed another can from the cooler. Last thing he needed was a smart-mouthed employee.

"If I knew how to drive that thing," he said, "why would I need you around?"

"Hell, Herschel, if you got something to say, go ahead and say it."

"Just be careful, is all. You might talk yourself out of a job."

"You know what? I'd probably be better off if I did. Wouldn't have to listen to your shit."

"I think it's the other way around. You're the one with an attitude lately."

Clayton had half a sandwich in his hand. He tossed it into the brush. "That's because you don't appreciate anything I do for you. You treat me like a goddamn wetback. We used to be friends, but now you're always ordering me around, and bitching when I don't do it fast enough."

"I'm your boss, remember?"

"Yeah, I know, but that doesn't mean you have to be an asshole."

Herschel took another gulp of beer, giving himself time to come up with a response. He thought of one. "Considering what I pay you, you oughta just keep quiet and deal with it."

Clayton shook his head, like, *I can't believe what I'm hearing.* "Yeah, right. *You* pay me."

"What's that mean?"

"You don't pay me, your daddy does."

Herschel was getting hot. "*I* run this place."

"For your daddy."

"Yeah, so what? My dad owns the ranch. What does that have to do with anything?"

"You're a spoiled kid who never had to work for anything in his life."

"You shut your fucking mouth."

"The funny thing is, you *complain* all the time. You complain about your dad, you complain about the wetbacks, you complain about the hunters who pay you a fortune to lease this place out. Christ, just get over it, will you? You've got it made. Fucking grow up."

Herschel's face was burning. He dropped his beer can and stepped forward. Clayton hopped nimbly off the tailgate.

"You wanna try me?" Clayton said. "Well, come on, buddy. I been looking forward to this for a long time."

Herschel was too angry to think clearly. He swung a looping punch at Clayton's head, but Clayton backed away and dodged it. He assumed the stance of a boxer. Herschel stepped forward and threw another haymaker. Nothing but air. Clayton danced effortlessly out of reach.

"Too slow," he said. "You're out of shape."

"We'll see."

"You bet we will."

Herschel decided to try a different tactic. He lowered his head and charged, hoping to wrestle Clayton to the ground—but Clayton simply stepped to one side and popped him in the kidney as he passed. The pain was intense. He was beginning to breathe heavily.

"You're out of your league, *boss,*" Clayton said.

"Fuck you."

"Ooh, good one. Clever as always."

Herschel moved forward again slowly, raising his fists. One good shot, that's all he wanted. Enough to knock that smirk off Clayton's face. Put him in his place. But Clayton kept feinting, moving side to side. Thought he was

Muhammad Ali.

Herschel said, "Why don't you—"

Clayton smacked him in the lip with a stinging left jab. Herschel could immediately taste blood.

Clayton said, "Hey, *boss*, you better call this off before you really get hurt."

Herschel spit a wad of red saliva into the dirt. "Why don't you quit being a pussy and fight like a man?"

Clayton laughed. "Is that what *you're* doing? Doesn't seem to be working out so good. You can't—"

Herschel rushed him again, intent on getting a grip on Clayton's lanky frame—but he wasn't fast enough. He didn't have the speed or the skills. As he charged forward, he knew he'd made a mistake. He saw Clayton begin to rotate his torso, leading with his right shoulder, followed by a big right hand. Herschel saw it coming, but he didn't have time to stop.

The impact was enormous.

He could feel Clayton's knuckles slamming squarely into his nose, his head whipping backward. His knees buckled and he fell onto his butt, blood gushing over his mouth, down his chin, onto his shirt. His ears were ringing. His eyes were watering. He was suddenly very tired.

"We about done here?" Clayton said. He was taunting Herschel. Sounding smug.

"Fuck off."

"Because if we are, there's something you should know. That border agent? Warren Coleman? Last night he stopped me at the Home Depot and asked if I knew anything about a shooting on the ranch."

How had this day turned shitty so fast? Herschel waited. Clayton didn't say anything more. So Herschel had to ask. "What'd you tell him?" His voice sounded different, like he had a head cold.

Clayton took his sweet time answering. Got a beer from the cooler, popped it open, took a long drink. Then he said, "I told him I had no idea what he was talking about. He tried to come on as a hardass, but I told him to shove it. I said there was no truth to it all, and if he didn't like that, he could go fuck hisself."

"Think he bought it?"

"I think so, yeah, but that's not even the point. I *lied* for you, man, even though you've been treating me like crap. *That's* the point. Next time, I might not feel so loyal."

"What, are you threatening me?"

"What do you expect? I've been putting up with your bullshit for too long."

Herschel wiped his nose with his sleeve. Lots of blood. He struggled to his feet, still feeling a little woozy. He'd lost his Stetson in the scuffle, so he picked it up, dusted it off, and put it back on head. It was clear what he had to do. There was no way around it.

"You're right," Herschel said. "I'm sorry. I really am. Dealing with the hunters and my old man and all that—it really puts me in a bad mood. I've been taking it out on you. I apologize for that. Seriously."

Clayton didn't respond.

Herschel said, "We okay, man? You whipped my ass good. Isn't that enough?" He stepped closer and stuck out his hand. Clayton hesitated. Left him hanging. Then he finally nodded and shook Herschel's hand.

"I lost my temper," Clayton said.

"Me, too." Herschel laughed. "Damn, I need some aspirin. You really nailed me good."

He walked from the rear of the truck to the driver's-side door. Opened it. His hands were beginning to tremble. His holstered .45 was there on the seat, right where it always was. Never know when you'll need a weapon in a wild place like this. Rattlesnakes. Trespassers. Traitors.

He didn't allow himself to think about it. *Just do it. Take care of business.* He came back around with the revolver feeling as heavy as a brick in his hand.

Clayton was tipping his beer back, drinking, and he didn't see what was coming. Herschel shot right through the bottom of the can into Clayton's head.

&

"Being a Border Patrol agent," said Eddie Bustamante, leaning back in his office chair, searching for the right words, "is like being a piglet roasting on a skewer. You catch heat from every side. We got the so-called patriots who think we're too soft on the illegals, and we got the liberals who think we're nothing short of a modern-day Gestapo." He paused for dramatic effect. "Screw 'em all, that's what I say. You can't please everybody. I guess you've been watching the news? You've heard the latest?"

"No, sir," said Warren Coleman. "Not since Friday night. To be honest, I got tired of it."

Eddie nodded gravely. "Understandable. Well, it's nothing to worry about, really. Some lefty pinhead went on Larry King last night and called you an oppressor, a tool of the police state. He said what you did was nothing short of an execution. You believe that? This asshole has none of the facts—he wasn't *there* when it all went down—yet he feels qualified to give an opinion. Called us all a bunch of jackbooted thugs. Ridiculous. 'Jackbooted thugs.' How trite is that? Anyway, that's not why I called you in."

Warren waited patiently. He wasn't worried. He had no reason to be.

"You've been officially cleared on the shooting," Eddie said. "Just like we all knew you would be."

"That's good to hear."

"We're all very proud of you, Coleman. A man died, yeah, but it was outstanding work on your part. By the book, with no policy violations. A situation came up, and you did what you had to do. In the process, you reminded all of America what we're up against."

"I, uh ... thank you, sir."

"You're free to go back on duty immediately, but I'd like you to take a few more days off. Get your head on straight. Decompress. Settle your nerves."

"Actually, my nerves are pretty good."

Eddie smiled, but there was something patronizing about it. "I'm sure they are, but, well, you've got some vacation time coming, and we'd all like to see you take some of it. There's no reason to rush back to the front lines. You earned a break. Go. Enjoy yourself."

Warren took a deep breath. Now was the time. "I've been thinking about a longer break than that, to tell the truth. A permanent break. In fact, I'm giving two weeks' notice."

Warren felt like he'd just stuck a needle into a beach ball. All the pressure was gone. Eddie looked stunned. His smile slowly faded. "I didn't expect this at all. What—"

"I'm going back to Hebbronville," Warren said. "Back to my old job."

"Do you—"

"I've been thinking about this for a long time, Eddie, way before the shooting. I appreciate your support, but the fact is, I've had enough. I've done my time. I'm tired of catching noodles. I'm tired of colanders and sieves. I don't want to be a piglet on a skewer anymore."

domingo

EIGHTEEN

"I'M NOTHING BUT AN OLD POLACK," Howard said. "My granddaddy was born in Warsaw in 1887. Factory worker. He came over in 1910, through Ellis Island, like everybody else. Millions of them, coming from damn near every country you can name. Funny thing about that island. Did you know it's mostly manmade? They built it out of landfill—thirty-two acres of it."

It was ten before eight on Sunday morning. Tomás was still sleeping. He had taken a pain pill early in the morning. Ricky and Howard were sitting in the kitchen, drinking coffee, talking, as rain pounded the metal roof.

The threatening skies of the day before had held overnight, until an hour ago, and now it was coming down in sheets. The street in front of the house was already flooded. Very few cars had driven past. Everybody seemed to be holing up and waiting it out. Howard's back yard looked like a small lake. Despite feeling poorly, Ricky had hoped to get out today and look for day labor, or maybe try to find a job as a busboy or a dishwasher, but the weather had put a stop to those plans.

There was some good news, though: the saucepan on the floor was empty. So far. Ricky knew that it could take a while for a leak to start dripping. Sometimes water had to pool in the attic or a crawlspace before there was enough to come through the ceiling. But he was optimistic that he had fixed the roof.

Howard said, "Anyway, there weren't many restrictions back then. Unless you were flat-out crazy or diseased or a convict, they let you in. Nobody was an 'illegal immigrant' because there was no such thing. Well, except for the Chinese. No Chinese were allowed since the 1880s. Then, in 1924, they passed some quota laws against other types of people. They wanted to keep out all kinds of Orientals, plus the southern and eastern Europeans, especially the Jews and Italians."

"What if you were from Mexico?" Ricky asked.

"No limits on Mexicans. They could still get in. The border wasn't even guarded. You could come and go as you pleased."

"How do you know all this? You weren't even born yet."

"My uncle—my daddy's brother—tried to come over in 1936. At that time, I was eleven years old. They wouldn't let him in."

"Because he was Polish?"

"Because he was Jewish. So he stayed in Poland. My daddy got a letter from him dated in June of '38, and that was the last anyone ever heard of him."

Ricky had read enough about the Holocaust to know what had happened to Howard's uncle. He kept silent for a respectful moment, then said, "What was the reason for the quotas?"

Howard shook his head. "Oh, they gave a lot of reasons, but most of it was bullshit. Part of it—very few people said this outright—but the big part of it had to do with some people thinking the superior races came from northern Europe. There was a book—*The Great Race*, I think. No, *The Passing of the Great Race*. Can't remember the writer's name, but he said all the best things mankind had ever done, it was the Nordic people who'd done it. They were the best of the best, and they shouldn't mix with other races."

"This was an American writer?"

"Yep. That surprise you?"

"That sounds like what Hitler would say."

"You bet it does."

Ricky was mesmerized by this discussion. He had never heard these things before. "People in the United States believed that?"

"A lot of folks did, at least in part, including Calvin Coolidge. He was the president when those quota laws got passed. Boy, he said some things that ... well, if a president said them today, he'd get tossed out of office for being a racist. Hell, somebody would probably burn the White House down. But things were different back then. Being a bigot wasn't such a big thing, because everybody was griping about one group or another. Same old arguments, too. Immigrants bring wages down. They won't learn English. They're all a bunch of criminals. They're stupid and inferior. People were saying stuff like that two hundred years ago, and a hundred years ago, and they'll still be saying it when we're both dead and gone. Except they probably won't be bitching about the Mexicans by then. It'll be some other group—maybe Canadians or Australians or who the hell knows. It ain't ever gonna end. It's just natural for people to want to keep things the way they are. We got it good here. People are always afraid someone's gonna come along and ruin it. What they forget is, we're *all* immigrants. Well, unless you're a native Indian. They're the ones who shoulda had an immigration policy, if you ask me. They shoulda been waiting there at Plymouth Rock, checking for passports."

Ricky smiled. It was a funny thing to picture, the Pilgrims being turned away because they didn't have the proper documents. What would this country be like today if that had happened? What would the world be like if America hadn't been peopled with such a variety of immigrants? How would that have changed the course of history?

Neither man said anything for several moments. Ricky didn't feel the need to speak. He was comfortable here, out of the rain, listening to the ruminations of an old man who'd seen so many things.

"Just when I think it can't come down any harder," Howard said, "it does." Ricky glanced at the saucepan, and Howard saw where he was looking.

"Not a drop, by God!" the old man said, and he roared with laughter. "I *told* those sonsabitches it just needed some caulk in the right place."

∞

Cris Ruiz had done some research yesterday, just to see if she was over-reacting.

Psittacosis—also known as ornithosis or parrot fever—was much less serious, and far more uncommon, than it had been before the advent of antibiotics. Confirmed human cases numbered no more than four or five dozen in the U.S. every year, primarily among bird dealers and hobbyists, pet shop and zoo employees, veterinarians, and, of course, poultry plant workers. Like Ricky Delgado and Rocendo Ochoa. There were likely many other cases that went unreported or were misdiagnosed.

The manner of presentation varied wildly. One patient might be asymptomatic, while another experienced a raging fever that peaked and disappeared in just a few days. A third patient might suffer a fever that climbed and fell repeatedly over the course of several weeks. He thinks he's getting better, then suffers a relapse.

Rarely, psittacosis could lead to complications—endocarditis, myocarditis, keratoconjunctivitis, hepatitis, encephalitis, or pneumonia severe enough to require intensive-care hospitalization. With proper treatment, chiefly doxycycline or tetracycline, the mortality rate was fairly low—from one percent to five percent, depending on how early the case was caught. But the risk was much greater for those who received improper care or no treatment at all. Especially those patients who were experiencing more serious symptoms, like Delgado. *Assuming he even has psittacosis,* Cris reminded herself. But if he *did* have it, he needed to start a course of antibiotics immediately.

Which was why Cris was currently sitting in the office of Wayne Skaggs, the plant manager at Kountry Fresh Chicken. Skaggs, Cris noticed, had a battery-powered singing fish on a plaque behind his desk. Cris had seen those fish before—they were a popular novelty item several years earlier—and she had wondered what sort of person would own such a tacky piece of junk. Now she knew: a man like Wayne Skaggs.

She didn't like to make snap judgments about anyone, but Skaggs was easy to pigeonhole. Just your average garden-variety redneck. Can of Copenhagen on the desktop. Several trophy deer mounted on the wall. Photos of Skaggs, clad in camo, posing with those trophy deer right after he assassinated them.

He'd called her "darlin'" a moment ago, as in, "What can I do for you, darlin'?" Giving her a big smile. More of a leer, really.

She hadn't expected to end up in the manager's office—she'd never even heard Skaggs's name until five minutes ago—but when she'd gone to the front office of the plant, asking questions about Ricky Delgado, the woman there had suggested that Cris should talk to him. That woman had then called someone named Carmen, and Carmen—a beautiful young girl—had come to the front office and led Cris down several hallways to this office. Now ... here she was, face to face with the plant manager, which seemed a little odd. Why would the plant manager concern himself with something like this?

In answer to Skaggs's question, Cris said, "Thanks for seeing me. I was asking the woman up front about an employee named Ricky Delgado. I need to get in touch with him, and I was thinking somebody in Personnel could help me out."

Skaggs gazed at her for a long moment. "Nobody back there today. Those folks work five days a week. What do you need to know?"

There were no windows in the office, but Cris could hear thunder. It had been pouring when she arrived at the plant, and the weather forecast called for rain all morning, clearing up in the early afternoon.

She said, "I understand Mr. Delgado doesn't work here anymore, and I was hoping he might've left a forwarding address, or even a phone number."

Skaggs continued to eyeball her, starting to grin again. Very patronizing. "You mind if I inquire as to what this is about? We got some sort of problem?"

She tried smiling back at him. "Well, it's a confidential matter."

"'A confidential matter.'"

"That's right."

He chuckled. He appeared very amused. "'Confidential,'" he said again. "I have to hand it to you, sugar. That's about as vague as it gets. I mean, come on, I don't even know who you are. There's privacy laws about this stuff. I can't just open up the personnel files to anybody that asks, even when they's as good-looking as you are."

A clumsy compliment, yes, but there was more to it than that. Since the plant obviously employed illegal aliens, Skaggs had to be wondering if she was a federal agent. A Border Patrol agent. So she'd have to reveal who she was and, to some degree, why she was looking for Ricky Delgado. Fortunately, she had doctor-patient privilege to fend off some of the more invasive questions. She tried to put him at ease.

"Okay, here's the situation. I'm a nurse at Dr. King's office. Mr. Delgado had an appointment last week. His condition requires some minor follow-up care, but we haven't heard from him. So I'd like to speak to him."

"Condition?" Skaggs said.

Cris nodded, but she didn't say anything.

"What sort of condition?"

"I'm afraid I can't say. Just like you, privacy laws."

"From what I saw, the boy had the common flu. Blew chunks all over my office."

This guy was a regular silver-tongued devil.

"Do you have a lot of workers out with the flu right now?" Cris asked. The flu was easily passed from person to person. Psittacosis was not.

"Just a couple," Skaggs said. "We run a clean house. Disinfect the snot out of everything, top to bottom, after every shift. Tends to knock the crap outta any bug that might be going around." Skaggs was very proud of that fact. He wasn't lying, either, because the entire facility smelled like bleach, or some other disinfectant. In fact, she'd smelled it from the moment she stepped out of her car in the parking lot. Even in the rain, she'd smelled it.

"That's good to hear," Cris said. She waited a few beats, then said, "So, you think you can help me out?"

He shifted in his chair, which squealed under him. The man could stand to lose some weight. "Well ... yes and no. Yes, for you, I'll fudge a little and tell you what I know. And what I know is, we don't have nothing in his file. Don't know where he went or how to contact him. You gotta understand, most of these guys are drifters. He could be halfway to California by now."

∞

If someone had asked what he was doing, Warren wouldn't have been able to explain himself. He was on his way to see Danny, but he found himself driving toward Herschel Gandy's ranch instead. What was motivating him, exactly? Was it the fact that a crime had occurred, and that Warren felt obliged to uphold the law? Or maybe he simply thought it was a shitty situation, that Tomás Delgado had gotten shot for illegally crossing the border. He honestly couldn't figure it out, and it made even less sense when he considered that he was putting himself in jeopardy by looking into it.

You've got integrity, Coleman. That's what it is. You're a man of deeply held convictions.

Yeah, right. That's why he'd never told Danny, or Eddie Bustamante, about his on-the-job misgivings.

Maybe he *did* have convictions, but not the ones he'd always thought he'd had.

Whatever the case, here he was, on Highway 83, heading toward the Gandy place in the middle of a thunderstorm. He realized, without having thought about it, that his goal was to speak directly to Gandy this time. Ask him about

Clayton Dupree. See how he reacts. Most people can't lie worth a damn. If Herschel Gandy knew anything about the shooting—including whether Dupree was involved—Warren figured he'd be able to tell.

There were a lot of possibilities.

Maybe Dupree had done the shooting, and Gandy didn't know anything about it.

Maybe Dupree had done the shooting, and Gandy *did* know.

Maybe *Gandy* had done the shooting.

Maybe Gandy and Dupree had done it together.

Maybe neither of them were involved at all.

Maybe Tomás Delgado had made the whole thing up.

Maybe this was a wild goose chase. Maybe, as Warren had decided yesterday morning, he should forget about it. Quit wasting his time. Stop being so obsessive. It wasn't healthy. It made sense to let it go. Okay, then.

He was about to make a U-turn when he saw a large white object on the horizon, distorted by the rain on his windshield. As he got closer, he saw that it was a vehicle on the side of the road. A Ford truck—Clayton Dupree's truck—and the problem was a flat rear tire on the passenger's side.

Warren slowed, thinking Dupree might be in the Ford, waiting for the rain to let up. But the truck was empty. And when Warren neared the entrance to the ranch, the gate was closed, which was unusual. Gandy, like a lot of local landowners, usually left his gate open for the illegal aliens. Not as a courtesy, but an act of desperation. Give them an easy path, so they won't cut your fence. Not that it worked. Open gates also gave agents like Warren easier access to private property, so they could do their jobs more efficiently.

Warren pulled into the entrance and saw that the gate wasn't just closed, it was chained and padlocked. Good possibility that Herschel Gandy was out of town.

What now? Hike all the way up to Gandy's house in this downpour, only to find that he isn't home? Screw that.

NINETEEN

H ERSCHEL THOUGHT IT STILL SEEMED UNREAL, like when you wake up to the lingering remnants of a disturbing dream. For those first few seconds, you're still in panic mode, thinking you're really falling, or you're naked in public, or you went ahead and married that bitchy ex-girlfriend. But in your bones, you *know* it's not real, and all you have to do is chill out and wait for your head to clear.

But this *was* real, and the proof—Clayton's body—was still lying where Herschel had left it, ten yards from the Bobcat. Herschel had hoped his problems might simply disappear overnight, but nothing had changed.

Why not? Why hadn't the pigs, coyotes, and buzzards ripped him apart? Leave a deer carcass sitting out and it would always be gone by morning. But the beasts hadn't touched Clayton. Maybe the human scent had kept the varmints, predators, and scavengers at bay.

Which meant Herschel would have to fix the problem himself, right in the middle of this shitty weather. Raining like a son of a bitch, turning the *sendero*s into muddy bogs. Thank God for four-wheel drive.

Herschel parked his truck and stepped outside. He was dressed in rain gear, but he'd end up drenched and there was no use worrying about it. Just get it done.

He climbed into the enclosed cab of the Bobcat and fired up the machine. That part was easy. Just turn the key, like a car. Gas pedal on the floorboard. Release the parking brake. Now to figure out these joysticks. One for each hand. What the fuck was wrong with a regular old steering wheel? Why make things complicated?

He knew one of the joysticks operated the motion of the vehicle itself, while the other controlled the rotary saw or the bucket or whichever piece of equipment you had attached up front. But which joystick was which? Why weren't they clearly marked?

He eased the left stick forward and the Bobcat began to roll. Okay, good. Ease it to the right and the Bobcat veered in that direction. This wasn't as difficult as it seemed. Sort of fun, actually. Like a big toy.

Now all he had to do was drive it back to the utility barn, attach the backhoe implement, and he'd be in business. Dig a hole and bury Clayton good and deep. The rain might even turn out to be a blessing. It would literally cover his tracks.

"You got a good-looking nurse named Cris?" Wayne Skaggs asked over the phone.

Dr. David King could tell that Skaggs was angry. "Yeah, I do. Why?"

"She was just here."

"Where?"

"Here, at the plant. She was looking for Ricky Delgado."

"Damn. Damn, damn, damn."

"Yeah, I know. You need to put a leash on that gal, and I mean quick."

ଛ

Warren had never been to Danny's apartment, but it was like a million other apartments in America. Two-bedroom floor plan. A sliding glass door that opened onto a small patio. Beige carpet. Off-white walls painted with semi-gloss so they could be wiped down easily. In the hallway were several framed photos of Emily, Danny's six-year-old daughter.

"You look good," Warren said from his spot on the couch, and it was the truth.

Danny was in a recliner, his feet up, wearing jeans and a loose T-shirt. No shoes. He had a large bandage across his forehead. The TV was on with the sound turned low. Football again. The Cowboys were in Philly, stomping the Eagles on their own turf. Romo was having an excellent day.

"I *feel* good," Danny said. "But check this out." He lifted his shirt slowly, wincing a little, revealing a bruise that resembled a purple cloud spreading across the horizon at sunset.

Warren said, "I'm surprised they don't have you in some sort of cast."

Danny grinned, like a kid showing off an injury from a failed bicycle jump. "They were thinking about it, that or a brace. But it's just a hairline fracture, so I talked 'em out of it."

"How's the pain?"

"Not so bad. Good meds."

Condensation was forming on the beer bottle Warren was holding. It was raining hard outside.

"I gave two weeks' notice yesterday," Warren said, just to get it over with.

Danny looked blank for few seconds, then he said, "Oh yeah?"

"Yeah."

"You fuckin' with me?"

"Nope. Sorry."

"Wow. I wasn't expecting that."

"I wanted you to hear it from me."

"I appreciate it. You sure that's what you want?"

"It is. And I've got vacation time coming, so I'm using it. Which means I'm done. I won't be going back."

Danny shook his head and took a drink from his own bottle of beer, then carefully placed it on the table beside the chair. "I guess I understand, but I'm gonna miss working with you."

"Same here."

"What're you gonna do now?"

"Go back to Hebbronville. I already got it lined up. It's been on my mind for a while. Several months."

Danny nodded slowly. "I'd been wondering."

"You could tell?"

"I knew something was up. You've been, I don't know ... less gung-ho than you used to be. I know you're not lazy, so it had to be something else." He seemed a little spacey from the pain pills. His eyes were glassy. Or maybe it was the combo of meds and beer.

Lightning crashed nearby, and thunder rumbled a moment later. Warren could hear the glass door rattling in its frame.

He said, "What happened was, my heart wasn't in it anymore. I tried not to let it affect my work, but sometimes it did, I guess. I wanted to apologize for that."

"Affected it how?"

"Sometimes I didn't see things I should've seen. Because I looked the other way."

Danny stared at him for a long moment, as if he couldn't quite comprehend what Warren had said. "For real?"

Warren nodded.

"That's fucked up, man."

Warren nodded again.

Danny shifted his gaze to the TV screen. It was halftime. Terry, Howie, and the other guys were exchanging witty banter and manufactured insults.

"Look," Danny said, "I know it's a weird job we do out there. So much power. We're playing God, if you think about it. People want into this country, and we keep 'em out. It's easy to feel bad about that, if you let it, but I don't. The way I look at it, it's like being in a life boat."

Christ, Warren thought. *Everyone has an analogy. Noodles. Life boats.*

"The boat represents safety and security," Danny continued. "But it can only support so many people, right? If you're one of the lucky people on that boat, man, and too many people are trying to climb aboard, they're putting your life at risk. It's that simple. So there comes a point when you have to start saying no. You have to start fending 'em off, hitting 'em with paddles, or the whole boat's gonna sink. Sure, that sounds harsh, but that's the way I feel about it." Danny grimaced as he propped himself on one elbow, facing Warren, starting to get worked up, even angry. "See, the thing is, people have been climbing into our fucking boat for years, and we've already reached our limit. We're taking on water, and if we don't do something about it, right this minute, we're all gonna be screwed. You can already see the signs. The quality of life in this country is going to hell, and I care too much to let it go any further. I've got a little girl to think about. I want her to have everything I had, and more. The American dream. Good schools, a good job, affordable housing, and all that stuff. I don't see how anybody can argue with that, but they do, and I'm getting sick of it. The bleeding hearts always say the illegals just want a better life. Well, maybe they do, but they're not gonna get it at the expense of my little girl, you know what I'm saying? I'll die before that happens. So, yeah, if you're not ready, willing, and able to do the job, maybe it's time for you to move on. Let somebody else take your spot."

Warren could feel his face burning with the flush of shame. This was a big mistake. He shouldn't have come here. He shouldn't have said anything. He set his beer down, still half full, and stood.

"I should go," he said. "You need to get your rest."

஋

It was nearly midnight, and the rain had finally let up. Every so often, a great gust of wind would sway the pecan tree towering over Howard's house, and a cascade of water would land on the roof.

Not a drop, by God!

Howard's comment had made Ricky feel good. The repairs had held throughout the storm, which meant the caulk would likely hold for years to come.

The old man was still up, watching television in the living room. Tomás, too, was awake. Ricky could hear him occasionally stirring on the floor, on top of the inflatable air mattress that was serving as his bed. He had insisted that Ricky take the real bed, since it wasn't wide enough for both of them. Howard had said they'd squeeze another bed in there as soon as he found one at a garage sale. Maybe bunk beds, he'd said. That would be more practical.

Tomás thrashed some more and let out a deep breath.

"You need to stop worrying and get some sleep," Ricky said.

"I can't. My mind is racing."

Ricky could understand. Tomorrow was a big day. The lawyer had a plan.

"Everything will turn out fine," Ricky said.

"I hope so."

"It will. You have to trust Mr. Wynn."

Ricky heard laughter from the television. It was tuned to a talk show, the one with the host who was from Scotland. Ricky watched it sometimes, but he had a hard time understanding everything the man said.

"Ricky," Tomás said, "I don't want to ruin things for you."

"What are you talking about?"

"What if they arrest us both?"

"They won't. They can't."

"How do you know?"

"That's what Mr. Wynn said."

The Scottish man was interviewing Salma Hayek. Ricky knew that she was born in Coatzacoalcos, a port city in Veracruz, but she came north to pursue her acting career. Funny how that worked. If you could act or sing or excel in sports, they'd let you in. People like Gloria Estefan and Sammy Sosa and Wayne Gretzky could come to this country legally.

Tomás sat up on his air mattress, obviously agitated. He said, "What if Mr. Wynn is wrong?"

·

lunes

TWENTY

D R. KING CALLED CRIS INTO HIS OFFICE first thing Monday morning. When he closed the door, she knew she'd been busted.

"Did you go out to the chicken plant yesterday?" he asked.

It meant Wayne Skaggs had called to complain, or to verify that she was who she said she was. Fortunately, Dr. King's tone wasn't as accusatory as she might have expected. There was even a slightly amused smile on his face.

"I did, yes."

"To find Ricky Delgado?"

"Yes, sir."

"Why, exactly?"

"To see how he's doing. And to ask him to come back for tests, if necessary."

He nodded, but didn't respond for several seconds. Then he said, "Okay. All right." He sat down at his desk. "Look. At first, when Wayne Skaggs called me yesterday, I have to admit, I was pretty angry. But I've had a chance to think about it, and I've cooled off. In fact, I want to thank you. Because you were right—I should've been more thorough. I should've run some tests. See, when you've been doing this for as long as I have, it's easy to get complacent. It looked like the flu—and a case like that almost always *is* the flu—so I made the easy diagnosis. And maybe I was right, maybe he had the flu. I guess we'll never know for sure. But what you did—going out to the plant—that took some gumption, and it reminded me that every single patient deserves the best care we can give him. So ... thank you for that."

Cris was stunned. "You're welcome."

"So what I did, yesterday evening, I called Skaggs back. Yeah, Delgado is gone, but I remembered that other patient from the plant ... "

"Rocendo Ochoa."

"Exactly. With the skin condition. I decided we could run some tests on him, and then we'd have our answer, at least in his case."

Cris was impressed by Dr. King's change in attitude. "With his nodules regressing, isn't there a chance the tests would be inconclusive?"

"Well, yes, that crossed my mind, but I decided it was worth a shot. The problem is, he's gone, too."

"Gone where?"

"He was supposed to work this weekend, but he never showed. Skaggs said that happens all the time. It's a very transient business, apparently. No way to reach Ochoa, so we're out of luck. But I can promise you this, if we get another patient from the plant with any questionable symptoms at all, we'll do a full work-up. If there's a problem with psittacosis at the plant, we need to alert the proper people."

The "proper people" were with the state government, though she couldn't remember which department. Probably Agriculture or Health. If there was even a single case of psittacosis among workers at the plant, the clinic was required by law to report it. Which could very likely lead to a shutdown, or even a recall of Kountry Fresh products. Wayne Skaggs would have a coronary, but that was just too bad. The public health—and the health of the plant's employees—trumped any concerns of productivity at the plant. She was glad that Dr. King had finally begun to take the situation seriously.

∽

"Sheriff, you got a minute?"

That was the last thing Phil Lindeman wanted to hear on a Monday morning. There was always a mountain of e-mail and paperwork to wade through at the beginning of a new week. Nothing major, but things that needed his attention. Administrative bullshit that sometimes made Lindeman wish he was still a deputy on patrol. "Not really, no. What's up?"

His chief deputy, Brian Sloane, was standing in Lindeman's office doorway. "We got a complainant out here, and, well, I think you'd better hear this one."

∽

Herschel Gandy had the good sense to direct any forthcoming attention away from himself. He'd called Clayton's cell phone last night, after finishing with the backhoe, and he'd called it again this morning. Twice. Once right after sunrise, and another just a few minutes ago. So when the cops eventually began looking for Clayton—and they would, because Herschel would have to report him missing sooner or later—it would appear that Herschel had been looking for him, too.

Herschel had even been practicing his lines.

We cleared some brush on Saturday, and that was the last I saw of him. I think he was going into town yesterday, and I noticed that his truck is still gone.

The cops, of course, would know exactly where Clayton's truck was by then. Saturday night, Herschel had driven it out to the highway and parked it on the shoulder about half a mile from the ranch gate. Then he drove a nail into the rear passenger-side tire. Like Clayton had pulled over for a flat. Who knows what happened after that? Maybe Clayton tried to hitch a ride and got himself into some trouble. Maybe he made it into town successfully, got to drinking, and just hadn't come back yet. It was a real mystery, wasn't it?

Herschel figured it might even be wise to mention Warren Coleman to the cops. Casually throw it in, because it could be the perfect cover.

You know, on Friday night, Clayton said he got questioned by a Border Patrol agent. The agent said a wetback got shot somewhere around here. Now, I don't know anything about it, and I'm not saying Clayton was involved, but it seems kind of strange that he's up and disappeared ...

Meanwhile, Herschel was savvy enough to go about business as usual. That's why, at ten o'clock on Monday morning, he was in his office, paying some bills on his computer—creating an electronic paper trail, showing that he was not overly concerned by Clayton's absence—when the doorbell rang.

Totally unexpected, because the entrance gate at the highway was still closed and locked.

₮

Sloane ushered three people into the sheriff's office: Peter Wynn, an elderly local attorney, and two young Hispanic men, one with a bandaged hand. *Wetbacks,* Phil Lindeman thought immediately, even though the men were dressed in khakis and golf shirts. Didn't matter. Lindeman had always been able to spot a wetback. Maybe it was the weathered skin, the calloused hands, or maybe it was simply the way wetbacks carried themselves around cops. Eyes down, shoulders slumped. Always trying to blend in with the scenery, hoping to go unnoticed.

"Have a seat," Lindeman said, and they did, except for Sloane, who remained standing near the doorway. "Y'all want some coffee?" He offered out of deference to Wynn. The old man had been around for a long time and had earned some respect.

"*¿Quieren café?*" Wynn said to the other men.

Both shook their heads.

"Thanks, but we'll pass," Wynn said.

"Okay, then, what can I do for you?"

With an open hand, Wynn gestured toward the younger of the two wetbacks, the one with the bandage. "This man's name is Tomás Delgado. He is an illegal alien. He is also the victim of a violent crime. We're here to report it."

₮

Herschel's heartbeat picked up when he opened the door to find a deputy standing on his front porch. The man was tall and slender, wearing a straw

Resistol, and he had a revolver on his hip. The odd part was, he was also wearing tennis shoes. Sweat was streaming down his face, and his uniform was stained under the armpits. He was holding a manila folder. The circular drive in front of the house was empty. No vehicle, which meant the man had walked the three miles to the house from the highway.

They'd come for him. Somehow they knew what had happened, and they'd come to arrest him. But wait. Was this about Clayton or about the wetback?

"Mornin'," the deputy said. He was staring at Herschel oddly. "Damn, son, what happened to your face?"

That's right. The bruising around his eyes. The swollen lip. He needed a good explanation. "Horse threw me," he said, without any hesitation or unnatural pauses. He tried to look appropriately sheepish.

"I was you, I'd have a long talk with that horse. You Herschel Gandy?"

"I am."

The deputy reached into the folder, extracted an envelope, and handed it to Herschel. "I'm Joe Lovelace, the constable for your precinct. Sorry to ruin your day, but you've been served."

"I ... what?" Herschel was confused. A constable, not a real deputy.

Lovelace grinned. "Somebody's suing you, bud. Ain't that a bitch? Now I'm gonna need you to sign this." He thrust a pen and a single sheet of paper in Herschel's direction.

"What's this?"

"Acknowledgment that you were served, that's all."

Herschel began to read the document.

Lovelace said, "Sure am glad you was home. Hell of a walk up here. But that's why I keep tennies in my trunk, for times like this. Boots just don't cut it."

Herschel signed the paper and handed it back. "Who the hell is suing me?" he asked.

"Don't ask me," said Lovelace. "All the details are in that envelope—the citation and the plaintiff's petition. You've got twenty days from next Monday to respond." He slipped the pen into his pocket and tipped his hat. "Don't suppose you'd give me a ride to the highway? Awful hot out."

Gandy made up a quick lie. "Sorry, I'm waiting on an important call. Can't leave the house."

"All right, then. You have a nice day. Might want to stay off horses for a while. They don't seem to agree with you."

∞

Ricky felt certain he was imagining things. He had to be. Worry was turning him into a hypochondriac. Whatever the cause, as he sat in the sheriff's office, Ricky began to experience a strange sensation in his chest. Not just a sensation, but a pain. He felt as if his heart wasn't beating quite the way it was supposed to. Maybe it was an anxiety attack. He'd never had one before, but this was as good a time as any.

∞

"And this other gentlemen? Who's he?"

"Ricky Delgado. Tomás's brother," Wynn said.

Lindeman noticed that the older kid was about as white-faced as a Mexican could get. "He illegal, too?"

"No comment," Wynn said.

Obvious what that meant.

"Okay, then. What's the complaint?"

Wynn opened a briefcase and removed a yellow legal pad. He slipped some eyeglasses from his breast pocket and put them on. He studied the pad for half a minute, then looked up at Lindeman. "Six days ago, meaning Tuesday of last week, Mr. Delgado crossed the Rio Grande approximately seventeen miles south of Laredo. He was entering the country illegally, which he knew at the time, and he was trespassing. He was in the company of two other men, also Mexican nationals. None of them had weapons of any kind. It was late in the day, near dusk, when they came upon a deer blind. The elevated kind, a, uh ... "

"A tower stand?"

"Right, a tower stand. They couldn't tell if the stand was occupied or not, so they hesitated. The last thing they wanted was any sort of confrontation with the landowner or a hunter. They discussed their options, which included circumventing the blind by going through the brush, or simply waiting until dark before they went any further. They decided to proceed with caution. They had taken only a few more steps—they were still approximately one hundred meters from the deer stand—when they were fired upon. The first shot hit Mr. Delgado in the hand, completely severing his thumb. He was carrying a backpack, which he dropped immediately, of course. He and the other men began running back the way they'd come—*away* from the tower stand. They were obviously not a threat, nor had they presented any sort of threat earlier—yet the occupant or occupants in the stand continued to fire in their direction. Mr. Delgado counted three more shots. None of those shots hit any of the men."

The lawyer stopped talking. Removed his glasses. Apparently, he'd said his piece.

Lindeman didn't dive right in with questions. This was a touchy one. Could be a real headache. He had to handle it carefully, because there was a chance his actions would be scrutinized later—by the feds, by civil rights groups, by the press. No wonder Sloane had dumped this one in his lap.

"There's a lot of wide open country south of here," Lindeman finally said. "And a lot of deer stands. Unless he can tell us exactly where this happened—"

"He can," Wynn said. "Two days ago, he showed me the ranch where this incident took place." Now his glasses went back on, and he consulted his legal pad again. "I've done some preliminary research, and the property is owned by a man named Samuel Gandy. But his son, Herschel, has power of attorney and runs the place."

Sam Gandy, Lindeman thought. *Well, shit.*

∽

Attached is a copy of Plaintiff's Original Petition ...

This instrument was filed in the above-cited cause number ...
You have been sued ...

Herschel set the citation aside and began to read the petition, which was several pages long.

Comes now Tomás Antonio Delgado, Plaintiff, in the above entitled and numbered cause ...

Who the hell was Tomás Delgado? Gandy didn't know anybody by that name.

On or about Tuesday, October 14 ...
... Plaintiff suffered a debilitating and permanent injury as a result of a gun shot wound to the left hand ...

Gandy paused there for a second. He understood what he was reading, but it didn't add up. Tomás Delgado was the illegal alien. The thumbless wetback. That much was obvious. But how could an illegal alien—one who was trespassing, for fuck's sake—file a lawsuit in the American legal system? Surely the courts wouldn't allow something like that. Plus, if a wetback *could* file a lawsuit, he'd be announcing to the world that he was illegal, right? Wouldn't he get deported and that would be the end of it? None of this made sense. Herschel wasn't nervous, not really, just baffled. And getting angry.

He continued scanning the document and saw that it provided a pretty good description of what had happened that night. Three immigrants trespassing. Gunshots from a deer blind. Backpack dropped in the dirt. Et cetera.

He flipped to the last page, where the lawsuit would be bottom-lined. What would this guy want? Payment of medical bills? A few bucks for pain and suffering? His eyes fell to the last paragraph and he froze. What was written was so ridiculous, so outrageous, at first he assumed it was a typo.

... actual damages in the amount of at least five million dollars, exemplary damages as permitted by law, and such other relief to which Plaintiff shows himself justly entitled ...

Five million dollars.

They couldn't possibly be serious. Justly entitled? In whose twisted world would a wetback be justly entitled to extort that amount of money from a U.S. citizen?

Then something occurred to Herschel. If Tomás Delgado had the balls to file a lawsuit, wouldn't he also press criminal charges?

TWENTY-ONE

AN HOUR LATER, AS THEY WALKED OUT of the sheriff's office, then
across the parking lot toward Peter Wynn's Mercedes, Ricky kept waiting for this ridiculous charade to come to an end. Surely the sheriff had alerted
la migra and the federal agents would show up at any moment. Perhaps they
would pop up from behind a parked car or suddenly emerge from around a corner of the brick building. Maybe an unmarked vehicle would screech to a halt
and a team of armed, uniformed men would pile out and take him and Tomás
into custody.

But nothing happened.

Ricky, Tomás, and Peter Wynn simply got into the lawyer's car and drove
away, just as Wynn had assured them they would. Nobody spoke for several
moments. Then Wynn said, in Spanish, "I think that went well."

Ricky was in the passenger seat, waiting for his head to clear and his heartbeat to return to normal.

"You did a great job, Tomás," Wynn said, glancing in the rearview mirror.

"I was scared," Tomás admitted. "I need to piss real bad."

"Why didn't you go at the sheriff's office?"

"Man, I just wanted to get out of there. I didn't know it would take so long."

The sheriff had asked a lot of questions, taking notes as he did so, and
Tomás had answered as truthfully as he could.

Did you actually see who fired the shots?

Who were these two men you were with?

What was in your backpack?

On and on the sheriff went, asking about the most mundane details.

What's the number for your cell phone?

The sheriff was less accomplished as a speaker of Spanish, and there were
several times when he'd had to ask Tomás or Peter Wynn for clarification. He
paid no attention at all to Ricky.

When Tomás recounted the visit from the Border Patrol agent in the hospital, the sheriff appeared confused. *He wasn't in uniform? He questioned you, but
he didn't arrest you?* Tomás repeated what the agent had told him: that *la migra*
had captured the other two men and deported them. Peter Wynn then spoke
up, saying that the two men would be in the federal computer now. Their names
and addresses. The sheriff expressed skepticism that the men would've provided

accurate information. Wynn said it was worth checking.

At the end of the discussion, the sheriff asked Tomás where he could be reached. Peter Wynn spoke up again. *Sheriff, for the time being, you can communicate with Mr. Delgado through my office.* It was plain that the lawyer didn't want to reveal Howard's name. Or maybe his address.

As the Mercedes sat at a stoplight, Peter Wynn said, "As I mentioned before, the sheriff has very little chance of actually filing charges on anyone for the shooting. Someone would have to confess, or we'd need a witness that actually saw who did the shooting. But, if we're lucky, the investigation will provide some details that we can use in the lawsuit. And it might draw some media attention, which would be a good thing for us. It'd make Herschel Gandy that much more willing to settle."

Ricky didn't want to talk about any of this anymore. Not right now. He turned one of the air conditioner vents so that it blew directly into his face. The cool air felt wonderful. He was worried that his fever was returning again.

Wynn adjusted one of the control knobs on the dashboard. "Are you feeling ill?" Peter Wynn asked. "Or did meeting with the sheriff make you nervous?"

Ricky gave him a weak grin. "I think it must have been the sheriff." He just wanted to get back to Howard's house and lie down.

๛

The front door was locked, so Ricky reached for the doorbell. Then he remembered he had a key. He felt peculiar using it, but he didn't want to disturb the old man. No reason to make him stop what he was doing and come to the door.

Peter Wynn had parked in the driveway, saying he should come inside and tell Howard about the meeting with the sheriff. So Ricky swung the door open and stepped inside, followed by Tomás and Wynn. He could hear the small black-and-white TV in the kitchen.

Tomás went straight for the bathroom.

"You go ahead and lie down," Peter Wynn said to Ricky. "I'll tell Howard how it went."

"I'm okay," Ricky said. "I feel better now."

He didn't, but he thought it would be rude if he didn't take part in the conversation. Howard, after all, was the one who'd arranged everything. He'd introduced Ricky and Tomás to Peter Wynn. If Tomás were eventually granted citizenship, or even just a visa, he would have Howard to thank.

They stepped into the kitchen, and there was Howard, sitting in his regular chair at the dinette table. The TV was tuned to *The Today Show*, but Howard wasn't watching. His eyes were closed and his chin was resting on his chest.

Napping. That's what it looked like. But something wasn't right.

Peter Wynn sensed it, too. Ricky saw that Wynn had opened his mouth, probably to call Howard's name, but now he closed it without saying anything. He looked at Ricky, expressionless, then back at Howard. He stepped over beside the old man and put a hand lightly on his shoulder. There was no reaction at all.

"Howard?"

No movement.

"Howard?"

Wynn took Howard's hand and felt the wrist for a pulse. Several seconds passed. Then Wynn lowered Howard's hand and calmly turned off the television.

ℨ

Warren Coleman had decided to give it one more try. One more trip to Herschel Gandy's place. He was just about to leave when the phone rang. The home phone, not his cell phone. He'd turned his cell off yesterday and left it on the dresser. Too many members of the media were still calling, plus friends and coworkers who'd already heard about his resignation. Honestly, he didn't want to talk to any of them. He was sick of talking about everything.

He paused, though, then decided to go into the kitchen and check the caller I.D., just in case it was Ellen. She was planning to speak to the school principal today and give notice. Could be ugly. Principals weren't fond of teachers who resigned while school was in session. But the other options—Ellen remaining here for another seven months to finish out the school year, or commuting from Hebbronville every day—weren't practical. "No," she'd said, "I'll take my lumps if I have to."

But it wasn't Ellen. The caller I.D. display read: OLGIUN, DANIEL. Danny.

Warren's hand instinctively went toward the phone, but he stopped himself and didn't pick it up. Why subject himself to more verbal abuse? He'd been thinking about the things Danny had said, and his reaction had slowly changed from shame to anger. He'd started thinking, *Where does this rookie get off lecturing me? I save his life, and that's the thanks I get?*

After the fourth ring, the answering machine kicked on and Warren heard Danny's voice:

> *Hey, Warren, I tried your cell but you didn't pick up. And your voicemail is full, too, in case you didn't know. Anyway ... look, I wanted to apologize for yesterday afternoon. I was way out of line. My bad. I could say it was the pain pills, but that would be a bunch of bullshit. It was just me being an asshole, and I got worked up and shot my mouth off, and you didn't deserve for me to go off*

like that. You were a great partner. So I'm sorry, okay? I'll, uh, I'll call you back later. Maybe tomorrow. Or you call me when you get a chance. I'll be here at my apartment, kicking back, watching crappy daytime television. What else am I gonna do, right? Later.

The machine clicked off and the kitchen went silent. Well, okay. Big of him to call, assuming the pain meds hadn't simply swung his mood in the opposite direction. But he sounded straight and sober.

Warren erased the message and turned again for the door. Then he went back for his cell phone, in case Ellen called.

&

This time the patient was a Honduran man who complained that he had something in his right eye. He said it had been in there for about a week, and as a result, the eye was red and inflamed. He looked miserable, repeatedly dabbing with a tissue to blot up the discharge. It was driving him nuts, and he couldn't get the object out no matter how many times he flushed the socket with water. He didn't remember getting anything in his eye, it was just there all of a sudden.

Of course, he worked at the poultry plant.

Cris suspected right away that there was nothing in his eye at all. No, it just *felt* that way. Dr. King would take a look with a slit lamp microscope, but Cris doubted he would find anything. Because, if she was right, this patient was suffering from something else entirely—a condition that could be caused by psittacosis.

"Does the lid crust over at night?" she asked. "Makes it hard to open your eye?"

"Yes, exactly." He was nodding, pleased that she understood his problem.

"Does it itch?"

"Very much."

"Do you have a sore throat?"

"No."

"Allergies?"

"No."

"Have you been taking any medication recently? Prescription or over-the-counter?"

"No."

"Had any kind of respiratory infection? A cold? The flu?"

"No, I feel fine, except for my eye."

"What exactly do you do at the plant?"

"I work in the kill room. I take the chickens and—"

She waved him off. "That's okay. Do you wear protective gloves?"

"Yes."

"All the time?"

"Unless I'm on a break."

"Do you wear goggles?"

"Yes."

"All the time?"

"Mostly."

"But not always?"

"It gets so hot in there. Sometimes I go without. But not for long."

"Okay, hold on just a minute."

She went down the hall to Dr. King's office. He was doing something on his computer, but he looked up, and Cris said, "We've got another patient from the plant."

"You've got to be kidding me."

"Unfortunately, no."

"What are his symptoms?"

"He appears to have conjunctivitis."

"Okay, wait. Pinkeye? Are you saying psittacosis can cause pinkeye?"

"In some cases, yes."

"How do you know that? *Why* would you know that?"

"I've been doing some reading."

He laughed, but he seemed a little put off. "Well, you're the expert, then." He pushed his chair away from the desk. "Okay, let's have a look."

≈

The microscope confirmed that it was pinkeye, but that still didn't prove it was caused by psittacosis. The patient hadn't necessarily caught it from handling chickens.

Dr. King took Cris back to his office and said, "Okay, here's what we're gonna do. Normally, I'd just prescribe antibiotics and be done with it. But, considering the circumstances, and the promise I made, I'm gonna get serologies and see what we're dealing with. Don't get your hopes up, though. You know as well as I do that there are dozens of things that can cause pinkeye."

He was right, of course. The patient could be suffering from an allergy he didn't know he had, or perhaps he'd grown allergic to an irritant that hadn't bothered him before. The pinkeye could have been triggered by exposure to an excessive amount of dust, pollen, or smoke. Or, even if the cause *was* bacterial, as she suspected, it could be a different bacterium than the one that caused psittacosis. Or the cause could be viral, rather than bacterial.

Yeah, it could. But Cris's gut told her it was none of those other things.

TWENTY-TWO

ARREN WAS DRIVING AND TALKING on his cell. Or listening, mostly. "Yeah, he was pretty upset," Ellen was saying. "I could see it in his face. But he said he understood. I think he was afraid you might come down here and kick his ass if he caused any trouble. It's funny some of the things people have said about you. They think you're like this tough-guy cowboy."

Warren was too distracted to respond. He'd decided to let the random circumstances of fate determine his course of action at Gandy's ranch. If the gate was open, he'd drive up and have a talk with him.

"You there?" Ellen said.

"Yeah, sorry."

"Where are you?"

"Just taking a drive. Getting some fresh air. I had to get out of the house."

If the gate was still closed, Warren would turn around, go home, and never think about Tomás Delgado again. Period. End of story.

"Anyway, I'm glad to have it done with," Ellen said. "I told him two weeks, but honestly, if it takes a little longer to find a replacement, I'm willing to stay another couple of weeks. I think that's fair, don't you?"

"Definitely."

It was a smart plan, this gate thing, because, in a sense, he was putting the matter in God's hands. God could open or close that gate—whichever He chose—before Warren got there. So the future was entirely up to Him. And you couldn't go wrong by letting God make the decision, could you?

"On the other hand, there's so much to do," Ellen said. "We have to find a place to live, Warren. We haven't even talked about that yet. Not an apartment, okay? Or a duplex. Let's just rent a house at first, then we can think about buying something."

"Yeah, that sounds good."

Then Warren remembered something he'd said just four days earlier: *If he takes the next exit, we'll pull him over.* Talking about Herrera in the Ford van.

Leaving it up to fate.

That didn't work out so well, did it?

Well, that system would have to do, because Warren wasn't far from the ranch entrance, and he didn't trust his own judgment anymore. Sometimes he wondered if he was behaving in a rational manner. Why couldn't he let this thing go?

Up ahead, still on the roadside, sat Clayton Dupree's truck.

"I'd better get going," Ellen said. "The bell just rang."

"Okay, I'll see you tonight."

"I love you, Warren. I'm excited by all this."

"I love you, too."

He hung up.

As Warren passed Dupree's truck, he noticed an orange abandoned-vehicle sticker on the driver's-side window, slapped on by some highly efficient deputy. Which meant the owner had forty-eight hours to move it or the vehicle would be impounded. Odd that the truck was still there. Most abandoned vehicles were junkers, not nice trucks like this one. Why hadn't Dupree fixed the flat, or at least towed the Ford to the ranch? Out here, on the highway, it was a sitting duck for vandals and thieves. Sooner or later, someone would throw a rock through the window and take anything of value.

Warren kept driving. He realized he was holding his breath. Nervous. Palms sweating.

Then, finally, the entrance to Gandy's ranch came into view. Warren pulled in and stopped, then simply sat quietly for a few moments, staring through the windshield.

The gate was closed.

&

Herschel was sitting on the deck, still dipping into the Crown Royal, getting pretty loose, and every now and then—this was weird—he'd catch himself wondering where Clayton was. Just for a split second, thinking, *Where's he run off to? Why is it so quiet around here?*

Then he'd feel horrible, he really would. All he wanted was somebody to talk to. He knew it was partially the whiskey making him mopey, but what kind of man shoots his best friend? He wished he hadn't done it, no question. But Clayton hadn't left him any options. He'd threatened to snitch.

Now this damn lawsuit. Twenty-seven days to respond. He had his cell phone in his lap, preparing to call Brent Nielsen. Herschel was dreading that conversation, but it was unavoidable. Nielsen would have a cow.

Jesus, what about Dad?

Herschel knew he couldn't expect to keep the lawsuit from his father. In fact, he *shouldn't* keep it from his father. Herschel had to start thinking like an innocent man, and an innocent man wouldn't hesitate to tell everybody who'd listen. An innocent man would get indignant and say the lawsuit was a crock of shit.

Of course, the difference was, Sam Gandy would assume his son was lying.

"What do you think it was that killed him?" Tomás asked, reclined on one of the two beds in a motel room near the state highway. The TV was tuned to a soap opera on Telemundo. "He seemed so healthy, even though he was old. I wonder what it was."

Ricky was trying to sleep, but he couldn't. His chest still felt odd. "I don't know. Perhaps a heart attack. A stroke. Could've been a lot of things."

Back at Howard's house, several hours earlier, there had been no doubt that Howard was gone. Ricky had even felt for a pulse himself—hoping he might find the faintest heartbeat—but Howard's flesh had already begun to cool. He must have died right after Peter Wynn had come by to pick up Ricky and Tomás.

Wynn had handled everything as if he'd been in such circumstances before. He immediately placed a call to someone he knew "at the county," then the three of them went into the living room to wait for the proper personnel to arrive. It was a sad situation, leaving Howard in the kitchen by himself, but it would've been unsettling to stay there with him. Besides, he looked peaceful.

So they sat there quietly, surrounded by piles of clothing, small kitchen appliances in various states of disrepair, stacks of books, CDs, DVDs, and cassettes, an assortment of power tools, and several boxes holding unspecified contents. Howard most certainly had known what was inside each and every box.

Ricky was afraid he was going to cry, and he had to think of other things. Like where he and Tomás were going to spend the night. Staying here, even if Peter Wynn thought it was okay, was out of the question.

"He was a good man," Wynn said, breaking the silence, speaking in English now. "A good man. Led a long, full life. Traveled all over Europe when he was young. The war, you know. Sure had some stories."

Wynn was staring into space, as if remembering one of Howard's tales, then he suddenly looked at Ricky. "He ever tell you he received the Distinguished Service Cross?" Before Ricky could answer, Wynn said, "No, I'm betting he didn't. He wouldn't have mentioned it. He hadn't talked about that stuff in years."

Ricky didn't know what the Distinguished Service Cross was, nor had Howard spoken of it. A medal of some kind, apparently. Ricky didn't translate the conversation for Tomás.

Wynn looked as if he were about to say something else, but Ricky said, "Do you think we should go somewhere before anyone gets here? My brother and me?" He asked the question in Spanish, so Tomás could understand. Ricky had visions of the house filling with all sorts of government officials. It made him tense.

Peter Wynn thought about it for several moments. Then he said, in Spanish, "I hate to say this, but that's probably not a bad idea. I hadn't thought about that."

They agreed that Ricky and Tomás would find a motel for the night. Peter Wynn tried to offer some money to pay for it, but Ricky refused. He had some cash. Then, tomorrow, they'd talk by phone and discuss what would happen next.

The motel room smelled of mildew, the floor was dirty, and the bed linens were stained, but the price was only thirty-four dollars a night. North of the border, that was a good deal.

"I hope it was quick," Tomás said. "When I go, I want to go quick, with as little pain as possible. Don't you?"

"Tomás?"

"What?"

"Please be quiet. I need to sleep."

martes

TWENTY-THREE

W AYNE SKAGGS PULLED INTO THE PARKING LOT of a crummy little diner on the outskirts of Rugoso. He locked his SUV and walked inside, carrying a brown paper sack. Not a big sack or a small sack, just a medium sack. The kind of sack that could comfortably accommodate five thousand dollars in fifties, twenties, and tens.

There were maybe twenty customers inside, scattered at tables and at the counter. Skaggs could smell the rich aroma of bacon, and his mouth began to water. He hadn't come here for breakfast, but he might have to grab a quick bite.

Dr. David King sat in a booth near the back. Skaggs slid onto the vinyl bench across from him, involuntarily letting out a small grunt as he did so. His lower back always complained when he sat down, or when he sat for too long. He'd gotten Carmen to order him one of those ergonomically correct chairs for his office, but it hadn't arrived yet.

King was sipping from his coffee mug, eyeballing Skaggs over the rim. He placed the mug on the table and said, "Well. Thanks for coming."

A waitress appeared, carrying a coffeepot. She was young and sort of cute, but her hips were a tad wide. On the other hand, broad hips often meant big tits, and Skaggs didn't mind the tradeoff. It appeared she was packing some nice ones under her uniform.

"Coffee?" she asked. Skaggs nodded. She poured. "Y'all want anything from the kitchen?"

Skaggs said, "You serve a decent BLT?"

"Sure do. It's yummy." She had a nice smile.

"Okay, gimme one with extra bacon."

"Want some avocado on that?"

"Now why would I ruin a perfectly good BLT with avocado?" Flirting a little, just because it felt good.

She smiled again. Then she looked at King, who said, "Nothing for me."

She nodded and turned for the kitchen.

As she walked away, Skaggs got a good look at her backside. "Speaking of yummy," he said.

King didn't say anything, so Skaggs handed the bag to him. The doctor placed it on the seat beside him, without even looking inside.

"So what's the story?" Skaggs asked. "You have a talk with your nurse?"

∞

The telephone in the motel room had no dial tone, so Ricky went next door to the Waffle House. The short walk left him out of breath. His chest felt tight. He wished he could go somewhere and lie down for a week, until he recovered completely from the flu. No time for that right now. Peter Wynn had asked Ricky to call him first thing in the morning.

Pay phones were becoming harder to find, and on those occasions when Ricky managed to locate one in working order, there was often a fellow immigrant using it. When it was Ricky's turn, he would see a variety of phone numbers scribbled on the phone's housing, and there would be depleted calling cards scattered in the vicinity. Nobody used these phones except *mojados* and very poor citizens.

Fortunately, there was a pay phone near the front door to the diner. As Ricky dialed, he decided that he would take the advice Peter Wynn had given: he would buy a cell phone today. Just a basic prepaid phone, like the one Ricky mailed to Tomás to carry on his journey north. No monthly charges, no frills, no hidden fees. Wynn said it would be a good idea for Ricky to carry one, so they could stay in touch. The lawyer said the next few days would be critical.

∞

The first time Skaggs and King had ever spoken, it had been over the phone, nearly two years earlier. At first, Skaggs had refused the call—he told his secretary to take a message—because he didn't *know* anyone named Dr. David King. She buzzed back a few seconds later saying the doctor insisted that it was an urgent matter.

So Skaggs had reluctantly taken the call, and the first thing King said, after introducing himself, was, "I have a patient here who works at your plant. A young man from Nicaragua. He appears to have tuberculosis."

Skaggs felt like somebody had punched him in the belly. He knew, of course, what a case of TB could do to a poultry plant. A shutdown. A recall. Not to mention the potential hassles regarding illegal workers. The federal authorities would swarm the place and start digging around. Could be devastating. Skaggs had been the plant manager for less than a year at that point, and he couldn't afford such a disaster—even though it clearly wasn't his fault. The only thing the higher-ups cared about was productivity. Quantity. Raw tonnage. Packaged meat out the door.

Before he could respond, King continued, saying, "The good news is, it isn't the drug-resistant kind. The other good news is, the patient said he's been working at the plant for less than a week. He said he's a keep-to-himself kind of guy, so he's had very little interaction with his coworkers, and he wears a mask most of the time. Which means there's a decent chance that the disease hasn't spread.

"By now, it had occurred to Skaggs that this was a highly unusual phone call. Why was the doctor talking to him, rather than to the health department? Why was he keeping his voice low?

Then Skaggs got his answers. He said, "What now?"

And the doctor said, "Just to be clear, you understand that I'm required to report each and every case of TB. It's the law."

Skaggs said, "Yeah, I understand that."

After a long pause, King said, "Unless you can think of a way to talk me out of it."

Skaggs did think of a way, of course. He talked it over with his boss, the regional supervisor, who was equally eager to keep the Rugoso plant up and running. Together, they were able to assemble an attractive "incentive package."

The doctor had been a team player ever since.

∽

"I've got some bad news," Peter Wynn told Ricky. "Right after you left yesterday, I called Howard's son Anthony to tell him of his father's passing. Once we got past that, I explained the situation to him—how you and Tomás had been staying with Howard—and I was hoping he'd allow you to remain in the house for a few more days. Unfortunately, he didn't go for it."

Ricky was disappointed. He and Tomás would have to find a new place to stay. Thirty-four dollars a night at the motel was okay for one night, but he couldn't afford it for very long.

"It gets worse," Wynn continued. "Did Howard ever give you the title for that truck?"

Ricky knew what was coming. "No, not yet."

"I told Anthony you'd bought the truck from Howard, and for how much, and he got very upset. He accused you of taking advantage of his father. I tried to convince him that wasn't the case, but he wouldn't listen. He said the truck better be sitting in the driveway when he gets there or he'd report it stolen. He caught the first flight out from Dallas this morning, so it would be best if you returned it right away. I'm sorry about that, but we don't need another complication right now."

Ricky tried to maintain a good attitude, but it was difficult. Twenty-four hours ago he had a decent vehicle and a good place to live. Now he had neither. He told Wynn he would take the truck back immediately.

"Did you get a cell phone?" Wynn asked.

"Not yet. I'll do it today."

"Please do, and call Maureen with the number, because I might need to reach you. It wouldn't surprise me if I hear from Gandy's attorney today. He'll probably want to settle this thing as soon as possible."

℘

"Yeah, I talked to her," King said, answering Skaggs's question about Cris. "I had everything contained. Then a third patient showed up." King gave the name of a Honduran man who worked in the kill room.

Skaggs was starting to feel a knot of panic in his chest. "When?"

"Yesterday afternoon."

"And?"

"Things don't look good. He has pinkeye, most likely caused by psittacosis. I put him on antibiotics."

"Shit."

King spoke quietly. "Look, it isn't time to freak out just yet. We could still keep a lid on it. He could be the final case."

"Man, I hope so. I'll fire his ass, just like the others. Today."

"Well, yeah. Of course you will. Get rid of him. Also, just so you know, Cris insisted that we get serologies, meaning run a blood test, and I couldn't think of a way to put her off any longer."

"Christ, she's a pushy bitch, ain't she?"

"She's headstrong, yes. I sent the sample out this morning."

Skaggs was confused. "Wait a sec. You sent it where?"

"A laboratory in Laredo."

The knot was growing. "Shit, doc, that means I'm screwed, doesn't it? If they know the results, won't they be required to report it?"

"Normally, yeah, they would. But don't worry, I fixed it."

"Fixed it how?"

King grinned. "I drew some of my own blood and sent it in instead."

He was expecting Skaggs to compliment him on the clever tactic, but the plant manager was distracted by something out the window. He gestured with his chin and said, "Look who's here."

℘

Sheriff Phil Lindeman had approached the Tomás Delgado case from a couple of different angles.

He'd talked to the district attorney the previous afternoon, the topic being a search warrant for the Gandy ranch. Lindeman was hoping to locate the missing thumb, or some bloody rags where the wetbacks had spent the night, but the DA said there was no chance of a warrant yet. The probable cause wasn't there. No witnesses, no hard evidence, nothing but the testimony of an illegal alien.

Then, first thing this morning, Lindeman had called the Border Patrol sector supervisor—a man named Bustamante—and asked if any of his men had visited Delgado in the hospital. Bustamante said, far as he knew, none of his agents even knew where Delgado was—but he'd look into it. He also agreed that it would be next to impossible to track down the two illegals Delgado had been traveling with. Good luck finding them in Mexico.

That left Lindeman little choice but to resort to step three, which meant going out to have a chat with Gandy. Lindeman wished he had more to confront him with, but who knows, Gandy might cop to it right off. Stranger things had happened, especially among the anti-immigrant crowd, who sometimes seemed to think they were above the law. Or maybe Gandy would consent to a search. That would make things easier.

Lindeman took Sloane along, and when they arrived at the ranch, the gate was closed and locked tight. Hell if he was going to walk.

"You got your cell?" Lindeman said.

Sloane pulled a phone from a small leather holster on his hip.

☙

Ricky hung up the pay phone and heard somebody say, "Mr. Delgado?"

He turned and came face to face with the doctor from the clinic. Dr. David King. He was wearing a suit.

"How are you?" Ricky said.

The doctor made a gesture toward the diner. "I was having breakfast, and I saw you out here, so I thought I'd come out and say hello. You feeling better?"

"Not yet, no. I'm beginning to have pain in my chest. I have very little strength."

The doctor glanced around the parking lot, as if he were embarrassed to be speaking to a *mojado* in public. "Have you been taking the tetracycline?"

Ricky shrugged. "I lost the prescription slip." Actually, it was still in his wallet, but it was easier to fib. Ricky hadn't filled the prescription because he knew that an antibiotic wouldn't help cure a virus like the flu. Didn't Dr. King know that?

Apparently not, because he said, "I'll write you out another one. I have a pad in my car. You really need to get it filled this time. It'll help you feel better."

Amazing, Ricky thought. *Even in the United States, there are doctors who don't know what they're doing.*

TWENTY-FOUR

"AND RIGHT OUT HERE, through the sliding glass doors, there's a lovely veranda that catches the late afternoon sun. Perfect for a cocktail at the end of the day."

The real estate agent—mid-forties, wearing too much makeup and a pants suit—was stretching it. The "veranda" was nothing but a concrete patio, and—because the backyard was treeless—the patio would be only slightly cooler than the inside of a kiln when summertime rolled around.

Still, Warren thought the house was okay. Three bedrooms and a large living room. Just under two thousand square feet total. Well kept overall, though the exterior could use a coat of paint. The neighborhood was decent, not far from where they had lived before. Five minutes to the police station, maybe seven to the middle school. It would do until they found a place to buy. Six hundred bucks a month, all bills paid, so they'd be able to stick some money aside every month for a down payment.

Linda Jean, the agent, said, "How soon are you planning to move?"

"We're ready now," Warren said, and he meant it. The sooner the better. That's why he'd gotten up early, driven to Hebbronville, and called the number in the first newspaper ad that caught his eye. It would be ideal if he could get their things moved before he started at the department.

"What line of work are you in?" she asked. Trying to sound casual, but she was probably wondering if he'd pass the credit check.

"Used to be with the Border Patrol, but I'm going to work for the police department here in Hebbronville."

"Oh, really? Wonderful. I'm sure the owner will appreciate having a police officer in the house. And your wife?"

This was getting tedious. This lady didn't really care. She was just doing her job, which was to sell. "Eighth-grade teacher."

"Isn't that wonderful, both of you in public service. There are times when I wish I'd been a teacher myself. My grandmother and my mother were both teachers, and my sister is a counselor at a—"

Warren's cell phone rang. Excellent. "Excuse me a minute," he said, and stepped out onto the "veranda." He hadn't received a call from the media in twenty-four hours—they appeared to have given up—so he was thinking it might be Ellen calling, curious about his house-hunting progress.

But the caller I.D. said it was Danny again.

∽

"You want a drink or anything?" Herschel Gandy asked.

"It's ten o'clock in the morning," Brent Nielsen replied. They were standing in the middle of Herschel's den.

"I meant like orange juice or coffee," Herschel lied. He was aware that he'd been telling a lot of lies lately. The truth was, he was feeling downright shitty from the whiskey he'd drunk yesterday, and he could use a little hair of the dog.

"I'm fine," Nielsen said. "What in the world happened to your face?"

"Got thrown off a horse." Same thing he'd told the constable. When you lie, be consistent. Find one story and stick to it.

"I didn't know you had horses on the ranch."

Oops.

"Happened at a friend's place. Mean old bay. Never was properly broke. You ride?"

"I do, some, yes."

"Western?"

"English."

Figures, Herschel thought. "Then you know how unpredictable they can be," he said.

Nielsen nodded but didn't say anything. It was awkward. The attorney had the conversational skills of a fence post.

"Okay, well, let's talk," Herschel said, and they sat at either end of a long leather couch. Herschel had no idea how to approach the subject, and he realized it didn't really matter how he said it. Just say it. "Remember last week when I told you about that wetback? Me and Clayton fired a warning shot near him and his buddies?"

Nielsen nodded again. No expression on his face.

Herschel said, "Well, this is total bullshit, but he's claiming I hit him. In the hand. Actually, he's not claiming *I* hit him, because he doesn't know who fired the shot, but he's saying *somebody* on the ranch fired at him, and now he's suing me. You believe that?"

Herschel had been wondering what Nielsen would say first. Would he be judgmental? Maybe have a told-you-so attitude? Would he ask to see a copy of the citation? It turned out to be none of those things.

What Nielsen said was, "Has the sheriff been in touch yet?"

Before Herschel could answer, his home phone rang.

∽

Warren took the call.

Danny said, "Hey, man, where are you right now?" Sounding serious, or maybe upset.

"Looking at a rental house in Hebbronville."

"Can you talk?"

"Sure. I got your message yesterday, and I was gonna call you back, but—"

"Don't worry about it, okay? I'm calling about something else. I think you got a problem, Warren. Do you happen to know a wetback named Tomás Delgado?"

Warren suddenly had a hollow feeling in his stomach. "Shit. What's happening?"

"I talked to Eddie this morning, and he said the sheriff called him about an illegal named Tomás Delgado who'd gotten shot. Remember those two illegals who told that story to Darrell Simmons? Turns out it was true, and this wetback Delgado filed a report yesterday, saying where it happened and when. But here's where it gets bad. Delgado said one of our agents—*not in uniform*—came to see him in the hospital. So Eddie's been asking around. He's wondering who this agent was and why he didn't arrest Delgado. After what you told me Sunday night, I kinda figured it might be you."

Warren was starting to feel sick. Apparently, Tomás Delgado had changed his mind and decided to press charges. Four days ago, that's what Warren had wanted. Now, though ... he wasn't so sure. A lot had changed since then—switching jobs, moving back home. He was ready to begin a new chapter in life.

"You there?" Danny said.

"Yeah, I'm here."

"This is bad, dude. Way fucked up."

"What'd you tell Eddie?"

"That I had no clue."

Which made Warren feel even worse. "I wish you hadn't done that. You don't need to get sucked into this."

"You're my partner. We stick together. Okay?"

"Yeah, okay. I appreciate it, Danny. I really do."

Neither man spoke for a few seconds. The rental agent was eyeing him covertly from the kitchen window. She probably thought he was talking to his wife, making a decision about the house. Good ol' Linda Jean, hoping to close the deal, earn a commission, and celebrate with a margarita at lunchtime.

Then Danny said, "This Delgado, he must've been one of those people you 'didn't see,' right?"

"Look, Danny, the less you know about it—"

"But that was you in Delgado's hospital room? I deserve to know."

"You're right, you do."

"So?"

"Let's talk in person, okay? I'll tell you everything, but not on the phone."

ഇ

Sheriff Lindeman heard only one side of Deputy Sloane's conversation.

Sloane said, "This is Chief Deputy Brian Sloane of the Webb County Sheriff's Department. Is this Herschel Gandy?"

A pause.

Then, "That's fine, Mr. Gandy, but the Sheriff and I just—"

A much longer pause. Sloane glanced over at Lindeman and shook his head, apparently on hold. He was about to say something, but then his attention went back to the phone. He listened for a moment, then said, "I understand that, Counselor. We're sitting down here at the gate. We came out as a courtesy."

Counselor. So Gandy had a lawyer up there at the house.

Sloane said, "No, just some questions at this point. All we're trying to do is find out what happened. We're interested in hearing your client's side of the story."

Another long pause.

"We would appreciate that. You can call this number whenever you're ready. The sooner the better, as far as we're concerned."

Sloane disconnected the call. "Gandy's got Brent Nielsen working for him, and Nielsen says Gandy doesn't know anything about Tomás Delgado. Nielsen wants a chance to review the lawsuit and talk to his client, then they might be willing to talk."

"When?"

"Couple of days."

Lindeman wasn't surprised. Smart move by Gandy, lawyering up. Can't force a suspect to talk. If he kept his mouth shut, the case would likely go nowhere. The word of an illegal alien—or even three of them, if Delgado's pals could be found—wouldn't carry much weight with a Webb County grand jury.

ഇ

Ricky pulled the Nissan into Howard's driveway and killed the engine. There were no other cars in the driveway or along the curb in front of the house. Howard's son Anthony hadn't shown up yet, which was a blessing.

He climbed out and locked the truck door. What to do with the key? Leave it in the mailbox? Under the porch mat? He had a key to the house, too. Maybe he should leave both of them inside and lock the doorknob behind him as he left. That made sense.

He let himself in through the front door and walked past the stacks of secondhand goods to the kitchen, trying not to think about Howard. He would become sad if he thought about the old man. Ricky had been lucky. Everybody deserved to know a man like Howard, but few people did.

Ricky placed the two keys on the dinette table beside the small television. Should he leave a note? Let Anthony know that Ricky appreciated everything that Howard had done for him? No. Definitely not. Anthony might get angry that Ricky had come inside the house. Which meant that leaving the keys inside was a bad idea. *Mierda.* This was getting complicated. Maybe he should just give the keys to Peter Wynn. Okay, then. That was the best idea.

He stood for a moment, taking one last look around. The house was so quiet. Just a low hum from the refrigerator. The saucepan that Howard had used to catch raindrops was washed and resting on the stovetop. And there on the counter was the Folgers coffee can.

Ricky told himself that he hadn't been looking for it specifically, but he knew that wasn't exactly true. He'd been thinking about something. If he didn't get to keep the truck, didn't he deserve his nine hundred dollars back? He thought that was reasonable, and Howard would certainly agree.

Ricky stepped to the counter, lifted the plastic lid off the can, and was startled by the large wad of rolled bills inside. Howard called it his petty cash fund, but there was nothing petty about it. Ricky removed the rubber band that encircled the roll and thumbed through the bills. No singles. Not even any fives. Just tens and higher. Ricky took a moment to count the money.

More than twenty-six hundred dollars.

Ricky peeled off nine hundred dollars and stuck the bills in his jeans pocket. Then he replaced the rubber band, put the rest of the cash back into the can, and snapped the lid on tight. He reluctantly set the can on the counter.

Better go now. His bicycle was on the side of the house, and he'd have to ride it back to the motel, where Tomás was waiting. After that, who knows?

Ricky exited the kitchen, walked through the living room, and got as far as the front door. Then he stopped. He couldn't do it. He quickly returned to the kitchen and opened the can again. Anthony would never even know the money existed, so how could he miss it? No sense in taking just a little, either. A crook is a crook, whether he takes one dollar or twenty-six hundred. Ricky forced the roll into his front pocket, creating a large bulge.

I am going to hell, no doubt about it.

Once again, he turned to leave—and he heard the front door open.

Ricky froze.

TWENTY-FIVE

BRENT NIELSEN HOPED HERSCHEL GANDY would now comprehend the full stupidity of his actions. The shooting was being investigated, and the victim had filed a lawsuit. Deep down, Nielsen couldn't help but feel a certain amount of satisfaction.

"You've got yourself into a real mess, Herschel," Nielsen said. "You're going to need a good criminal attorney."

Gandy didn't react. Just sat there staring into space. He looked hung over. He smelled like booze.

"I can refer you to someone," Nielsen said. "Best guy in the county."

"I'm not worried."

"You should be."

"I'll look guilty if I hire some bigshot lawyer."

You are guilty, Nielsen thought. He wanted to gather his things and leave. Let Gandy deal with this fiasco himself.

"I saw a TV commercial for McDonald's the other day," Gandy said.

What in the world are you babbling about? Nielsen wondered.

"It had a couple of Mexicans in it. They were selling some kinda chicken sandwich, but they didn't call it chicken, they called it *pollo.*"

Nielsen was starting to have serious concerns about Gandy's mental condition. "What's your point?"

Gandy shook his head, "Boy, you just don't get it, do you?"

Nielsen treated it as a rhetorical question and didn't answer.

After several moments, Gandy said, "What about the lawsuit?"

"What about it?"

"What's it gonna take to get it thrown out?"

"What makes you think it's going to be thrown out?"

"The guy's not even a U.S. citizen. He was trespassing."

"That makes no difference."

Gandy gaped at him. "It doesn't?"

"Of course not. Delgado has rights, too, just like you and me. I tried to tell you that the other night, at dinner. Didn't you ever hear of a group called Ranch Rescue?"

Gandy hadn't, so Nielsen told him the full story. As Gandy listened, an expression slowly crept onto his face. Rage? Anguish? Incredulity? But he didn't say anything. He looked down. His shoulders were slumped. He looked like a boxer lingering on his stool after a losing night.

Nielsen said, "I'll contact Delgado's attorney and get negotiations going. Your best bet is to settle the lawsuit as quickly and quietly as possible. Go to court and you never know what's gonna happen. Plus, if they like the settlement, there's a good chance they'll drop the criminal charges. They can't come right out and promise that explicitly—it violates state bar rules—but it happens anyway. Sort of an implied part of the deal."

"Sounds like fucking blackmail."

Nielsen shrugged. "I guess you could look at it that way." He rose to leave.

But Gandy wasn't done. "Look," he said. "I didn't tell you the complete truth."

What now? "How so?"

"When I said it was me and Clayton in that deer blind ... it wasn't. It was Clayton, all by himself."

Nielsen reluctantly sat back down. He didn't know what to believe. "Why did you lie?"

Gandy took a moment before answering. "Clayton was my friend, so I wanted to back him up. See, if I was there with him, I could swear that it was an accident. But I wasn't there. He didn't tell me about it until later. He said it was a mistake, but ... Christ, you think I'm hard on Mexicans, Clayton was even worse. He mighta shot Delgado on purpose. He started all this bullshit, and now he's gone."

"Gone where?"

"I don't know. Just gone. I haven't seen him since Saturday afternoon. I called his cell phone a couple of times, but no answer. I think he took off. Left me to deal with this clusterfuck. You need to tell the sheriff. It was all Clayton."

"So you're saying he's the one who fired the shots?"

"Yeah. Weren't you listening?"

"You weren't there, and you're willing to swear to that in court?"

Gandy looked up. "What, you don't believe me?"

It wasn't easy, but Nielsen managed to say it. "Yeah, I believe you, Herschel. Now tell me everything Clayton told you about the shooting. Don't leave anything out."

&

It had to be Anthony.

Ricky didn't know what to do. His heart was booming. He was trembling all over. The door to the carport could provide an escape route, but Anthony would hear it open.

Ricky waited, still holding the coffee can, afraid to set it down. Nothing was happening. No movement, no sounds.

Then a voice said, "What are you doing?"

And Ricky realized it was hopeless. Anthony knew he was inside the house. Ricky started to say something when he heard the voice again.

"I said what're you doing?" Then, inexplicably, Anthony laughed. "Yeah, it's here. The hood's still warm, so he must've just dropped it off."

Ricky realized his mistake. Anthony was talking to somebody on his cell phone! Talking about the Nissan in the driveway.

"Anyway," Anthony said, "I'm here. Just walked in the door. Place is a goddamn mess. Shit stacked everywhere. I knew Dad was a pack rat, but this is ridiculous."

The coffee can—which couldn't have weighed more than a few ounces—was beginning to feel as heavy as a cinderblock.

"I'm gonna need a trailer to haul all this stuff off. All kinds of old books and magazines and just all sorts of crap."

If Ricky bolted through the carport door, could he outrun Anthony? He sounded like a big man. Big and slow. But Ricky was ill, and he doubted he could run far.

"Yeah, okay. I'll call you tonight, after I get a handle on things." A pause, then, "Love you, too."

Ricky heard a rustling sound—a cell phone going back into a pocket—then a heavy sigh.

"Well, shit," Anthony said.

Nothing for several seconds.

Then movement. Floorboards creaking. Going *away* from the kitchen, down the hall.

Ricky still didn't move.

Nothing again, then he heard the sound of Anthony urinating urgently into the toilet. Now was the time to move.

Ricky delicately placed the coffee can on the counter. He stepped nimbly across the tiled floor and eased the carport door open.

Quiet.

He stepped through the doorway and gently closed the door behind him. He didn't lock it, but that was the least of his concerns. His bike, too. He'd have to leave it behind. But he could buy a new one, and one for Tomás. He had plenty of money now.

He scurried between the exterior wall and Howard's large American car, then proceeded down the driveway, past a small sedan, which had to be Anthony's rental car, and when he reached the street he finally took a breath.

It was a brief article, no more than six column inches on the fifth page of the metro section. But the headline caught Cris's eye as she sat alone eating lunch: ILLEGAL IMMIGRANT ALLEGES SHOOTING ON AREA RANCH.

The victim, of course, was Tomás Delgado. The article didn't mention his brother Ricardo. The facts were scant. Delgado claimed that he and two other men had crossed the Rio Grande onto a private ranch, where shots were fired from a deer blind. Delgado sustained a permanent injury to his hand. A spokesman for the sheriff's department said they couldn't comment on an active investigation.

Cris read it a second time. Not much to latch onto. But at least she had a way to track down Ricky Delgado if she needed to. If the Honduran patient's blood test came back positive for psittacosis.

Ricky used the plastic card key to open the motel room door. Tomás was sitting at the foot of the bed, watching *Lola, Érase una Vez*. He immediately rose to his feet.

"Where have you been? I was starting to worry. Are you okay? You look horrible."

Ricky had walked the three miles from Howard's house. He was sweaty and exhausted. He'd had to stop to rest several times. At one point, he'd felt as if he were going to faint. Normally, a walk of that distance wouldn't have even winded him. Now his lungs could hardly keep up with his heart, which was racing. Ricky had had the flu once before, when he was in his late teens, but it had never gotten this bad. It was as if someone had a firm grip on his heart and wouldn't let go. His breathing was raspy and wet. He went straight to his bed and lay down.

"Will you get me some water, please? And three aspirin."

"What happened?"

"Please."

Tomás went into the bathroom and came back with three Advil and a plastic cup full of water. Ricky downed the pills, drained the cup, and asked for more. The second cup went down just as quickly.

Tomás placed a hand on Ricky's forehead. "You are on fire. You need to see a doctor."

"No more doctors. I'm tired of doctors. No doctors, no hospitals. Let the Advil work."

"But you—"

174

"I'll be fine. Just let me rest."

"We have to check out by two o'clock."

Ricky shook his head.

"So we're staying here again tonight?"

Ricky nodded.

"Then I need to go pay for it."

"Hold on a minute. Just let me catch my breath."

❧

He woke, unsure how long he'd been sleeping, but Tomás was still sitting in the same spot. It couldn't have been more than a few minutes. Maybe thirty at the most.

Ricky slowly sat up. He felt a little better. Not as hot. "I need you to do some things. Are you listening?"

"Yeah, sure."

"First, go pay for the motel room. Pay for two more nights. We'll see what happens after that. Then go to the Wal-Mart and get us a cell phone. Call Peter Wynn's assistant Maureen and give her the number. Also, buy a good bike. Just one for now. We'll get another one later, when I'm feeling better. Can you ride a bike with one hand?"

"I think so."

"Buy some medicine for the flu, too. Nyquil or Theraflu or something like that. And get some food for later." Ricky wasn't hungry, but he knew he should eat.

Tomás was nodding, listening intently, but he said, "How am I going to pay for it all? I thought we only had a few dollars."

Ricky dug into his front pocket and extracted the huge roll of bills.

Tomás sucked in his breath sharply.

❧

It had been less than an hour since Brent Nielsen had left the Gandy Ranch, but now Herschel sounded drunk on the phone. Nielsen didn't like that. Drunk people weren't reasonable. They had no capability for logic.

"Are you free tomorrow morning at ten?" Nielsen asked.

"For what?"

"A meeting with Tomás Delgado's attorney."

"Shit, already?"

"I told you it would be best to take care of this as soon as possible."

Gandy didn't say anything for a moment, and Nielsen thought he heard ice cubes rattling against a glass. "Yeah, okay," Gandy said.

"After that, we need to speak to the sheriff. We should tell him exactly what you told me about Clayton Dupree."

"I've been thinking about that," Gandy said. "Clayton's gone, right? So maybe we should just leave it alone. Who's gonna know? This wetback can say it happened on my ranch, but how's he gonna prove it?"

The booze. Gandy couldn't think clearly.

"What if they find Dupree? What if he tells them that you knew about the shooting?"

Gandy laughed. "They ain't gonna find Clayton."

"How do you know that?"

"Trust me."

"Do you know where he is?"

More ice cubes rattling. No answer.

"Herschel?"

"Where's the meeting?" he said.

ℂ

When Tomás returned several hours later, the room was dark, the TV was off, and the air conditioner was set to sixty degrees. Ricky was sleeping soundly in his bed, snoring deeply.

Tomás leaned the new bicycle against the wall, placed his new backpack on the floor, then walked over to his brother's bedside. He placed a hand on Ricky's forehead. Still hot. Maybe not as bad as before, but still very hot. Tomás knew that he'd likely catch the flu, too, being in such close quarters with his brother, but so far, he felt fine.

He stripped his clothes off and took a long shower. It felt great, though he had to hold his injured hand overhead, out of the stream, the entire time. Also, he'd learned that it was sort of awkward to towel yourself off with one hand. You couldn't get your back very well. When he opened the bathroom door, the cold air rushed in and gave him goose bumps. Ricky was still sleeping.

Tomás got dressed, which also was difficult with one hand, then grabbed the backpack, took it back to the vanity, and worked the zipper open. Inside were various flu medicines, plus a box of Triscuits, four cans of tuna, two cans of sliced peaches, a large bag of beef jerky, a tube of Pringles potato chips, and two chocolate bars. If they needed more than this, Tomás would run next door to the Waffle House and order some things to-go.

Tomás was hungry, but he wanted to wait so they could eat together. Plus, even though he'd been smart enough to remember to buy a can opener, he doubted he could operate it. He tried to open the bag of jerky, just to have a snack, and he couldn't even seem to do that either. He grabbed the upper part of the bag with his teeth and was trying to tear it open, when Ricky said, "Need some help?"

Tomás stopped what he was doing. "How are you feeling?"

"About the same. Maybe a little better. You get all the stuff?"

Tomás waved an arm proudly at the bike. "See my new ride?"

"Nice. How about a phone?"

"Got one. I called Maureen."

"Good."

"You know what she said?"

"What?"

"We have a meeting tomorrow morning with Herschel Gandy and his law-yer."

෪

After Warren sat down—same place he'd sat last time, on the couch—Danny said, "Look, first things first, I was way out of line the other day. I owe you a major apology."

"No, you don't."

"Yeah, I do, and it's been bothering me for two days, so just let me say it, okay? I'm sorry. That's how I treat the man who saved my life? I shoulda kept my mouth shut. I get carried away sometimes."

A large bouquet of flowers rested on the coffee table. Some thoughtful soul, wishing Danny a speedy recovery. A single helium balloon floated above the flowers: GET WELL SOON!

"Don't worry about it," Warren said.

"Well, I *am* sorry."

"I appreciate that, but I don't blame you for getting pissed off. There was a time when I would've felt the same way."

Danny nodded his head slowly. "You want a beer or something?"

"No, I'm good, thanks."

It was quiet in the apartment. No TV this time.

Warren said, "I want you to know, if this thing with Tomás Delgado gets messy, I'll make sure everyone knows you had nothing to do with it."

"That's good. Thank you. So you still haven't heard from Eddie?"

"Nope."

"Weird."

"I know."

If Warren were in Eddie's shoes, he'd speak to every agent in the sector. Especially any agent whose performance had been slipping lately.

In the last two months, you've had a steady decline, week after week, Eddie had said on Thursday. *You're down about thirty percent. Got any explanation for it?*

Wasn't it blatantly obvious who'd visited Tomás Delgado in the hospital— *without* arresting him?

On the other hand, what about the bad press? If the truth came out, the average citizen would be infuriated. *Why aren't the Border Patrol agents doing their jobs? This is an outrage!*

"What changed?" Danny asked.

"What?"

"You said there was a time when you would've felt the same way as me. What changed?"

Tough question. Could he even give a voice to the feelings in his head? He owed it to Danny to try.

"Ever wonder what you'd do if you lived in Mexico?" he asked. "If you were born down there?"

Danny shrugged. "Not really."

"I have, and I know what the answer is, at least for me. I'd come up here. No question about it. We've got so much more than they do. Can you imagine how tempting that is?"

"But it's against the law."

"Yeah, I know, and I'd cross anyway. I think most people would."

"I wouldn't. Not illegally."

"Would you try to come up here legally?"

"Maybe. Probably."

"So what would you do when you got turned down?"

Danny opened his mouth, started to say something, then changed course. "I don't want to get into an argument about it, Warren."

"Yeah, me neither. That's not why I'm here."

"No, it's not. You were gonna tell me about Tomás Delgado."

Warren took a breath. "It was Wednesday of last week, when we were staked out on Eighty-Three. You were reading your book, and I saw three of them cross. I looked through the glasses and I could tell that one of them had an injured hand."

Danny smiled. "You never said a word."

"No."

"Hey, in my own defense, I was only glancing down for a few seconds."

It was longer than that, of course, but Warren didn't say anything.

Danny said, "And later, when I told you what Darrell Simmons said about those two illegals ... "

"I knew it had to be the same guys."

"So how did you know where to find Delgado?"

"That was dumb luck. I was visiting you. I didn't know Delgado was in the hospital until I saw him."

"Why'd you talk to him?"

"Because if somebody was really shooting at illegals, I couldn't just let it lie. But Delgado wouldn't talk. He was too scared."

"Well, I guess he changed his mind, huh?"

"I guess so."

"Eddie said Delgado was also suing the landowner."

"Really?"

"Yeah, he hired some local attorney." The look on Danny's face said he found the whole thing repugnant.

Warren thought about that. "The funny thing is, I'd be a good witness. I can back up his story. Or part of it."

"Man, you're crazy. You'd have to admit everything you just told me. Might as well kiss your career goodbye. You'd never wear any kind of badge again. Would you really do that?"

Four days ago, yeah, he would've come forward. But now, he didn't know what to do. The gate to Herschel Gandy's ranch had been closed. That was supposed to seal the deal. "I don't know," he said.

"How many times did you do it?" Danny asked.

"What, look the other way?"

"Yeah. Let illegals pass."

Might as well tell the truth. He already knows everything else. "Maybe fifty times in the past six months."

Danny was smiling again, even laughing a little, when he said, "You know, since we're being all honest and everything, I gotta say that makes me fucking sick to my stomach."

miércoles

TWENTY-SIX

MAYBE IT WAS BECAUSE ELLEN spent all of her time on her feet, burning energy at the front of a classroom, or because she'd always had a light appetite, or maybe she simply had a high metabolism, but she still had the same lean, trim figure she'd had twenty years earlier when they'd started dating.

She had her back to Warren, sleeping on her side, the sheet pulled over her shoulder. He reached out and placed a hand on her hip. So warm and soft. This was what it was all about. Right here.

Ten minutes 'til six. Still no morning light coming through the windows. He hadn't slept well, thinking about Tomás Delgado. Warren's testimony could add a new dimension to Delgado's case.

Forget about it. It's not your problem.

He ran his hand down the outside of Ellen's thigh to her knee, then back up. Slowly. She stirred ever so slightly. She was awake. He slid his palm down the curve of her waist, then along her rib cage, then to her back, where he traced the length of her spine. He caressed her buttock, and he could feel his erection swelling rapidly.

Ellen moaned with appreciation and stretched her arms, simultaneously arching her back and thrusting backward toward him.

಄

Sheriff Lindeman had just sat down with his first cup of coffee when Deputy Sloane appeared in the doorway and said, "Yesterday I talked to a guy who used to hunt on Gandy's place. He said Gandy has a hired hand named Clayton Dupree."

"Yeah?"

"Well, that name kept ringing a bell—knew I'd heard it somewhere—then this morning I remembered I stickered his truck a couple days ago. It's still out on Eighty-Three with a flat tire, not far from the ranch. Or it was yesterday, when we drove by."

"Interesting."

"Yesterday I hadn't placed the name yet. Anyway, Brent Nielsen called just now. Get this. He said Herschel Gandy is gonna come in this afternoon and make a statement saying it was Clayton Dupree that shot Delgado, and it was an accident. Supposedly Gandy didn't know about it until later."

Lindeman said, "So where's this Clayton Dupree?"

"Nielsen says Gandy hasn't seen him since Saturday."

"Where does Dupree live?"

"There on the ranch, I think."

"Well, find out for sure. 'Cause if he does, now we've got enough for a search warrant. For the truck, too. Tow that son of a bitch in."

&

Ricky woke to the sound of a shower running. Tomás's bed was empty. Quite a bit of light was showing around the edges of the curtains. He checked the digital clock on the nightstand and saw that it was twenty minutes past eight.

The shower stopped.

Ricky was having a hard time focusing. Tomás had a meeting this morning in Laredo with Peter Wynn, Herschel Gandy, and Gandy's attorney. To talk about a settlement. Wynn would be coming by shortly to pick Tomás up.

Ricky simply lay quietly for a moment, assessing his condition. Did he feel worse? No, not really. Did he feel better? Absolutely not. Still feverish. His chest was still tight. Breathing was an effort. If he didn't know better, he'd think he was having heart trouble, which was ridiculous. He was too young for that.

He swung his feet to the floor and sat up straight. The room tilted for a few seconds. He was lightheaded, bordering on nauseous.

Tomás stepped out of the bathroom, a towel wrapped around his waist, and saw Ricky. "What are you doing?"

"Getting ready for the meeting."

"Ricky, no. You should stay here and rest."

"I'm going with you."

&

The solution came to Warren unbidden. An epiphany of sorts. He wasn't looking for it. In fact he was specifically trying *not* to think about the Tomás Delgado situation. After all, he didn't have to make a decision right this minute, did he?

Ellen had left for school, and he was scanning the Laredo newspaper, drinking coffee, just zoning out. Reading some sports scores. A couple of book reviews. He skipped the metro section, because he didn't want to see another article about himself. But he checked the world briefs.

Top story: another typhoon in south-central Asia. Relief organizations were mobilizing to assist the survivors. Airlifting food and fresh water and medical supplies. A group of British doctors was dropping everything and flying over to help. *Now that's dedication,* Warren thought. Most physicians wouldn't go that far—literally and figuratively—and very few people would expect them to.

And he had to laugh when he realized the same damn thing applied here. Metaphorically speaking, Tomás Delgado was a flood victim and for a week now, Warren had been acting like a British doctor, going above and beyond the call of duty. What's more, Warren had already offered his help—when Delgado was in the hospital—and Delgado had turned it down.

So how much more did Warren owe him? Not as a Border Patrol agent, but as a fellow human being. The answer, as Warren now saw it: very little.

Was Warren obligated to contact the sheriff? To voluntarily sully his own reputation? To tell the full story, and make himself look like an immigrant sympathizer? He felt he could honestly say no.

But there was something else he could do. A middle ground. He could help Delgado, maybe in the most relevant way possible, without completely screwing himself—and that seemed like a reasonable compromise at this point.

Warren left the newspaper where it lay and went in search of a phone book.

৯০

After Ricky showered and got dressed, he wiped the steam from the mirror and saw a scary face staring back at him. He looked terrible. Weak. Diseased, almost. He took two more Advil and the last of the antiviral medication. He was sweating, but he didn't check his temperature. Why bother?

"You don't need to be there," Tomás said. "I can handle it myself."

Ricky put both hands out and braced himself against the vanity. He decided that if he still felt this way tomorrow, he would go see a doctor. Not David King, though.

There was a light knock at the door. Peter Wynn had arrived.

৯০

The Rugoso phone book was perhaps three-quarters of an inch thick, and that included both business and residential listings. Warren flipped to the yellow pages—to the "A" section.

According to Danny, this guy Delgado was suing the landowner and had hired an attorney.

Warren knew that a lot of lawsuits were settled before going to trial. And sometimes, when a lawsuit was settled, criminal charges were dropped. Which meant that Warren could come forward—tell Delgado's attorney what he'd seen—without getting involved with the criminal case. In fact, Warren could insist on it.

I'll tell my story, he'd say, *but not to the sheriff.*

That was fair, wasn't it? Delgado could twist Gandy's arm for a big chunk of cash. Hit him where it hurts—in the wallet.

Rugoso was a small town. Population: four thousand and eight hundred. Total number of attorneys listed: four. The first in line: Stanley Billings.

Warren grabbed the phone and dialed.

ɛᴏ

It was a slow morning, very few patients, so Cris was catching up on paperwork when the call came in. It was Cathy, phoning from the lab in Laredo. The two women had never met in person, but Cris had spoken to Cathy dozens of times.

"That rush job you sent on Monday?" Cathy said. She always sounded friendly but professional. Very organized and capable.

"Yeah?"

"The IgG and IgM levels are all within normal ranges."

It seemed so anticlimactic. *Normal.* The Honduran patient didn't have psittacosis. Which meant, by logical extension, that Rocendo Ochoa and Ricky Delgado didn't have it either. There was no outbreak at the poultry plant.

Cris had been wrong all along. She resisted the urge to say, "Are you sure?"

Cathy said, "You want the specific numbers now?"

"No, you can just mail them," Cris said. "There's no hurry."

ɛᴏ

Three law firms down, one to go. One final chance. Warren made another deal with God: If Delgado's lawyer wasn't this fourth guy—a man named Peter Wynn, which was a funny name for an attorney—Warren would let it drop again, this time for good. No ifs, ands, or buts.

Warren dialed and a woman answered on the third ring. He used the same spiel he'd used on the other three: "Hi. My name is Warren Coleman. What's your name?"

"Uh, Maureen. Maureen Hobbs."

"Okay, Maureen. I need to ask you a question out of the blue. Can you tell me if Mr. Wynn has a client named Tomás Delgado?"

But this time, unlike with the other three calls, there was a pause. Then Maureen Hobbs said, "I'm sorry, what was your name again?"

"Warren Coleman. I know this is sort of weird, and I know there's that whole confidentiality thing to consider, but I need to know if your boss has a client named Delgado. I assure you it's important."

"I'm afraid I can't—"

"Maureen, please listen to me. I have information that can help Tomás Delgado. I'm willing to share it but, honestly, I'm not gonna jump through a lot of hoops. You want the information, that's fine. If you don't, that's fine, too."

There was another pause, this one much longer. She was obviously thinking.

"Maureen?"

"Yes?"

"Why don't you just let me talk to your boss?"

"He's not here right now."

"But he does represent Delgado, right?"

Maureen Hobbs took a breath. "Let me put it this way. I won't say that he doesn't."

"Okay, great. Now we're getting somewhere. When do you expect him back?"

"Probably this afternoon."

"Good enough. I'll call back then."

Warren was just pulling the phone from his ear when he heard Maureen say, "Wait!"

Warren said, "Yeah?"

Maureen said, "I have a hunch that Mr. Wynn would want to speak to you right away."

"You could give me his cell phone number. Or call him and ask him to call me."

"He doesn't carry a cell phone."

"You're kidding."

"He's nearly eighty years old. I can hardly get him to use a computer."

"Okay, I'm not in a rush. I'll call him back—"

"He has a meeting in Laredo in thirty minutes. Between you and me, it might just concern ... well, I'd better not say too much."

Warren understood. Peter Wynn was already moving on the Delgado case. Something big was happening this morning. Something urgent enough that Maureen was seesawing back and forth, wondering how much she should tell. Or wondering if Warren really had anything of value.

He said, "Look, I might as well lay it on the line. I saw Tomás Delgado and two other men cross Highway Eighty-Three last Wednesday morning. They came from Herschel Gandy's ranch. Delgado had a bloody hand."

Maureen made a sound. Sort of a quick intake of breath. A wow-that's-really-good type of reaction. She then told Warren exactly what was happening in half an hour.

The ornate sign in the reception area said the name of the law firm was Nielsen, Gray, Cauley, Turpin & Hughes. Beneath those names were even more names, maybe sixty or seventy of them, in alphabetical order.

Abbott, Acosta, Anderson, Birdwell, Bocanegra, Brizendine, Campos ...

An army of influential attorneys, doing business out of a fancy glass high-rise on the outskirts of Laredo. Judging by the décor—everything was done up in brass and leather—the army was quite successful. Warriors who were used to winning. But Peter Wynn did not appear intimidated, and Ricky tried to draw confidence from Wynn's positive demeanor.

It wasn't working very well. Ricky found himself wondering what Herschel Gandy would look like. Probably a typical Texas rancher—large and powerful, with rough, calloused hands and a loud voice.

They continued to wait, just the three of them, in the reception area. The receptionist, Ricky noticed, was every bit as beautiful as Carmen, except this young woman actually smiled. She was cordial and charming, and she didn't seem to understand that Wynn, Tomás, and Ricky weren't here on a friendly mission. Or perhaps she didn't care. Perhaps it was her manner to smile at everybody.

Ricky and Tomás were both wearing the same type of outfit they'd worn to the sheriff's office—a golf shirt and khaki pants. Wynn was wearing a gray three-piece suit and wingtip shoes.

At five minutes before ten, the receptionist cheerfully escorted them into a conference room, which featured a mahogany table that was nearly as long as the trailer in which Ricky used to live. The room was empty. The receptionist offered coffee, which they all declined, then she departed, closing the massive door behind her.

"Lovely girl," Wynn said, and that was all.

They waited some more. The temperature was pleasantly cool, but Ricky's forehead was still warm and damp. His chest ached with a dull but constant pain. After this meeting, he would return to the motel and sleep for the rest of the day. He might even fall asleep in the back seat of Wynn's car.

"What I want you to do," Wynn said to Tomás in Spanish, "is keep your bandaged hand in view at all times. Just rest it there on the tabletop. A little reminder of what this case is all about."

Tomás nodded.

Ricky could see the anxiety on his brother's face. Apparently, so could Wynn, because he said, "There's no reason to be nervous. You have every right to be here. You are the victim. Keep in mind that Nielsen will probably speak as if our case has no merit at all. Just ignore those remarks. Don't say anything, even if he asks you a direct question. Let me do the talking. Okay?"

Tomás nodded again. "Gladly," he said. "Whatever you think is best."

"Something else you should know: Ethically, we can't use the criminal case as leverage. In other words, we can't offer to drop those charges in order to reach a favorable settlement. But believe me, they understand what's at stake. It goes without saying."

The room fell into silence.

After several minutes, Wynn said, "Also, this is just an initial meeting. I seriously doubt we'll reach a settlement this afternoon. But that's okay. After today, we'll know where we all stand."

The room went quiet again.

At ten minutes past ten, Ricky heard voices outside.

The door to the conference room swung open.

TWENTY-SEVEN

ERSCHEL GANDY WAS NOT A BIG MAN. He was perhaps an inch taller than Ricky, and slender, with soft features and an unshaven jaw. Both of his eyes, Ricky noticed, were blackened, and his lower lip was swollen. He wore starched jeans, a cowboy-style shirt, alligator-hide boots, and a straw Stetson on his head. He seemed out of place in this sleek, modern conference room.

A tall man—middle-aged, blond, in a gray suit—had preceded Gandy into the room, and a younger man in a blue suit followed behind. Peter Wynn rose from his chair and amiably greeted the tall man, who was named Brent Nielsen. Gandy's lawyer. It appeared that Wynn and Nielsen knew each other. Then Wynn introduced himself to the younger man, who was named Kyle. Probably also a lawyer.

Then Wynn introduced Nielsen and Kyle to Ricky and Tomás. Everyone was friendly but cordial. Ricky noticed that nobody introduced Gandy, who kept his distance, standing several feet away from the group. Nielsen offered coffee, which Wynn declined, then everybody sat down—Ricky, Tomás, and Wynn on one side of the table, Gandy and his lawyers on the other. Ricky noticed that Gandy was staring at Tomás. Not just staring, glaring. Tomás was avoiding his gaze.

Brent Nielsen said, "I appreciate y'all driving over."

"Not a problem," Peter Wynn said. "My client wants to get this wrapped up as quickly as possible. I'm sure yours does, too."

They were speaking English. Ricky could keep up, but Tomás wouldn't be able to understand what was happening. Perhaps that didn't matter.

Nielsen said, "Let me start with something that could have an impact on the proceedings today, if you don't mind."

"By all means," Wynn said.

"After our meeting this morning, my client and I plan to sit down with the sheriff and make a formal statement about the incident on the ranch. In case you didn't know, Herschel has a former lifelong friend named Clayton Dupree."

"Yes, I was aware of that," Wynn said.

Was he really? This was the first time Ricky had heard that name.

"I say *former* friend because Herschel has disassociated himself from Dupree. Dupree used to live in a small cabin on the ranch, but I've drawn up eviction papers as of this morning. They will be posted on the cabin door this afternoon. I'd serve the papers directly, but my client hasn't seen Dupree since Saturday."

"What does Dupree have to do with this?"

"Bear with me," Nielsen said.

Ricky noticed that Tomás had both hands in his lap. He was forgetting to rest his bandaged left hand on the tabletop. Gandy was still glaring steadily at Tomás. Ricky tried to glare equally hard at Gandy, but Gandy was oblivious. Tomás would meet Gandy's gaze for a moment, then look away, obviously intimidated. The lawyers didn't seem to notice any of this.

Nielsen continued. "The reason for the eviction, well ... the truth of the matter is, Dupree might have been responsible for your client's injury."

Ricky was surprised by the admission, and he assumed it would greatly help Tomás's case. But he couldn't tell from Wynn, who was pokerfaced. Wynn said, "He fired the shots?"

"It looks that way. Last Tuesday evening, Dupree was hunting feral hogs on the ranch. When he came back to the house afterward, he told Herschel that he had fired several warning shots at three trespassers—after giving the required verbal warnings in both English and Spanish. I should also mention that the property is fenced and properly posted on all sides with NO TRESPASSING signs. My client was, of course, very concerned about the situation. He asked Dupree if he'd hit anyone, and Dupree said no, absolutely not. Then Herschel told Dupree he could no longer hunt or even carry a weapon on the ranch. If he'd known that anybody had been injured, he most certainly would've called it in immediately."

Wynn was taking notes. He said, "Dupree said he warned the men before firing the shots?"

"He did, yes."

That's a lie! Ricky wanted to shout. Tomás would have mentioned that.

"And the men did what?" Wynn asked. "They ignored the warnings of an armed man?"

"They kept coming forward, yes. Dupree told them to turn around and leave the ranch, but they did not."

Wynn kept writing for several moments, then placed his pen down. He smiled. "Clayton Dupree isn't just a friend, he's an employee."

So Wynn *had* been aware of this man named Dupree.

"*Was* an employee," Nielsen said. "But he was not acting on Herschel's behalf."

"Doesn't matter," Wynn said. "We both know your client incurs a certain amount of liability."

Nielsen didn't respond to that directly. Instead, he said, "Look, we might as well cut to the bottom line."

"I'm all for it."

"Mr. Gandy is willing to cover all of your client's medical costs, plus one year of living expenses. We're estimating that to be twenty thousand dollars, which is probably generous. We would also ask that you and your client not speak to the press. Ever. About any aspect of the settlement."

Take it! Ricky thought. *Take it!*

But Wynn shook his head. "What's he going to do after that first year? The injury prevents him from doing any type of manual labor."

"Well, Mr. Gandy can hardly be expected to support your client for the rest of his life. He's making this offer today merely out of a sense of good will. He feels bad about what happened. Mr. Delgado will have a solid year to adjust to his physical condition, and to find a job that suits him. We feel the offer is more than generous."

Gandy was still staring at Tomás, who had his head down. Ricky was getting angry.

Wynn said, "I think a jury would be even more generous. I mean, look at the result from the Ranch Rescue case—"

"Which never made it to trial."

"Right, and a judge awarded a default in the amount of eight hundred and fifty thousand. The court made it clear that it won't tolerate vigilantes along the border."

"Oh, come on, Peter. This is not a case of vigilantism."

Wynn let out a snort.

"We could go round and round on this all day," Nielsen said.

"We could."

"Or, in the interest of putting this behind us, you could make a counter offer."

There was no hesitation on Wynn's part. "Four hundred thousand."

Nor on Nielsen's. "No offense, but that's ludicrous."

"It's fair, Brent."

"If you were suing Clayton Dupree, yes, it would be fair, but Herschel wasn't involved."

"The sheriff might think differently," Wynn said.

Gandy looked so smug, daring Tomás to look him in the eye. Ricky couldn't take it any longer. He nudged Tomás and quietly said, *"No se asuste de él."*

Don't be scared of him.

Tomás looked at Ricky.

The lawyers were still bickering.

Ricky gestured with his chin toward Gandy. *"Mírelo. Él no es nada."*

Look at him. He is nothing.

Tomás did as Ricky asked. He looked at Gandy. Several seconds passed. Neither man looked away.

Then Gandy smirked and said, "You goddamn wetback."

The lawyers abruptly stopped talking.

Nielsen said, "Herschel, what are you—"

"You shut your mouth," Ricky said to Gandy.

Peter Wynn placed a hand on Ricky's arm.

Gandy, still focused on Tomás, said, "Why don't you haul your sorry ass back to Mexico?"

Ricky rose to his feet. "This used to *be* Mexico, before you stole it away from us."

But Gandy didn't react. "I'll even give you a ride."

"Gentlemen—" Brent Nielsen said.

"We'd better call it quits for today," Peter Wynn said, closing his notebook.

Gandy leaned toward Tomás—an aggressive move. "It's time for people like you to quit leeching off America. Speaking of which, who paid to fix that little boo-boo on your hand? You pay for that yourself?"

"Stop it, Herschel," Nielsen said.

Gandy was ignoring everybody but Tomás. "Or are the taxpayers footing the bill? You even understand what I'm saying, *Tommy*? You speak English at all?"

"You're behaving like an ass."

The smirk again. "My truck's right outside, *Tommy*. Come on, I'll drive you to the bridge. It's the least I can do."

"Leave my brother alone," Ricky said. His face was red hot, and it wasn't the fever this time.

"And if you don't wanna go, maybe I'll just kick your ass back across the border."

Nielsen said, "Christ, Herschel, just shut up."

"Go home," Gandy said. He, too, rose to his feet. Tomás remained sitting, with no expression on his face at all. "Go home!" Gandy shouted. "*¡Vamanos!*"

Tomás didn't move.

"Don't make me come around this table," Gandy said.

"He's not scared of you," Ricky said.

"Fuck you."

"He's not scared of you."

"He should be."

"He's not."

"He sure as hell was last week!"

The room went silent.

Brent Nielsen began shaking his head.

଼

Warren was on Highway 359, speedometer at eighty-five, just a few miles from Laredo. Maureen Hobbs had told him where the settlement conference was taking place. He knew exactly where it was. A new highrise on the edge of town. No more than five minutes away.

His cell phone rang. He checked the caller I.D. and saw that it was Linda Jean, the real estate agent. He answered, and she said, "We've got a problem."

"What's up?"

"Look, I—you didn't tell me who you were."

"What do you mean?"

"I knew you were a Border Patrol agent, but I didn't know ... what happened. That you shot a man last week."

"What difference does that make?"

"To me, none whatsoever. But the owner recognized your name and refused the application."

∞

It took Herschel Gandy a half-second longer than everyone else to figure out what he'd just admitted. Then his expression changed. His face went red.

Brent Nielsen said, "Herschel, I swear, you've got to be the dumbest son of a bitch I've ever known." He was actually chuckling.

Gandy finally broke eye contact with Tomás and looked at his lawyer. "This doesn't change anything."

"Go on home," Nielsen said. "I'll call you later."

"We're not giving him a dime." Gandy's teeth were clenched.

Nielsen didn't reply. He appeared embarrassed.

Gandy turned back toward Ricky and Tomás. There was no mistaking the hatred in his eyes. Ricky was ready. If Gandy made a move around the conference table, Ricky would meet him halfway. He didn't know if he'd have the strength to fight well, but he'd do what he could. Gandy pointed at Tomás, who still had not risen from his chair. Tomás didn't flinch or avert his eyes. He simply sat and calmly looked at Gandy.

Then, without another word, Gandy turned around, opened the door, and stalked out of the room.

Nobody moved for several seconds. Nobody spoke.

Then Brent Nielsen said, "I apologize for my client's behavior, but I know that doesn't even begin to cover it."

∞

"Yeah, it sucks," Warren said, "but I'm sure I can find something just as good, or even better."

"Can the owner really do that? Just change his mind?"

He was talking to Ellen on his cell phone, and pulling into the parking lot of the highrise. Twenty after ten. The meeting was probably just getting started. Lawyers—or at least the ones Warren knew—never stuck to a schedule.

He made a left and looked for a spot. The lot was crowded.

He hadn't told Ellen exactly what Linda Jean had said, that the landlord didn't want to rent to him *specifically*. Instead, he'd said the landlord had decided not to rent the place out after all. A little white lie to keep the peace. Otherwise she'd have raised hell. It was easier this way.

§

Herschel Gandy used his anger to propel himself forward. Down the elevator, out the glass doors, across the parking lot—each step fueled by the knowledge that he understood what was right and what wasn't.

If you're not part of the solution, you're part of the problem.

Herschel had read that on a website, and he knew in his heart that it was true. Too many people were unwilling to take action. Too many Americans were afraid to challenge the status quo. They were cowards.

But he wasn't.

§

Warren braked for a pedestrian who suddenly stepped out from between two vehicles, not watching where he was going. Wearing a Stetson and boots, walking fast, like he had somewhere to be, or something important to do.

"I'll call you later, okay?" Warren said. He found a spot in the far reaches of the lot.

He also hadn't told Ellen that he was in Laredo. She thought he was already on his way back to Hebbronville. Warren didn't know why he hadn't told her what he was doing this morning. Probably because she would've told him to forget about it, that he didn't owe anybody anything.

§

Ricky, Tomás, and Peter Wynn rode downward quietly in the elevator. Ricky noticed that his hands were trembling. His knees felt weak. His heart was still beating heavily, and there seemed to be an irregular rhythm to its workings. The confrontation was to blame. Too much adrenaline was coursing through his system. He realized now how afraid he'd been.

"You okay?" Tomás asked.

Ricky nodded.

"You look ill," Tomás said.

"I don't feel good," Ricky finally admitted. "I need to lie down."

"Still dealing with the flu?" Peter Wynn asked.

Ricky nodded again.

"You should've gotten a shot," Wynn said. "I get one every year. I never get the flu."

The elevator slowed and came to a stop on the ground floor.

§

It was more clear than ever that his country needed him. It was time to take a stand. To show that some people were still willing to fight for our way of life. If that meant he had to be a martyr, so be it.

Herschel thumbed the remote and popped the locks on his truck. Jerked the passenger door open. Leaned in and opened the glove compartment.

§

"Why don't you wait here," Peter Wynn said, "and I'll go get the car."

Ricky didn't object. He sat on the curb at the edge of the parking lot. It was late October, but it was still very hot and humid. Ricky lay backwards on the carefully trimmed grass. He was very thirsty.

Tomás knelt beside him. "Are you okay?"

"No. I don't know what's wrong."

"No more arguing. You need to go see a doctor."

§

Warren was halfway across the parking lot when he saw the same man in the Stetson, thirty yards away, walking back *toward* the building, weaving through a row of cars. Something familiar about him.

Well, of course. It's Herschel Gandy.

Warren hadn't thought about that, that the lawyers might not be alone, that their clients might be present for the meeting.

Did it matter? Not really.

Would Clayton Dupree be here, too? Warren walked more slowly. He didn't want to ride in the elevator with Gandy. He watched him, noticing the way Gandy was striding purposefully, confidently, assuredly, as if he couldn't wait to sit down with the enemy and tell them what's what.

Then there was a flash of reflected sunlight, a quick glimpse of an object in Gandy's hand as he passed between a Tahoe and a Camry.

∽

"You want me to get you some water?" Tomás asked.

"I just want to go," Ricky said. He could barely speak. He couldn't get enough air into his lungs.

"We should go back inside the building where it's cool. I'll call for an ambulance."

Ricky struggled to sit upright. "No. Ask Peter Wynn if he will take me."

∽

Warren froze. Had he really just seen it? A gun in Gandy's hand? Absolutely.

He instinctively reached for the revolver on his hip, but it wasn't there, of course. No radio, either. Just a cell phone. Didn't matter. There wasn't time.

Warren broke into a stealthy trot. Couldn't let Gandy enter the building. Too many innocents. He'd have to talk him out of it, or physically stop him. But how?

Then Warren saw something else, and his stomach dropped. Two dark-skinned men were sitting at the curb, maybe forty yards ahead. The Delgado brothers, it had to be. They were oblivious to the approaching danger. Gandy had no intention of going inside. His target was right here.

Warren yelled and began to run.

∽

"Hey!"

Ricky heard the shout as Tomás was saying, "I'm worried about you."

"Look out!"

Why was somebody yelling?

Tomás turned and Ricky shielded his eyes, searching for the commotion. He was gazing east, into the sun. A man was marching this way. It was Herschel Gandy. There was another man running up behind him.

"*¡Él tiene una pistola!*"

Tomás immediately sprang to his feet. Ricky tried to stand, but he couldn't.

"Ricky?" Tomás said.

Ricky realized he'd made a mistake coming here. Not just to the lawyer's office, or to Rugoso, but to the United States. There was nothing but trouble here.

Ricky said, "Run, Tomás."

"No."

Gandy was twenty yards away when he raised his arm, still walking, and fired the pistol in his hand. The roar was immense.

Ricky was suddenly flat on his back, staring at the sky. There were no clouds to shade him.

He heard another shot, then a scream.

A third shot.

And nothing more.

&

Warren hit Herschel Gandy hard around the midsection, wrapping him with both arms, driving him to the ground. The big revolver bounced and skittered across the blacktop.

Gandy didn't resist. Warren had him pinned, one hand on the back of his neck, grinding his face into the pavement. He grabbed one of Gandy's hands and yanked his arm behind his back. Gandy grunted with pain.

Warren looked toward the two men at the curb. Both of them were down. Neither was moving.

An old man in a suit emerged from the sea of cars, an expression of disbelief on his face.

"Call 911!" Warren shouted. "Now!"

TWENTY-EIGHT

Four hours later.

Same emergency department. Same damn waiting room. Warren even recognized some of the doctors' and nurses' faces as they passed in the hallway, going about their business with hurried efficiency.

The television mounted on the wall was tuned to a Mexican *telenovela*, and many of the people in the room—almost all of them Hispanic—were watching it. Or maybe it simply gave them someplace to look while they awaited word of a loved one.

Warren wondered when somebody from the agency would show up. Somebody would, that's for sure. Maybe Eddie Bustamante, maybe somebody else. And then the full story would come out. It was unavoidable now. Warren would have to tell them everything, all the details, starting with Tomás Delgado crossing Highway 83 eight days ago.

Why'd you let them pass, Coleman?

How often did you do something like that?

When did it start?

Those things seemed so unimportant right now.

"You'd think someone would come out and tell us what's happening," Peter Wynn said.

The elderly attorney was sitting to Warren's right. Both of them had remained at the crime scene for several hours—giving their eyewitness accounts to city cops, county deputies, then the sheriff—until Warren said he'd had enough and he was going to the hospital. *If you need more, you can call me later, but I'm leaving now.* Nobody tried to stop him. Wynn had followed him over. They'd been waiting for an hour. They hadn't spoken much.

"No news is good news," Warren said. How fucking trite was that? He didn't even know if it was true. Just because they hadn't heard anything, that didn't mean things were going well. Maybe both of the brothers were dead. Things hadn't looked good at the scene.

Ricky had taken one to the shoulder, just below the collarbone, so he might be okay. But Tomás ... he was a mess. Entry wound about three inches above the navel. Gut shot. That was never good. Internal bleeding. Organs damaged. Even if surgery was successful, there was a huge risk of infection. And what about the spine? Had it been hit? Warren was trying to remember if Tomás had moved his legs at all.

"What you did back there—" Wynn said.

"You told the nurses who you were, right? That you're their attorney?"

"I did, yes."

"So they'll tell us when there's news."

"They said they would. I'm sure they will."

℘

Sheriff Phil Lindeman said, "Four hundred feet. If that office building had been just four hundred feet closer to town—*inside* the city limits—this mess wouldn't be in my lap. But it is, so I guess I have to deal with it. It's a shame, 'cause I know your daddy, and he's a good man. Now I gotta get him on the phone and tell him how bad his son fucked up. It's pretty much a slam dunk, too, no doubt about it. Multiple eyewitnesses. Physical evidence out the wazoo. I've never had it this good. Even your own lawyer said you threatened Tomás Delgado a few minutes before you shot him. You said you might just kick his ass back across the border. Then you got even dumber and mentioned how you'd scared Tomás Delgado last week—more or less admitting you were the one that shot him from the deer blind."

Herschel Gandy didn't respond. Just sat there trying to look bored. Like he had better things to do. They were in a tiny, windowless interrogation room, nothing but a small table and two chairs. Every word and movement was being captured on video. Earlier, Gandy had waived his rights, including his right to an attorney, saying attorneys did nothing but cause trouble and send huge bills. He'd had a few choice words about Brent Nielsen in particular.

Lindeman was the first person to question Gandy since he'd been taken into custody. Lindeman had wanted to get statements from the witnesses first, and to see what turned up during the search of Gandy's ranch and his truck. They'd found some good stuff so far, and they weren't done yet.

"Truth is, I don't really need you to say anything," Lindeman said. "I've got everything I need. Prosecutor told me so. But I was thinking you might want to give your side of the story. Help us understand why you did what you did. Maybe show some remorse, assuming you regret it."

Gandy finally made eye contact. "Remorse? You kidding me?"

"You don't feel bad about shooting those boys?"

"Would you?"

"Look, I'm only trying to help you out, son."

But there was more to it than that. Gandy's lawyer, Brent Nielsen, had said something interesting during his interview. It had to do with the first shooting, the one on the ranch. Gandy told Nielsen that Clayton Dupree had done it, and when Nielsen asked where Dupree had gone, Gandy said nobody would ever find him. According to Nielsen, Gandy said it in a way that made the lawyer wonder whether something had happened to Dupree. Gandy probably thought a comment like that was covered by lawyer-client confidentiality, but it wasn't.

Gandy didn't respond to Lindeman's last comment. So the sheriff said, "Let's switch gears, then. You still saying Clayton Dupree blew Delgado's thumb off?"

"Damn right."

"Delgado said he was carrying a backpack. You ever see that backpack?"

"Nope."

"Did you even *know* about the backpack?"

"Nope."

"Delgado also had a cell phone. It was inside the backpack. Ever see that phone?"

Gandy started to say something, then changed his mind. He was on shaky ground and he knew it.

Lindeman said, "We found that phone in your office, tucked in a desk drawer. Had your fingerprints on it. Got an explanation?"

Gandy took a few seconds to answer. "Yeah, Clayton gave me a phone. Said he found it. We figured a wetback dropped it. I didn't know you were talking about that phone."

Decent story. Gandy was fast on his feet. Except it didn't make sense.

Lindeman said, "Why would Dupree tell you about shooting Delgado, but make up a lie about the phone? That phone was the least of his worries."

Gandy shrugged.

Lindeman said, "You don't have an answer for that?"

"You'd have to ask him."

"We pulled the records on that phone. Somebody used it to call the chicken plant two days after Delgado lost it. You know anything about that?"

"Nope. Must've been Clayton."

"Next day, Delgado's wife called and somebody answered. This person, whoever it was, said her husband was dead."

Gandy actually smiled. "That's pretty funny."

"You did that?"

"Nope."

"And you never saw the backpack? Even after Clayton told you he'd shot Delgado, he never showed you the backpack?"

"Nope."

Time to lower the boom. "Thing is, we found that backpack in the toolbox in the bed of Clayton's truck. With blood on it and everything. I'm guessing he was gonna ditch it somewhere but never got around to it."

Lindeman let that sink in for a few seconds. Gandy was trying to stay cool, but it wasn't working. There was worry in his eyes.

Lindeman said, "There were several things in there, most of them unimportant, but we found four casings from a two-seventy. Your prints were on those, too, along with Clayton's. Funny, because Delgado says four is the exact number of shots fired at him and his buddies."

Gandy could easily cop to this shooting, too, and say it had all been an accident. Say he hadn't meant to hit Delgado, that he'd only fired warning shots. But he was smart enough to know there were other implications. Reasons not to admit he'd been there.

Lindeman said, "Here's my theory. You and Clayton were in that deer blind together. You fired the shots. But that's okay, because you didn't mean to hit anybody, and even if you did, you damn sure didn't expect a wetback to file charges. But he did, plus a lawsuit, and suddenly you realized that Clayton could be a problem. He was the only one who could pin it on you. He could really screw you over good."

Now there was outright panic on Gandy's face, and Lindeman knew he'd hit pay dirt.

"We noticed you'd been clearing some brush out on the ranch," he said. "But when we looked at your Bobcat, there wasn't no rotary cutter or brush saw hooked up to it, there was a backhoe instead. Lots of fresh mud on it, too. Now why would you be out digging in the rain?"

Gandy didn't reply.

Lindeman waited a full minute, then stood up and said, "I'll be right outside. When you're ready to answer, you let me know."

❧

An hour later—still with no word about the Delgado brothers—Warren saw Eddie Bustamante coming down the hallway. It was hard to miss the uniform.

Eddie stopped for a moment, as if he'd lost his directions, then he spotted Warren through the glass partition and stepped through the open doorway. The reaction inside the waiting room was almost comical. Conversations ceased. Heads turned away. People suddenly became very interested in the magazines resting in their laps. *La migra* had arrived. A couple of men near the doorway discreetly slipped into the hallway and disappeared.

Eddie nodded at Warren and walked over. "Coleman," he said.

"Hey, boss. Fancy seeing you here."

Eddie shook his head. "Just can't keep a low profile, can you?"

"Guess not."

Eddie was glancing around the room, at the people who were actively ignoring him, then at the television, then back at Warren. "We need to talk."

"Yeah, I guess so." Warren was glad Peter Wynn had excused himself to the restroom a few minutes earlier. The forthcoming conversation might be awkward.

Eddie made a gesture with his head. "Why don't we find a place a little more private?"

"Works for me."

♫

Cris Ruiz had just given a tetanus shot to a construction worker who'd stepped on a rusty nail when the girl from the front office asked her to take an urgent call.

"Who is it?"

"An ER nurse from the county hospital in Laredo."

Cris took it on the extension in the supply room.

The ER nurse said, "We have one of your patients here—a man named Ricardo Delgado?"

"Yeah, he's one of ours."

"He was shot this morning and we—"

"Wait, he was shot?"

"In the shoulder. EMTs found a script for tetracycline in his wallet, and we were wondering what that was for, because his vitals don't look so good. He should be stable by now, but he isn't."

Cris was too stunned to speak.

"You there?"

"Yeah, sorry. That script was from this office?"

"Sure was. Dr. David King."

Cris went from puzzled to furious in less than a second. "Give me a number. I'll call you back in five minutes."

♫

They were at a table to the rear of the hospital cafeteria.

"So who called you?" Warren asked.

"The sheriff."

"What'd he say?"

"That my one-man crime-fighting force was on the loose again. That you tackled and subdued a gunman, but not before he shot a couple of illegal aliens."

Warren waited for Eddie to continue. He didn't.

Warren said, "Guess you're wondering why I was there. Outside the law office."

Eddie looked him in the eye. "Not really. I already *know* why you were there."

Warren was puzzled by that remark. Earlier, when the county investigators asked Warren what had brought him to the highrise in Laredo, he'd simply said he'd had business with an attorney in the building. That seemed to satisfy them. So how could Eddie know the details?

Eddie shared the answer. "Danny Olguin came to see me this morning."

TWENTY-NINE

WHEN LINDEMAN STEPPED BACK into the interview room, Gandy said, "Can I get something to drink?"

Lindeman said, "You're a sorry son of a bitch, you know that? I oughta bring that dog in here and let him rip you a new asshole."

"What're you talking about? What dog?"

"That Catahoula hound. It was penned up outside Clayton's cabin. How long since you gave him food or water?"

"I—how was I supposed to know?"

"You said you ain't seen Clayton since Saturday. Today's Wednesday. You never thought once about that dog?"

"I figured Clayton took him along."

Lindeman grinned. Men like Gandy always thought they were smart, but their mouths tripped them up. It had happened at the lawyer's office and it happened again now.

Lindeman said, "So you never checked the cabin? Your friend just up and disappeared, and you never even went down to the cabin to look for him? I find that hard to believe."

Gandy kept silent. He looked down at the table.

"If you *had* checked the cabin," Lindeman said, "you'd have known the dog was there. He was howling like a banshee when Sloane drove up. Water bucket was bone dry."

Gandy didn't move.

"On the other hand," Lindeman said, "maybe it's because you knew you wouldn't find Clayton at the cabin. Because you know where he really is."

Gandy made no effort to deny it.

Lindeman said, "The good thing is, that dog gave me an idea. With all the rain on Sunday, we're having a hell of a time figuring where you dug with that Bobcat. But they got dogs specially trained to find a body. A foot deep, six feet deep, it don't matter. If it's down there, they'll find it. Just a matter of time. We got one of them dogs coming over from Laredo right now."

The expression of despair on Gandy's face was unmistakable.

Lindeman said, "I know a guy who did something like what you did this morning. Shot an unarmed wetback. DA filed for attempted murder, it got pled down to assault with a deadly weapon. Judge gave him four years, he was out in two. You might get lucky like that—assuming the Delgado boys live. So your biggest problem might just be this thing with Dupree. You tell us what happened—and where we can find him—that'll help you out in the long run. You think about it."

∞

Cris stepped into Dr. King's office and closed the door behind her. He looked up from his computer, annoyed at the interruption, but she spoke first.

"You've got some kind of deal with Wayne Skaggs, don't you?"

She had to give him credit. He did his best to appear confused, hanging on to the ruse. "What the hell are you talking about?"

"That's why we see so many patients from the plant. When one of them gets sick—something that needs to be reported—you cover it up."

"Have you lost your mind? What the hell do you—"

"I just got a call from the ER at county. They've got Ricky Delgado there with a gunshot. He had a script for tetracycline in his wallet. A script from *you*. You wrote it. You signed it."

Under other circumstances, she might have savored the way his expression changed. He was always so cocksure of himself, so smug. But not anymore. The arrogance slowly melted away. Now she saw began to see desperation. And panic.

"I don't—Cris, I—"

"It's time to quit screwing around. I need to know right now—what's the tetracycline for?"

"But I can't—I don't remember—"

"Bullshit! It's all over, don't you see that? No more games. The man's life is in danger. You tell me what he's got or I call the state medical board."

"But I—"

"Then the cops, of course. They'll need to know."

"Please don't do that. Please, Cris. Let me explain." Sounding like a scared kid. Pathetic.

She said, "It'll look a lot better if you cooperate. Maybe you won't go to jail."

His head was down.

She said, "It's psittacosis, isn't it?"

After a long moment, he nodded.

∞

Eddie Bustamante said, "Actually, I started piecing it together when the sheriff called on Tuesday. I figured if one of my agents had given Tomás Delgado a free pass, well, considering your performance lately ... "

Warren lowered his head. His future was hanging in the balance.

"My first inclination," Eddie said, "was to nail your hide to the wall. Make an example out of you. What you've been doing is inexcusable. You should have resigned six months ago, when you first started having doubts."

Warren was wise enough to keep his mouth shut. What exactly had Danny told him? Everything, apparently.

"But," Eddie said, "I thought about it some more and I started to change my mind. Couple of reasons. For starters, you're leaving the job, so I know this bullshit you've been pulling has come to an end. And second—I'll admit it— we don't need the bad publicity. In the eyes of the press—most of them, anyway—you're a goddamn hero. Our recruitment rate has soared in the past few days, all because of you. So, yeah, I decided to let the whole thing slide. Then along comes your partner this morning." Eddie shook his head, like he'd seen just about everything. "See, Olguin got it in his head to play undercover agent. When you went over to his apartment last night, he recorded your conversation. Used one of those little digital jobbies. Hid it in a vase full of flowers." Eddie laughed. "Not the way they do it in Internal Affairs, but surprisingly effective. So I pretty much know every last detail."

Warren closed his eyes. He couldn't remember ever feeling more betrayed. He thought about how apologetic Danny had been last night, and the questions he'd asked. Now it made sense. Danny had masked his anger. He'd been setting Warren up.

"I don't know what to say," Warren said. His stomach was beginning to knot up. He thought about Ellen and their new beginning in Hebbronville. "What happens now?"

Eddie poured a packet of sugar into his coffee. Stirred it. Took a sip. "Frankly, that depends on Olguin. He was pretty worked up. Said you were guilty of dereliction of duty and maybe even treason. He was way up there on his high horse. I tried to talk him down a bit."

Warren sensed a glimmer of hope. "You did?"

"Not that he doesn't have a good argument," Eddie said. "On the other hand, I told him I wasn't sure the recording would even be legal in court. I told him he'd look like a major asshole for snitching on the man who saved his life. And last, I asked him about a certain remark you made—about him reading a book—and I mentioned that reading a book on duty could be grounds for dismissal. I said I'd sure hate to see him lose his job over such a minor infraction."

Warren suppressed a smile. "I appreciate that."

Eddie shrugged. "You were a hell of an agent. Most of the time. You're not the first to go a little soft, and you won't be the last."

"What did Danny say?"

"That he had to think about it. He'd cooled off quite a bit by the time he left. But if he decides to pursue it, I'll have no choice but to go along."

"I understand."

They sat quietly for a moment. Then Eddie gulped the last of his coffee and rose to leave. He stuck out a hand and Warren shook it.

℘

Lindeman came back into the cramped conference room a third time. He was carrying a Coke in one hand and a Dr Pepper in the other. He placed both cans on the table. As far as he could tell, Herschel Gandy hadn't budged in thirty minutes.

"Help yourself," Lindeman said.

Gandy reached out slowly and grabbed the Coke. He popped the top and took a long drink.

Lindeman sat down and waited.

Gandy stared at the middle distance. Then he took another drink—a long one—draining the can.

"Want another?"

Gandy shook his head. He let out a muffled belch. Wiped his mouth with the back of his hand. "Here's the problem," he said. "I could tell you what happened, but you wouldn't believe me."

Finally, Lindeman thought. "Try me."

"Your job is to call me a liar. No matter what I say."

"Not if you tell me the truth. I've been doing this a long time. I'll know if you're telling the truth."

Gandy considered that for a while. He changed his mind and reached for the Dr Pepper. Opened it and took a sip. Placed it on the table.

"Clayton got in the habit of firing warning shots at wetbacks. Sometimes he liked to shoot right at their feet or just over their heads. I was never there, but he bragged about it. I said he better quit before he got in trouble. This time, he got fancy and shot at the guy's backpack. The wetbacks ran off, and when Clayton went down there, he found the backpack with blood on it. He told me all about it that night. He showed me the backpack, and the cell phone that was in it, but that was the only time I saw any of that stuff. I didn't want anything to do with it. He was worried the cops might show up, and he wanted me to be ready to lie for him, to say we were together that night and neither of us had gone out on the ranch. I told him I wouldn't do it. I wouldn't lie. But, yeah, I agreed not to call it in. I figured Clayton might've just grazed the guy—no big deal—so why get the cops involved? Besides, those wetbacks were trespassing."

Lindeman sat stock still. No questions. If he asked questions, Gandy might clam up.

Gandy took another drink and continued. "The next night, I got together with Brent Nielsen and told him about it, to see what might happen legally. I'll admit, that's the one time I did lie. I said it was me who fired the shot, because Brent was my lawyer, and I knew he had to keep everything confidential. I didn't know if that applied to Clayton or not. So I said it was me. Then, things were fine for three days. Smooth sailing. We figured the wetbacks were long gone and Clayton was home free. Then, on Friday night, Clayton came back from town and said a border agent asked him about the shooting. That was all I could stand. I told him he needed to come see you and say what happened. Tell you it was all an accident. But he wouldn't listen. He said nobody could prove anything, especially if I gave him an alibi."

Lindeman kept his face free of expression, but he figured everything he was hearing was bullshit. It was easy for Gandy to blame a man who couldn't refute it.

Gandy said, "We were clearing brush the next morning and we got into an argument. I was starting to worry that I'd get in trouble for not reporting what happened, and I damn sure didn't want to go to jail for something Clayton did. So I told him if he didn't come see you, I would. That—that set him off. That's when he—"

Gandy looked down. His face was bunched with emotion, real or manufactured. He said, "That's when he went to the truck and came back with my forty-five. He was gonna *shoot* me, you understand? Best friends for more than twenty years, and he was gonna shoot me. I didn't have time to run, so I rushed him. We wrestled for the gun and he punched me a couple of times with his free hand. That's what happened to my face. I had both hands on the gun and you better believe I wasn't gonna let go. I finally got it twisted around facing him, and I warned him, but he wouldn't stop fighting. So I closed my eyes and pulled the trigger. I felt him drop."

Lindeman was glad he was getting all of this on videotape. With any luck, he might be able to pick the story apart later. Find inconsistencies. Contradictions. Outright lies.

Lindeman waited some more, but it was obvious that Gandy had said his piece. So Lindeman asked, "Where'd you hit him?"

"In the head."

"Then what? You buried him?"

"The next day, yeah."

"Why? It sounds like self-defense."

Gandy sniffed. "Just like I said. I didn't think anybody would believe me. I figured you'd say it was just the opposite—that I shot Delgado and I killed Clayton to shut him up."

"So then you parked his truck out on Eighty-Three?"

"Yeah."

"How did your fingerprints get on those two-seventy casings?"

"It was my ammo. My rifle. He borrowed it all the time."

Lindeman saw that Gandy had all the holes pretty well plugged. If he stuck to his story, he just might get away with it. He'd almost certainly do time for the shootings this morning—assuming the grand jury wasn't filled with people just like him—but he'd probably dodge any charges for killing Clayton Dupree.

Lindeman could only think of one more question. "Why did you say what you said at Nielsen's office? About scaring Tomás Delgado last week. That makes it sound like you were in the deer blind."

"Honestly, Sheriff, I wanted to shut his brother up. He was pissing me off. It was just something to say."

⁊⧽

As Warren neared the waiting room, he saw Peter Wynn and a middle-aged Pakistani or Indian man in scrubs off to one side of the hall, apparently concluding a conversation. By the time Warren reached Wynn, the man in scrubs had ducked through a doorway and disappeared.

"News?" Warren asked.

"Yeah," Wynn said. "They're still working on Tomás. He has a perforated colon but no other major injuries. Extremely lucky. The prognosis is good as long as he doesn't develop an infection."

"And Ricky?"

"The damnedest thing. The gunshot wound is the least of his problems. They've got that under control. But they say he has a disease from working in the poultry plant. Something called psittacosis, or parrot fever, and that led to myocarditis, which is an inflammation of the heart. He thought he had the flu, but he was in the beginning stages of heart failure."

"Is he going to be okay?"

"They don't know yet. But the doctor said it was ironic, because Ricky probably would've died without treatment. Getting shot might've saved his life."

tres días más tarde

THIRTY

RICKY WOKE.

Groggy, but he knew where he was. He remembered what had happened, to a point. Leaving the office building. Waiting at the curb. Herschel Gandy approaching with a gun. Aiming it. Ricky recalled an overwhelming sense of despair and futility. Intense pain in his shoulder and chest. The shrill sirens of many different emergency vehicles, both near and far. And that was all.

He'd awoken earlier several times, but none of those episodes had lasted longer than a few seconds, and he wasn't fully coherent for any of them.

Tomás.

Had his brother visited him, sitting bedside in a wheelchair, or was that Ricky's imagination?

And Peter Wynn, telling him about Howard's funeral.

Also ... Cris. The nurse. Had she been here? The memory of her looming over him was too sharp to be a fantasy.

Wasn't it?

He couldn't keep his eyes open.

❧

Deputy Sloane appeared in Sheriff Phil Lindeman's doorway.

"I just talked to the lab in Austin," he said. "I think we got something good."

Today was Saturday. Lindeman had interviewed Herschel Gandy on Wednesday. They'd dug up the body of Clayton Dupree on Thursday morning. The medical examiner had conducted the autopsy yesterday. The results seemed to support Gandy's story, except for one odd detail.

"Talk to me," Lindeman said.

"Those microscopic metal fragments around the entry wound? Aluminum. They came from a beer can."

❧

Ricky woke again.

He sensed that somebody was in the room. He raised his head which took a monumental effort—and saw a man he didn't recognize sitting in a chair. White guy, mid-thirties, dressed in jeans and a casual shirt.

The man smiled.

Ricky tried to speak, but his mouth was dry.

The man rose from the chair, saying, "I'll let them know you're awake."

∞

The county jail was right next door, so Lindeman walked over to see Herschel Gandy. When the jailer brought him in to the visiting room, Gandy saw who was waiting and said, "What, no Coke this time?"

Back to his old cocky self.

"Have a seat, Herschel. We need to talk."

Gandy sat. The jailer closed the door as he left.

Lindeman punched a button on the digital recorder he'd brought along. "How's jail so far?"

Gandy obviously couldn't tell if Lindeman was being sarcastic or not. "No big deal. My attorney thinks the judge'll grant bail soon."

Gandy had finally hired a criminal attorney. Actually, his father had. Some high-priced mouthpiece from Houston.

"Speaking of which," Lindeman said, "you don't mind talking without him being here, do you?"

"Nope. I've got nothing to hide."

"Good. Bet you're looking forward to going home, huh?" Lindeman said.

Gandy frowned. "You came here to ask me that?"

"Sorry. Just being friendly. I'll get right to it. You said you and Clayton Dupree were fighting for the gun. You got the upper hand, and you warned him to let go. He wouldn't, so you had no choice but to shoot him. That sound about right?"

Gandy stared at him for a long moment. "Pretty much, yeah."

"Well, if I've misstated it in any way, please let me know."

"No, you got it. That's exactly what happened."

"Okay, good. That's fine. So can you explain why we found tiny shards of aluminum embedded in Dupree's face?"

Gandy looked down at the table. He didn't reply.

Lindeman said, "I know this is a silly question, but he didn't happen to be drinking from a beer can when you shot him, did he?"

Nothing from Gandy, except a nauseous expression on his face.

"We found a beer can with a bullet hole in the bottom of it, but I guess that's just coincidental, right? 'Cause if it's not—if you shot a man who was simply enjoying a cold one—that wouldn't look like self-defense at all. That would look like murder."

"No more questions without my attorney," Gandy said.

"Yeah, that's what I thought."

♋

"Do you understand English?"

"Yes," Ricky said.

"Well, you might not understand mine," the doctor said, smiling, "so stop me if anything is confusing. My name is Vijay Malik. I performed the surgery on your shoulder, and you have nothing to worry about there. The bullet passed under—"

"Wait."

The doctor raised his eyebrows.

Ricky said, "Where is my brother?"

"Yes, of course. He is fine. He is in the room next door. A nurse will bring him in shortly."

"Thank you."

"You're welcome. As I was saying, the bullet passed under your clavicle and left a nice, clean hole in your scapula—the shoulder blade—but it should heal up quickly. You'll need to rest it, which means a sling for at least four weeks. You're probably not too sore right now because we have you on morphine, but it will give you some pain later. Less than you'd expect, though. But that's not the reason you were out for three days. You have a disease called psittacosis."

Three days? Ricky thought. *It's been three days?*

"Normally," the doctor said, "it responds quickly if you receive the proper treatment. You did not. The infection spread to the walls of your heart— a condition called myocarditis. I called in a heart specialist who performed a diagnostic test called an endomyocardial biopsy—a needle-puncture proce- dure—which allowed him to analyze tissue samples from your ventricle. What he looks for are lymphocytes, or white blood cells, attacking the heart muscle. You had plenty. He then treated you with powerful immunosuppressants and immune globulin. You went from critical condition to stable condition in thirty- six hours. As of this morning, all of your vital signs are normal. You can expect a full recovery, but you'll be with us for at least two more days." The doctor paused. "I know it's a lot to take in at once. Do you have any questions?"

"What was the disease called?"

"Psittacosis."

"How did I get it?"

"Almost certainly from working at the poultry plant."

"What is it? A virus?"

"No, it's a bacteria."

A bacteria. Now Ricky understood. That's why Dr. King had prescribed antibiotics. Working at the plant had made Ricky sick and Dr. King didn't want him to know.

"Anything else?" Dr. Malik asked.

"There was a man in here when I woke up earlier."

"I'm afraid he has already left."

"Who was he?"

The doctor smiled again. "I will bring you the newspaper article and let you read about it."

∞

The Kountry Fresh poultry plant was still operating and Dr. King was still seeing patients.

Cris hadn't blown the whistle yet.

She would—she'd decided that—but she'd been putting it off. After confronting Dr. King on Wednesday, she realized that taking her story to the authorities would have drastic consequences. Hundreds of plant employees would suddenly be jobless. Most of them would be rounded up and deported. Families would suffer. The town itself would likely shrivel up and die.

But it had to happen, no question. She'd been preparing herself mentally.

She'd left the clinic after Dr. King had admitted everything he'd done—including sending his own blood sample to the lab—and she hadn't been back since. He hadn't called her. She hadn't called him. Maybe he thought she wasn't going to turn him in.

The hospital where Ricky Delgado was being treated wouldn't report the psittacosis; it wasn't their responsibility. They would assume the primary caregiver, Dr. King, had already reported it.

Which meant it was up to Cris.

She dreaded it. She didn't want to be responsible for ruining so many lives.

Then she had an idea. A way to minimize the damage.

Saturday afternoon, she steered her Honda down the same rough gravel road to the cluster of mobile homes tucked behind the trees. In the daylight, she saw that the homes were even more rundown than she'd previously thought. Practically unlivable.

Half a dozen men were sitting at the picnic tables. She parked and walked over to them. She recognized the young man she'd spoken to on her previous visit.

He smiled and spoke to her in Spanish. "Nurse Cris. Good to see you again."

"How are you doing, Ignacio?"

"Better now. How are you?"

"I'm okay, but I'm afraid I have some bad news about the poultry plant. And I need you—all of you—to spread the word."

℀

Warren received a package in the mail on Saturday. Small. Light. No return address, but intuition told him who'd sent it. He hoped he was right. Lord, wouldn't that make life easier?

He slit the packing tape and opened the box.

No note inside.

Just a digital voice recorder.

℀

Wayne Skaggs couldn't figure it out. Something strange was happening, that was for damn sure.

It started on Wednesday night, when he was watching the news and heard the name Ricky Delgado. Yep, *that* Ricky Delgado. Delgado and his brother had managed to get themselves gunned down in Laredo. Apparently by some local rancher, but the reporter didn't say why.

Skaggs's immediate concern, of course, was whether the doctors at the hospital would realize that Delgado had parrot fever. If so, it wouldn't take a rocket scientist to figure out where he got it.

Skaggs called Dr. King. No answer, so he left a message. King didn't call back. Skaggs tried him again on Thursday. And Friday. And Saturday. Still no call. The doctor was ducking him. But why?

Then it got worse.

Sunday, Skaggs noticed that some of the plant employees were behaving oddly. Whispering amongst themselves. Clamming up when Skaggs walked by. Late in the day, on a smoke break, he spotted a kid from the deboning section toting an ice chest to the parking lot. Stealing, plain as day. The kid started his truck and took off before Skaggs could nail his ass.

At the end of the shift, Skaggs realized that it wasn't an isolated incident. More than half the employees had skipped out before their shift was up, and nearly three tons of freshly slaughtered chicken was missing.

Skaggs didn't get it. Why would so many employees suddenly rip him off and throw away their jobs? Nothing like that had ever happened. Sure, there was ongoing theft at the plant—and it wasn't uncommon for a worker to grab what he could and never come back—but Skaggs had never seen it on that scale.

It was like a goddamn mutiny or something.

As Skaggs drove to the plant early Monday morning, he knew it was going to be a rough day. None of the thieving employees would come back, of course. Skaggs would have to make do with a skeleton crew while putting out the word that he needed new employees. A bunch of them. Pronto.

He turned into the parking lot, thinking, *I'll get through this.* Hell yeah, he would. He wouldn't let a bunch of wetbacks ruin his performance record. He'd just have to crack the whip, and let everybody know that—

He hit the brakes. *Son of a bitch.* Normally there were maybe two hundred vehicles in the lot. Today he'd expected half that.

There were seven.

Nice cars, too, meaning they were owned by the front office staff. But the junky old beaters that the illegals drove? Not a one.

Skaggs let off the brake and began to coast forward. It was almost eerie. Like a ghost town. There wasn't another person in sight.

Looking back on it later, he realized he should've enjoyed those first few hours. The peace and quiet. Better yet, he should've hauled ass. Because right after lunch, the feds raided the place.

∞

The man from the newspaper articles came back to the hospital on Monday afternoon. Ricky had been wondering if he'd ever meet him. He decided that maybe the man didn't *want* to be met. Yet, suddenly, there he was, in the doorway.

"*Hola,*" said Ricky.

"*Hola,*" said Warren Coleman.

diciembre

THIRTY-ONE

Rɪᴄᴋʏ Dᴇʟɢᴀᴅᴏ ꜱᴀᴛ ɪɴ ᴛʜᴇ darkened movie theater in Laredo and wondered whether he smelled like chicken. It was, of course, a valid concern. Did he carry the aroma of deep-fried fast food?

For six weeks now, he'd been working as a cook at the Tastee Nuggets in Rugoso. He had been conducting himself as a model employee, and his boss had already hinted that Ricky would be a candidate for the next assistant manager position that opened up. The restaurant job was a vacation compared to working at the poultry plant.

Ah, the poultry plant.

Already it seemed so long ago. A lot had happened in the past two months. Herschel Gandy had pled guilty to two counts of assault with a deadly weapon and was serving six years. But he had larger problems, namely his murder trial coming in the spring. There had been several newspaper articles about the case, but Ricky hadn't read them.

He was again healthy and strong, and Tomás was almost fully recovered, too. For the time being, they were sharing a home in Howard's old neighborhood. Ricky had purchased it with his half of the settlement.

One point six million dollars. He felt it was obscene to receive that amount of money for a bullet wound, but that was how they did things here. Brent Nielsen and Samuel Gandy, Herschel's father, had readily agreed to the terms Peter Wynn had suggested. Ricky hadn't gone to that settlement conference.

Peter Wynn had suggested that Ricky should also sue Kountry Fresh Chicken for the conspiracy regarding his illness, but Ricky felt that wouldn't be right. He said he'd rather sue Wayne Skaggs personally, but Peter Wynn said Skaggs had nothing to take. The same was true of Dr. David King, who wasn't properly insured. He might've been a doctor, but he handled his finances poorly and owed many creditors. He had filed bankruptcy and left town. He would lose his license when the medical board finally took action.

The plant itself was slowly rebuilding. An experienced manager had been brought in from Arkansas. He was attempting to hire a new workforce, but it was a difficult task because the employees had to be legal residents. Few people wanted the jobs. The town, meanwhile, seemed to be holding on.

Peter Wynn had not yet managed to obtain U-visas for Ricky and Tomás, but he had performed some "legal wrangling" that allowed them to remain in the United States while the matter worked its way through the government bureaucracy. For Tomás, though, the end result would likely be of little consequence. It appeared doubtful that Sarafina would be granted citizenship, and Tomás would not remain in the States without her. He would return home—with one less thumb and a lot more money.

Ricky munched a handful of popcorn and waited for the movie to start. It was a Christmas comedy, but he wasn't sure what it was about. It didn't matter.

During the third preview of coming attractions, Cris finally returned from the lobby and took the empty seat beside him.

Ben Rehder is a freelance writer, novelist, and outdoors enthusiast who lives with his wife near Austin, where he was born and raised. He attended The University of Texas, where he received a bachelor's degree in English, while simultaneously pursuing a career as an advertising copywriter.

Rehder's love of the outdoors has influenced much of his writing, including his Blanco County comic mysteries revolving around a Texas game warden and a colorful cast of rural characters. Novels from that six-book series made best-of-the-year lists in *Publishers Weekly*, *Library Journal*, *Kirkus Reviews*, and *Field & Stream*. *Buck Fever*, the first in the series, was nominated for the Edgar Allen Poe Award for Best First Novel from the Mystery Writers of America.

Living all his life in Texas, Rehder has had a front-row seat for the ongoing culture wars surrounding illegal immigration. In *The Chicken Hanger*, Rehder explores from several perspectives the often symbiotic—and sometimes tumultuous—relationship between undocumented workers and U.S. employers and citizens.

Rehder's nonfiction articles and essays have appeared in *Newsweek*, *Texas Parks and Wildlife* magazine, *Texas Co-op Power*, and the *San Antonio Express-News*, covering topics ranging from hunting laws to pit bulls to healthcare reform. He has had one short story published in *Alfred Hitchcock's Mystery Magazine*.